MORTAL
FLESH

MORTAL FLESH

Gilbert Phelps

Random House   New York

Library of Congress Cataloging in Publication Data

Phelps, Gilbert.
  Mortal flesh.

  Published in 1973 under title: The old believer.
  I. Title.
PZ4.P539Mo3   [PR6066.H4]   823'.9'14   73-20596
ISBN 0-394-49147-5

Manufactured in the United States of America

2 4 6 8 9 7 5 3

First American Edition

To my wife

(Strong is your hold O mortal flesh,
Strong is your hold O love.)
"The Last Invocation"
Walt Whitman

MORTAL
FLESH

A MAN'S PAST is a landscape of erection. That's what I was thinking when I woke this morning—or was it yesterday morning, or the morning before that? After an operation you're full of the oddest thoughts and feelings and sensations. You aren't living and you aren't dying: you are somewhere in between, and it's bound to be a limbo.

You get all kinds of strange fads. Almost like a pregnant woman . . . I remember that Tanya spent a whole day collecting sea-shells on a beach deserted except for me when she was expecting our son . . . My fad is to write about myself—a ridiculous enough decision in my situation. I've got a collection of writing-pads in my locker. People used to bring them to me when I first came in here, thinking I would want to write letters. I used to have a lot of friends and acquaintances. Perhaps I still have. But I don't send letters any more.

I suppose this idea of a pregnant woman's fancies has something to do with the fact that it was my belly they operated on—I think. I'm not going into all the reasons why I think so. One of the advantages I enjoy now is that I can have a thought and even come to a conclusion—just like that. One moment it isn't there, the next it is, and that's all there is to it. It makes you feel like God. You can't be bothered with reasons and explanations though. You take it for granted that they exist, and you expect other people to do the same—and what the hell anyway!

Nobody, I suppose, writes about himself unless he thinks that his own self and his own body are the most important in existence. If it comes to that I haven't yet met anyone who didn't secretly feel exactly that, however much they dolled it up. How can you avoid it? You've only got you. Your body and yours alone is the wireless-set dumped down in the midst of all this chaos. It alone picks up—whatever it does pick up, and the ether's a big and mysterious place.

Some wireless-sets, of course, are better than others, and

5

some of us become more expert than our fellows at twiddling the knobs. I know, too, that when a man and woman are together they can teach each other a lot about tuning, and even lash up the two sets so that they get all kinds of distant places; Sydney, say, or Hanoi, or, if they're specially fortunate, signals from outer space. But even then, when there's the two of you humming side by side, you're each of you contained inside your own little cabinet of bone.

In any case in these circumstances I'm bound to be more aware of myself than usual . . . I once read somewhere, in one of those clever psycho-medical journals, that it had been "observed that old men *in extremis* revert to infancy and seek comfort by clutching the penis"—THE penis, you note, the definite article used in as indefinite a way as if it referred to something like the gold standard or the state of the nation. I've got news for the writer of that article. Boys and young men who are not *in extremis* do it too; and middle-aged men, and good men and bad men, and rich men and poor men—and even the author of that article. And they don't do it for "comfort." They don't even necessarily do it for pleasure either (unless there's some good reason why they have to), but simply to say, 'This is me' and 'I am I.'

I put my hand inside my own pyjama trousers just before I decided on writing this: it must have been what started me off. I let go as soon as I realized I wasn't going to get an erection; but I left my hand there long enough to reflect that here was the one part of my body that hasn't changed one iota in all these years: in structure and texture, I mean: performance, I suppose, has become somewhat irrelevant.

The physical manifestations of that self, it is true, have undergone a sad diminution. My legs, for example, used to be as firm as tree trunks. They looked just the same when I was seventy as they did at seventeen. They're still not too bad below the knee, in the sense that the calves still bulge—though the muscles are knotted and it's difficult to tell where they end and the veins begin. It's the thighs that really infuriate me. I've always been a big man, and even now I haven't shrunk below the six-foot mark. But when I last got out of bed my thighs looked as long and narrow as crankshafts and they quavered beneath my weight like the legs of grasshoppers. It seemed hardly credible that there had been a time when I could jump a five-barred gate, and run for hours on end without the slightest twinge of fatigue.

6

I never put on too much weight, and when my belly began to bulge, it turned out that it wasn't fat. But the top layers of my body seem to have been washed away, like the earth on an exposed hill-side. My shoulders, for example, still measure a good way across, but they are mostly bony, with stringy lines on top of them. There are stringy lines along my forearms too, while my biceps are like balls of old twine. I look like one of those pictures you see in books of anatomy of a man who's been flayed by the artist in order to show all the nerves and sinews.

Surmounting my bony shoulders is a head like a lump of rock. I've always had craggy features; now they look as if they had suffered a land-slide. My nose is more like the prow of a ship than ever, only you'd go round in circles if you tried to steer by it—it was knocked sideways in a political demonstration when I was in my teens and no-one could ever seem to set it straight. I've got a chin like a ham-bone and a lumpy forehead; they haven't changed much, and there's still quite a lot of shaggy white hair . . . But as far as this one surviving area of youthful smoothness is concerned, I've noticed the same thing in women, no matter how old they are, though with them it can be one of a dozen different parts of the body. Sometimes it's the breasts, and sometimes it's only the nipples. Sometimes it's the lower belly, or the small of the back, or the insides of the thighs—and sometimes it's all of them.

I am surprised to find that now I can even think of Trudy as a natural feature of my sensual landscape. God knows, I was unhappy enough with her. But when you get to my age you can view love, happiness, and unhappiness in their proper perspectives. You no longer make the mistake of saying happiness equals love—or vice versa. I used to look back on my life with Trudy with nothing but pain and bitterness, and see it as a black waste. Now, as I'm writing this, I can detect a kind of gulf stream threading through it. It wasn't strong enough or warm enough to transform the surrounding blackness: on the other hand, it wasn't entirely swamped by it. I can see now that it wasn't wasted. It flowed somewhere . . .

In fact it has just struck me where it *did* flow—into my life with Tanya. How that would have infuriated them both! Though Tanya would have understood in time—if she'd had more time. Because it isn't a case of robbing Peter to

7

pay Paul. Every separate relationship has its own bit of the stream, which belongs to it and it alone. But the stream flows on, now narrow, now broad, now muddy, now clear, and the fact that it was impossible for Trudy and me to be happy together doesn't mean that there was no love at all between us, or that what there was, was lost . . .

One of the other advantages I have now is that I'm forced back to first essentials. Life revolves round meals and bed-pans—and, of course, pain; but pain isn't as bad as they make out: it bangs away like a drum—a marvellous re-minder of one's here-ness . . . Not that I don't think there's a there-ness of some sort too. But it will play quite different tunes, on quite different instruments, and I suppose you have to go through this rather crude and obvious prelude before you can hear them . . . Anyway, to find my body cornered in this way is to be filled with an even sharper respect for its sensuality. *That* has not diminished and *that* is the real seat of memory: that's where the most important things that have happened to you—oh, and I mean things you've waxed intellectual or philosophical or poetical about —are stored away. I'm not excluding thoughts of God either. They proceed from the same source, but when your body's upright and bustling with blood and health you don't realise it. You don't see how natural it is that the best things as well as the worst come from the centre of one's being. So, when I put my hand on my penis, I began to remember all that be-longed to it. Erections actual or imagined, welcomed or rejected, consummated or denied—or transposed into other forms, intó all the deeds and achievements of man's sojourn on earth.

Well, what I want to do is to re-create my past—or, rather, those parts of it which interest me or which choose to come back to me—as far as possible in terms of that centre of my being which first told me that I was a man, and which, until even that fails, will continue to assure me of my manhood.

*   *   *

Yesterday I watched the light on the wall from the mo-ment I woke up until I fell asleep. It's October (I think), so the days don't last very long. But it's one of those steady Octobers, when the sun seems to have forgotten what to do next. It goes on rising, shining, setting, in absent-minded brilliance. Everything else is absent-minded too. The flowers

8

go on blooming, or come out all over again. There are but-
terflies everywhere: I suppose they are new ones, but they
might just as well be left over from summer. The birds make
as much noise as they did two or three months ago, though
I imagine many of the noisiest have already migrated. I can't
remember exactly. I used to have little facts like that at my
finger-tips, but most of them seem to have drained out of me.

I couldn't see all this, of course, though I could certainly
hear the birds. All I could see was the light on the wall and
the occasional ripples of light and shade moving across it.
You couldn't say the wall changed colour, but it did change,
as if someone with a very good eye and one of those subtly
graded shade-cards house-decorators use kept on distemper-
ing it over and over again, experimenting first in one shade,
then another.

Light and colour are beginning to flow back into me too.
I am strong enough to make use of my organ of memory.

*   *   *

As a matter of fact I think it's the way everybody remem-
bers the past, though again hardly anyone will admit it. Yet
it's the secret experiences that form the real growing-points
of our lives. It's round those fertile spots that the seeds of
future good or evil cluster.

Perhaps if I had more time at my disposal—and I haven't,
not only because I'm pretty long in the tooth, but also because of this second operation I think I heard them whispering about—I could uncover all the tender nodes of sensation,
like violets or snowdrops under layers of leaf-mould. I would
write, too, about those indeterminate years when one's sensuality, although it has passed the stage of being one long,
continuous blanket with mother, father and everybody else
woven into the texture, still hasn't begun to sort itself out
properly . . .

Touch, touch, touch . . . Playing doctors in the loft;
wrestling in the mowing grass; bare knees touching in the
bus; riding a bicycle; sliding down a banister; your hand,
the hand of the girl or boy next door, the gnarled old hand
fumbling in the cinema, anybody's hand; the cat kneading
your lap, the dog snuffling at your crotch—all those stabs of
sensation which you and everybody else pretend to forget,
but which were the explosions of the rivet-gun welding the

9

person you became, the man or woman you now are. It seems to me that just to mention these moments is to smell the scorched flesh and to see the plumes of smoke rising down the long avenue of my past, like sacrifices at the shrine of a very ancient and neglected god . . .

I remember a discovery I made when I was about four years old. My grandmother was living with us at the time, and her widowed son-in-law, a skipper in the merchant service, was spending a leave with us—a large Irishman with a broad nose and hairy nostrils, a broad mouth, and a mahogany complexion.

He used to get up very late, and my grandmother would give him his breakfast. On this occasion I was sitting in a corner of the kitchen playing with some toy. My uncle, wearing gaudy pyjamas and a silk dressing-gown with dragons on it, sat slouched in his chair at the breakfast-table, his big face morose, his mouth turned down like an inverted horse-shoe. After a while I became aware that my grandmother kept glancing quickly downwards, in the direction of her son-in-law. I was puzzled why this glance should be so different from any other—different, for example, from that she would have directed at a ray of sunlight or a stain on the carpet. Where did the difference lie? She did nothing unusual. She had her habitual serene expression. She moved in the same unhurried manner that she always did, talking in her quiet murmur about the weather and the prices in the shops, as she poured out a fresh cup of tea for my uncle or propelled toast and marmalade in his direction, while he ignored her, as he always did. And yet that periodic lowering of the eyelashes intrigued and excited me.

Eventually I edged my way, unnoticed, to the other side of the table. I waited, my heart thumping, for the next downward glance. When it came, I sent one of my own after it. I saw that my uncle's dressing-gown and pyjama-trousers were gaping open. I snatched my eyes away so quickly that I was never afterwards absolutely certain what they had seen: but something dark, fierce, terrible lurking in a thicket. I was shocked and yet elated.

I pushed the memory out of sight as hard as I could, though I know now that I did so as if I were pressing a seed into the earth, confident that although it was hidden it had not been destroyed. I was not in the least disturbed, I remember, by my grandmother's curiosity. I accepted it as a

10

revelation of the adult world, and one that filled me with awe, pity and love.

At the same time there was a suspicion in some corner of my mind that I had only accomplished a part, and that the least difficult, of my initiation. There was a further revelation, even more horrifying and awe-inspiring—and yet ennobling and cleansing—that I still had to face one day. It was as if I knew that I had to look twice into the face of the Gorgon.

All children have experiences of this kind, and that kind of knowledge. But children are snatched away from them and forced down the long, icy aisles of a sterner and very different kind of initiation. It's not their fault that they forget so thoroughly. Everybody in the adult world is so busy giving them false starting points that they are lost almost before they begin. Time after time I've watched people struggling to explain their past to themselves, so that they can better understand their present. They stand staring back over the marsh, trying to pick out the tufts it's safe to travel by. Easy enough at first when the tufts are plainly visible. But farther back, where the mist thickens and weird shapes come heaving out of the ooze—that's where they hesitate and come to grief.

Lying here now I've felt a tremendous sense of relief and reassurance. I'm not a disgusting old sensualist smacking my lips over past experiences. No, I have managed to keep open the way back.

*   *   *

Other memories come swimming towards me out of the mist . . . I was still not much more than four when my mother took me to stay with a sister of hers who lived in a village about sixteen miles from us. There I discovered for the first time that I had a cousin named Amy about the same age as myself. She used to come into my bedroom in the mornings while our mothers were downstairs cooking the breakfast, getting the oven ready for the day's bake, filling jugs from the pump outside the back door.

Together we would climb into the high, old-fashioned bed. We would make tents and tunnels and caves. We would lie there, giggling and moving our legs up and down in a kind of threshing motion, like animals treading down straw.

Then one day, when it was time for my cousin to return to her room, we found ourselves standing on the bed facing

11

each other. Very slowly, with a questioning, apologetic smile, Amy lifted her nightgown and held the hem at the level of her chin. After a few seconds, with the same tentative smile, she lowered it, and I followed suit with my nightshirt.

For about a week this was a daily ritual between my cousin and myself. At the end of it we would nod peaceably to each other and then run off about our business, with the feeling that the day had started sweetly and well. Then one day my aunt suddenly entered the room at the very moment when we were standing half-naked on the bed, rising slightly up and down on the springs as if we were about to take wing.

Two sharp slaps, and a moment later my cousin was running, howling, to her room, while I was standing, holding my night-shirt tightly around my knees, feeling sick and giddy as I swayed on the bed-springs, fighting hard at my Adam's apple. I was determined not to cry: it would have seemed an act of betrayal. It wasn't so much the pain of the slap, though my aunt had dry, bony fingers, like a bunch of twigs, that made it so difficult to control myself, but the sight of her face, purple with rage, a frown creasing her forehead and drawing two clefts at the top of her nose and between the eyes. It was a face that haunted me for years. I've been getting nightmares about it again recently, as a matter of fact . . . I dream a lot nowadays—I suppose they've scooped so much out of me that there are great windy spaces that have to be filled somehow.

Perhaps it's not surprising that that nightmare had to come back. The devil takes advantage of one's periods of physical weakness. I'm not frightened of him, though. I wrestled with him then, as a child, and I'm still strong enough to do it again if need be. If I wasn't I'd die at once. I'd find some way of dying. The last thing I'm going to do is to give into him now. I didn't when I was a child, though I was shocked to find how strong he was, and how powerful his adherents. Between them they forced me to take refuge in the catacombs of my secret self. My cousin Amy they got then and there, for life. When I next saw her she scurried past with downcast eyes. But for my own part, I went quiet and mild and apparently indifferent about most things. They thought I was converted. But I was patient and cunning. I had become a recusant. I accepted as a fact of life (or rather, death) that it was no use looking for the kind of grace I had already experienced at home or in the usual places. I had faith, though, that it would visit me again when and where it could. I held myself in readiness.

*   *   *

Some time has passed. How long I don't know for certain. It must be several weeks because the light that gathers on the wall is a darker gold, and is more frequently agitated by shadows: long, angular shadows, quite unlike the dancing dots and waving sprays I saw before, and caused I presume by the flailing of branches that are now bare. I love that troubled, dark-gold patch with a tenderness that hurts, the kind of love I haven't experienced since I leaned over my new-born son . . .

To feel that pang again is to know that life is seeping back into me. I have the strength to sustain longer flights of memory. I feel as if I have a time-machine lying here beside me. I touch the buttons at random, or fall against them accidentally. No doubt the machine weaves its own patterns, but they are not neat chronological ones, and I am aware of no conscious control.

Now, for example, as I write, something has touched one of the buttons . . . I am carried back, back to a time when I was a young man, working in Brazil, in a place called Curitiba. At home I had won scholarships to grammar school and university, but after my father died the money ran out and a distant relation who was in the coffee business, and had important connections in Brazil, had got me a job.

It was while I was in Curitiba that I met Trudy—a most unlikely juxtaposition really, because Trudy looked, dressed, and for the most part behaved as if she were still in Surbiton. She was a tall girl with a beautiful body, but somehow, and in spite of the flimsy clothes, she managed to cancel it out. I still can't understand how she did it. The perfect lines of her bust—and with Trudy bust seemed the appropriate word: one would have hesitated to speak of breasts in the plural—were always visible through her blouse. She had a whole collection of blouses; they tended to be on the small side and she had a habit of leaving the top button undone, though it would never have crossed one's mind that it might have been done on purpose. It made not the slightest difference. Something stopped the eye really settling, but then for some reason it shot off. The blouses usually had a lot of frills

13

and flounces: perhaps there was something in the way they were arranged that trapped the eye in a kind of lacy whisk, and then flicked it off at a tangent. Or perhaps it was the way she held her body. It is true, she did hold it; it was a beautiful body, but she couldn't let it go the way it wanted; there was always something a little stiff about it, especially round the hips. As a rule when you put an arm round a girl's waist, you feel her body floating under your fingers, like a skiff on water, but with Trudy I always felt as if the skiff was filled with lead.

But Trudy yearned for the exotic, the unusual. The longing made so little difference to the carriage of her body or the expression on her face, that it was difficult to believe in it. There was plenty of determination behind it, though. She had horrified her parents by suddenly leaving her job at the bank where her father was manager (it really was in Surbiton) and announcing that she was going to work abroad. Abroad would have been all right, if it had been Holland, or Switzerland, or even France. But South America—and a part of South America nobody had ever heard of—that was a very different matter. But she had persisted. Once there, it is true, she encapsulated herself as far as possible in an atmosphere not so very different from that of Surbiton, for she had got herself a job in the British Consulate and lived in a chintz-curtained room in the Consul's house. Still, it was a considerable break and had demanded a great deal of courage.

While I was in Curitiba I also made friends with an ex-patriate Russian, a tall, rangy man with a neatly clipped, grizzled moustache, and a courteous voice and manner, which were quite genuine but went oddly with the bitter expression on his face. There was some mystery about his past. It was rumoured that he had once been a cavalry officer in the Tsar's bodyguard. After the Revolution he had apparently become a Professor of Languages in Germany. Why he had come to Brazil, and why he had gone into the coffee industry nobody knew. Anyway, my relative had written to him to ask him to keep an eye on me. I called him Ivan as everybody else did, and it was years before I discovered that this was in fact his first name, though it had once been accompanied by a good many others, including a high-sounding title.

As he was supposed to be teaching me something about

14

coffee we saw a good deal of each other. For the most part it was coffee we talked about, but one day he suddenly turned to me and said: "I'm going to show you some old-time Russians!" It was the first time I had known him show any excitement and I gathered that somewhere in the interior there was a Russian settlement of some kind.

The next morning we set out in Ivan's old Ford. We drove out of Curitiba and headed north into a landscape of bare, eroded hills, twisted into the shapes of ruined battlements, with palm trees growing on top of them like ragged banners. The sky was petrol blue: the sun blazed down until there wasn't a spot on the car that wasn't unbearably hot: my forearm stuck to the top of the door and whenever my knees brushed against the dashboard it felt as if they had touched a hot-plate.

Some hours later we came across an old man driving before him an ox as emaciated as himself. He was so unaccustomed to seeing strangers that he looked round wildly, as if seeking an avenue of escape. We asked him if he could direct us to " the Russians ". He stared at us, with a pained, bewildered expression.

" The men with boots and beards," Ivan said. The old man's eyes lit up, and he pointed to a faint track, leading over a bare, dry field.

We drove for several miles along the path, came to a fringe of eucalyptus trees and passed through them into another field, which was presumably under some kind of cultivation because the green skin had been peeled back, though all that was disclosed in the process was an expanse of brittle earth, glittering with chips of quartz, with here and there a bristly patch of green showing through.

This field stretched on and on as far as the eye could reach. I've never experienced anything so utterly desolate; not a house, not a soul in sight; a still, brassy sky; a horizon empty except for a solitary clump of wilting palm trees; and not a sound apart from the monotonous crunching of the car's wheels. I was a young man, but suddenly I found myself thinking of death more seriously then than at any other time of my life—even during the months I've spent lying in this bed. It wasn't morbidity, but something natural and inevitable, growing out of the silence and emptiness. When you're surrounded by people, houses, landscapes you know and recognise, you don't hear your life ticking away. If you hear anything at all it's a quiet, slow whispering which comes from the people and objects around you as much as it comes from yourself, like the burning of a banked-up fire through a long winter's day. But that car felt as if it was on a conveyor belt carrying us across an unknown landscape to an unknown rubbish-tip at the edge of the world. Ivan must have felt the same, for he gave me a quick look and said:

" Yes, I know—you get the same feeling on the steppes . . . back home."

Then suddenly I heard, of all things, the sound of a balalaika. A few minutes later we crossed a ridge and dropped into a village. At first I was convinced it must be a mirage: two parallel lines of single-storied wooden houses, each with a fenced-in yard, faced each other across a wide, dust road. Three boys, wearing wide-sleeved blouses, belted at the waist, baggy trousers tucked into high leather boots, and round Cossack caps, were squatting on their heels over a portion of the road that had become flattened and baked to the consistency of asphalt, trying to spin a top on it. A group of little girls stood watching them, each of them a bulge of skirts, petticoats and aprons, and their heads wound round with lengths of fringed scarf and shawl.

The children stopped their game and stared at us. Very slowly Ivan climbed out of the car and went up to them, a trance-like smile on his face. He put out a hand and laid it on one of the little girls' heads, immediately snatching his hand away, as if he feared she might crumble at his touch. Then he spoke in Russian and in a voice guttural with tenderness. The children burst out laughing, clapped their hands, and began chattering nineteen to the dozen. Several of them came over to the car, where I was still sitting, and dragged me out of it. We were hustled across the road in the direction of a hut from which the strains of the balalaika were coming, accompanied now by the throbbing rise and fall of Russian singing. None of the grown-ups was at work today, we were told: it was a holiday and a betrothal was being celebrated.

We were ushered into the hut. Brightly patterned curtains hung at the little windows; small cushions covered in the same material were scattered on the rough wooden settles and benches; there was a gaily quilted bed in an alcove. The room was dominated by a huge stove—and there was even a grandfather rolled up on top of it, fast asleep, a smell of

16

scorching rising from his beard, where it hung over the edge of the stove.

All the men wore beards, and the soft, fuzzy tufts of hair, like the stuffing in sofas, on the chins of the young men, were evidence that they had never even begun to shave—though I didn't know at the time that this was to do with their religion.

The atmosphere was stifling, what with the sub-tropical heat outside and the stove going full blast inside, and all the windows tightly closed. Within a few minutes I felt more dizzy than ever. At the same time there was a fresh and pungent smell in the room. Part of it I traced to the freshly baked oaten cakes which an old woman, whose natural dumpiness was accentuated by the voluminous skirts round her middle, kept piling on my plate. But there was another aroma that was not dissimilar, a kind of blend of new bread and oranges. It came from jugs filled with a cloudy liquid, which was in fact brownish-orange in colour. The taste itself wasn't unlike orangeade mixed with barley water, but more brackish. I was very thirsty and drained my glass at once. It was immediately refilled, amidst a roar of approval.

There was a great deal of laughing and chattering and stamping of feet. The man with the balalaika struck up again, and the room vibrated to the throaty yet liquid singing of Russian folk songs. Ivan joined in enthusiastically: it was the first time I had seen his face without its caustic, closed-in expression. As I knew little Russian I was excused the singing, but my glass was filled every time I emptied it. I was treated not just with courtesy, but with a kind of deference. I was addressed always by the word " stranger ", uttered in tones of the deepest respect. In a dim sort of way I realised that my unexpected advent must chime in with some folk superstition, and that it was regarded as a good omen for the betrothed couple, so that the liquid that was continuously being poured into my glass took on the significance of a libation. But a sensation of having strayed into the wrong space-time spiral—or, rather, into several spirals that had become entangled—increased every minute. At the same time another highly evocative Russian word—kvass—began to impinge on my muddled consciousness, and after a time it dawned on me that it referred to the cloudy-orange liquid in my glass.

The young bride-to-be was particularly attentive in seeing

17

to it that I had enough cushions, and that my plate and glass were always filled. She must have been about eighteen, with the kind of looks for which the clichés used in Russian novels—rosy cheeks, cherry lips, pearly teeth, black brows—seem peculiarly appropriate, somehow conveying an extra dimension of freshness and innocence. She was small but plump: in all those clothes it was impossible to tell *how* plump, though when she moved there was a quick, fluid motion and her small feet, in their elaborately embroidered slippers appearing under the long skirts, might have been mounted on castors.

What particularly fascinated me was the expression on her face. As long as I can remember I have been struck by the fantastic variety of the expressions that flow, almost continuously, across the faces of women, practically from the day they are born till the day they die. I think our own range must be infinitely smaller. Perhaps it has something to do with the effect of beard and bristles, which half conceal the features when they are present, and reduce the skin to the sensitivity of wash-leather when they're regularly shaved off. Or maybe something to do with the structure of the male face. Anatomically a man is a jutting sort of creature. It seems to me, in fact, that he acquires a dozen or so basic expressions quite early on, and simply rings the changes on them for the rest of his life. The dissatisfied lines round a man's mouth, for example, hardly ever alter. Similarly the humorous clefts round the mouth of a man who has had some experience and acquired some wisdom, they begin to form quite early on and then simply deepen with the years. It takes a really big shock to shift a man out of his few basic expressions. But a woman's face changes a hundred times a day.

The thing I remember most about the Russian girl's expression was the combination of innocence and knowledge. She blushed if anyone spoke to her: her lips were parted in a kind of amazement, but at their corners there was also a pucker of secret amusement, such as you see in the faces of old women who have lived through many vicissitudes. When her young man took her hand, she looked down at it in surprise, as if she felt it was beginning to live an independent life of its own and ought to be called back home; but she kept glancing up at him with eyes that flickered with mischief, tender mockery and a deeper expression which seemed

18

to be saying: "I'm a treasure-house—if you have the key? Have you? Have you?" He would look back at her as if he knew exactly what she was thinking, and was replying: "Yes, I *do* have the key"—and then they would smile at each other in a conspiratorial way, and she would blush again.

It was only when two of the older men offered to take us to their chapel to show us some ancient eikons and an equally ancient psalter that I realised that something was wrong with me. Ivan jumped to his feet at once, but when I tried to follow, nothing happened. My legs would not move. I looked down at them in astonishment. It was an extraordinary sensation. From the waist upwards I felt, apart from a slight muzziness in the head, unusually alert and active: below the waist I was apparently paralysed.

The whole room was rocking with laughter. The men came over to me and slapped me on the back. By now, though, the effort of trying to make my legs work had begun to affect the rest of my body. With each grunt and pressure I could feel alcohol flooding through my veins and up into my head, as if it had all this time been stored in my legs and I was now pumping it out.

The next thing I knew was that everybody had left the room except the betrothed couple, and that they were undressing me, very gently and for some reason taking a great interest in my garments, holding each of them up to the light and examining the makers' labels. Perhaps the English names and trade-marks fascinated them, but by the excited way in which they chattered about them one would have thought I was something that had dropped out of the skies.

When they had finished and I lay there as naked as the day I was born and far more helpless, they opened a chest, took out a voluminous night-shirt, yellow with age and smelling of tallow, and put it on me. I have a dim recollection of them lifting me up, and of my head pillowed on the girls' breast, while the young man took my legs. I know that when they moved in the direction of the stove I began to struggle feebly, presumably because I didn't want to share it with the old grandfather, who snored peacefully throughout. Anyway, they must have known what I was getting at, for the next thing I knew was that I was in an alcove behind a curtain, lying on a large bed with a very thick mattress, which made a rustling noise every time I stirred. A lemon-

19

coloured streak of light showed through the small window high up in the wall above the bed, and somewhere a cockerel was crowing.

The hut was deserted when eventually I awoke, and gingerly hoisting my legs on to the floor found them as good as new, apart from pins and needles in the ankles. By the time I had dressed practically the whole village had gone off to work in the fields. Ivan appeared from somewhere, and the old woman gave us a breakfast of eggs, oat cakes and coffee. Two of the Elders of the sect escorted us back to the car. They gave us pressing invitations to return for the wedding in a couple of months time. We promised to come, but as soon as we were out of sight of the village I knew we wouldn't do so. For some reason we were silent and depressed all the way back to Curitiba. It was only later that Ivan explained that the colony we had visited was one of several groups of Old Believers who had been allowed to settle in this remote area of Paraná (the state of which Curitiba is the capital) two years before. He told me something about the sect. I wasn't particularly interested in their religion as such, but I like that phrase " Old Believers ": it rang a bell of sympathy somewhere inside me, and it has stuck in my mind ever since.

*   *   *

One of the reasons why this episode, in defiance of all chronological order, has pushed its way into my memory is that this new nurse who has been looking after me since my operation reminds me of the Russian girl.

It's something about the way her hips and breasts refuse to be muffled by her uniform. Something, too, about her eyes and her firm, direct gaze. I had a bad day yesterday—I'm beginning to wonder whether I'm going to climb out of this pit. I couldn't sit up, and, yes, there was something wrong with my legs. I wanted to go on writing and I tried to do so lying on my back, but I couldn't hold the pen properly, so I pushed it and the writing-pad into the locker, and let go. I drifted off for several hours, so far away that the memories couldn't even get to me in dreams. I woke up quite suddenly, and heard a rustling noise. The nurse was standing by the locker. At once she began to straighten the bed, very brisk and business-like. But I think she had been reading my scribblings. She didn't say anything, but just before she closed the door she threw a quick look at me. I couldn't place it at all. But I know it didn't contain either disgust or condemnation.

*   *   *

Again I brush against a button of my time machine; again I am carried back to a segment of my past . . .

I was just turned sixteen. A friend of mine named Cartwright had organised a dance in aid of some school charity, and I was staying at his house for the night. Cartwright was a little older than I, a neat and dapper young man with very blue eyes, pink cheeks, red hair and a pinched-in nose. He was clever, possessed a good deal of charm, and had that blend of self-confidence, self-indulgence and cynicism that comes from being surrounded by too many doting women. His father rarely appeared on the scene, but his mother and his four sisters were plump, jolly and gregarious. The house took after them. There seemed to be tables in every room loaded with food and drink. The larder was always available to anyone who felt like raiding it. Somewhere there was always a kettle on the boil, and somewhere there was always someone brewing tea. The rooms abounded in corners, alcoves or window embrasures where it was cosily dark and private. There was a profusion of screens, wing chairs big enough for two, and high backed settees with deep cushions like maternal bosoms.

I had partnered Cartwright's younger sister Priscilla at the dance—and now my heart began to thud and to sink at the same time, as she piloted me to a particularly buxom settee in a particularly dark corner. At the dance I had been aware that Priscilla was wearing a dress that clung more efficiently than it concealed. I had, indeed, been proud of it, as a circumstance that would enhance my standing with my school-fellows, especially as Priscilla was two years my senior. But at that age two years seems a vast gap. The areas of flesh which she exposed, even the deep cleavage between her breasts, scented with a decidedly top-heavy perfume, had seemed no possible concern of mine. I had regarded them as a species of costume jewellery designed to attract attention rather than to provoke desire. In the dances I had held her gingerly, apologising because my hands were sticky. I had felt embarrassed by the softness of her stomach against mine, and slightly disgusted when, on making our turns, her thighs pressed against mine.

It was only now that it came home to me with a shock that

21

I was actually holding in my arms a young woman who had very little on. Suddenly I seemed to be surrounded by flesh: it cascaded around me like large soft, warm blossoms. I struggled like a drowning man. As she pressed her mouth against mine it felt as if my whole body was being smeared with peeled ripe fruit. My fingers, moving of their own volition from her shoulder blades, sunk into her well-covered shoulders. Her arms seemed extraordinarily naked. The forearms were unexpectedly long and slender, with a very faint dark smudge along them. But her upper arms were fully fleshed, the insides white and unused looking, and incredibly smooth and firm. She closed them over my hands, holding them tight against her ribs, as if to prevent them from moving towards her breasts. But when she released my hands it was so suddenly that the movement was in itself sufficient to dislodge the shoulder-straps of her dress, and a moment later my hands, fingers, lips, face were exulting among her breasts, like a swimmer buoyed up on the billows of a warm tropic sea.

I was hardly aware of what was happening to me. The rhythmic moans that came from both of us seemed to have no connection with our own bodies, but to be echoes of something that was happening far, far away. I could feel my hands trembling as, cautiously and clumsily, they continued their explorations. The insides of her thighs were slightly ridged and smoother, with a kind of polished smoothness, than any other part of her body. But from the moment when, suddenly, they fell apart, like mounds of snow melted in the sun, and I discovered that she was even more naked than I had supposed, and to a degree I had not dreamed possible, I was swallowed up in a series of shocks, which thundered through my being like heart-attacks.

Above all, there was terror, terror both of the unknown and of the forbidden—but forbidden not merely by the edicts of society but in a very special sense, which involved defiance and even the possibility of forgiveness for disobedience accompanied by sufficient courage. Much of the terror lay in the fact that everything—as far as the girl was concerned—seemed so much bigger than I had expected. I had suddenly become a Gulliver smothered in the cavernous embraces of a female Brobdingnag. I had the sensation of being driven forward by a hurricane and drawn in by a vortex. I was so overwhelmed that I lapsed into a kind of

22

unconsciousness. I didn't really feel what was happening to me at all. I only knew that some time later I seemed to emerge from a long subterranean journey. I had that languid but blissful feeling you get when you suddenly begin to recuperate after an illness—and at the same time there was somewhere at the back of my mind a secret sense of elation and achievement, as if somewhere along my subterranean journey I had passed one of those apparently impossible tests you get in fairy tales. As the various objects in the room, together with Priscilla's flushed cheeks, parted lips and damp hair, stopped swimming around me and suddenly came into focus, the memory of that childhood experience when I followed the direction of my grandmother's gaze flashed into my mind. It was as if I had followed up the one act of daring by another, and had looked for the second time into the face of the Gorgon. In some dim way I also had the feeling that half the terror had been exorcised, and that a time would come when there would be no fear left at all, or, rather, when fear had been replaced entirely by wonder. When I glanced at the clock on the mantelpiece and saw that only fifteen minutes had passed I thought there must be something wrong with it.

I saw little of Priscilla after that night. Neither of us seemed to want it. I knew it immediately when we met at breakfast the following morning. We smiled at each other, but there was something final about the smile. Whenever we met afterwards it was as strangers who merited an extra degree of kindness and consideration because of circumstances which we knew existed but had somehow forgotten.

It was almost as if I became two separate persons. On the one hand there was the I who every now and then found myself stumbling, groping, or simply being led—and in either case dazed and lost—into another adventure. This part of me was secret and secretive, almost furtive. But it was the furtiveness of the sleep-walker rather than that of the practised seducer. On the other hand, there was an I which was incredibly naïve. At school I could never understand half the dirty jokes and allusions, and those I did grasp made me blush, to the delight of my school-fellows. And when, feeling guilty at my backwardness, I tried to repeat some joke I had heard, I invariably made a mess of it . . . I've never gone in much for dirty jokes as a matter of fact, except when sometimes it has become a natural,

Rabelaisian accompaniment to love-making . . . How Tanya used to gurgle with delight at my stories in that odd, converted chapel-cum-studio in Cornwall. I always told my stories well when I was in bed with Tanya. But I was a middle-aged man before that happened, and I joined the two halves of myself together at last.

*   *   *

This morning I had a good look at the new nurse without my spectacles, and she looked more like Tanya than ever. She has the same sort of deceptive smallness—not much more than five feet tall and with small bones but at the same time a kind of opulence . . .

The nurse couldn't tell I was looking at her because without my spectacles my eyes have a misty, unfocused look. I gave her quite a shock when I suddenly said to her:

" If I die—when I die—I would like you to be here."

She didn't react in the usual tut-tutting way, but said quite matter-of-factly: " Why?" I got a bit confused then.

" Because it must be a woman," I said.

" Who . . . what . . . must be a woman?"

" I mean, it must be a woman who lays me out." She frowned.

" Now you're being morbid!" she said, but accusingly, even angrily, not at all in that jolly, rallying way in which nurses so often talk to their patients.

" I'm not thinking of death," I tried to explain, " but of life—the last bit of life in me. I hate the thought of my limbs being handled by some clumsy young internee, or, worse, by the rubbery paws of a male nurse."

" But why? What difference does it make?"

" It *ought* to be woman! We start with a woman, and we ought to end with a woman. That's how it always used to be. Any woman. I don't mind how gnarled and wrinkled an old crone it is . . ."

" Thank you," she said, with a faint smile.

" I didn't really mean it must be you—the thought just came into my head. But it *does* make a difference, to me."

But she wasn't listening. She seemed to be deep in thought. Then suddenly she raised her head and said, very seriously:

" Then I would need to know you much better, wouldn't I?"   *   *   *

Sometimes I see the faces of all the women I have known in my life ranged round my mind's eyes as in a family photograph. I am sure they are all there, but I couldn't read them off from left to right. What happens is that first one, then another, swims up to me from the sepia blur, grows brighter and brighter before my eyes, each feature piercingly distinct, until the whole image is transfigured by the exact quality of love and tenderness that had belonged to it and no other . . .

Oddly enough the dimmest face is that of Renée, the girl I first went to bed with—in the sense, I mean, that I really knew and felt what was happening instead of acting in a complete daze. She was rather thin, with crisp, black hair, and a white neck, very broad at the base, which gave her a Pre-Raphaelite look. She liked dramatic ornaments—huge bracelets, chains and torques, that kind of thing—and she always wore black.

I met Renée at a party in Griffiths' rooms. Cartwright and I were at the same college. Griffiths and Cartwright, in fact, were close friends, and collaborators in the relentless and, as it seemed to me, quite joyless girl-chasing which seized them like a fever in their youth.

The only other thing they really had in common was a near perfect command of German. Cartwright's mother was Swiss-German, and Griffiths had been born in Germany and spent his early childhood there; his father had been a chaplain with the British Army of Occupation after the First World War. Griffiths was taking German as one of his main subjects for his Modern Languages degree course, and I was in the same faculty. My languages, though, were Spanish and Portuguese, and I was only at the beginning of my second year when my father died and I had to leave the university. My languages stood me in good stead, though, in the rather odd business career I somehow drifted into. I could never take business seriously enough to settle down to some speciality and make a lot of money. But I quite liked getting to know about various commodities, especially South American ones—coffee among them—and I seemed to have a gift for bringing commodity to buyer, and *vice versa*. I was really a kind of go-between, which suited me very well because it left me free to keep myself intact in the middle.

Griffiths, incongruous though it seemed at the time, intended to follow his father into the Church himself eventually. He was very tall, with a large, plump face like a ripe plum. His body, too, was like a plum in shape, with a bulge which began just below the breast-bone, and which seemed made for clerical black. He wore horn-rimmed spectacles through which large, velvety brown eyes shone with a perpetually caressing expression. When he looked at a girl the lenses of his spectacles seemed to increase in strength, so that the pupils grew to enormous size. At the same time they would become suffused with a kind of oily fluid, which seemed to exercise an extraordinary hypnotic effect, especially with highly respectable girls like Renée. You could watch them practically drowning, like midges that had blundered in.

Griffiths wasn't always efficient administratively, though. He often found himself with two girls at the same time, and then he had to make a rapid choice before he ushered one or the other of them out of the way before they created a disturbance.

On this occasion I had burst into his rooms to borrow a packet of tea, at the exact moment when he was about to exercise his Judgment of Paris. Perhaps Renée suspected that the verdict would go against her (Griffiths' spectacles were gleaming in the direction of the other girl) and was determined to forestall it. At any rate, she picked up her coat, came up to me as I stood goggling in the doorway, rose on her toes, kissed me, and said:

" Let's go to your rooms, shall we?"

I was so taken aback that I got into a worse panic than usual. On the way back to my rooms I kept getting in Renée's way or tripping over my own feet. As I opened the door I dropped the packet of tea, which burst. Later I scooped up most of the tea with a fish-slice, but the remains crunched underfoot for days afterwards.

I was aware of the next half hour only in spasms, as if I was going in and out of tunnels on a sunny day. I remember noticing for the first time that when a woman is lying flat, with the upper part of her body tilted slightly backwards, her breasts practically disappear and the rib cage takes on an extraordinary prominence, though the curves are somehow as rich as ever and the nipples spread out like water-lilies. As I ran my fingers up and down Renée's body I experienced an extraordinary sensation of languor and freedom, as if I

26

were wandering, alone but content, across an interminable stretch of smoothly corrugated sand. The image was broken by a scrap of black flotsam, which resolved itself into the fact that Renée, no matter how often I tried, would not allow me to remove her black stockings. For a moment this interposed a barrier between us. For me, the presence of the stockings struck a discordant, even sordid, note; for Renée it somehow acted as a guarantee not only of the respectability she valued so highly, but also of her selfhood and independence.

I had never seen a woman entirely naked, and I was disappointed out of all proportion by my failure to do so now. My hands remained for some time in the stockinged part of her legs, in a sulky dumbness, as if I suspected I was being cheated of something crucial. But when eventually I reluctantly raised my hands higher, I was seized by a piercing access of new pleasure as they encountered the smoothness, like that of oiled glass, of the insides of her thighs above the black stockings. A moment later she raised her legs in a bucking motion, and suddenly the thudding of my heart, which had seemed to be distending the whole of my body, subsided; my head cleared, and for the first time I was aware, in full clarity of consciousness, of penetrating a woman. Whereas with Priscilla it had been a haze of fearful sensations and guilts, now everything was clear-cut and intense, like a tropical midday when the sun seems motionless and each shadow has a cutting edge as sharp as a knife.

For the first time, too, although it seemed to take place a century later I was aware of ejaculation, not as a swamp-like melting of the flesh but as a triumphant projection—an extension not a diminution. I felt hollow, yet excited by a sense of newness and renewal, as if a spring had been struck from the rock in an empty cavern.

There was still something lacking, but whatever it was, I knew it was at present beyond me. I was still too young and selfish and greedy. It may have been the black stockings. I was dimly aware that they were something more than the trivia of sensuality, that they represented some small clash of the will, some small conflict of desire that isolated the experience and would prevent it from going any deeper. I knew that between Renée and myself some minute but vital need had somehow or other been ignored or outraged; a touch, a holding, a pressure ignorantly or carelessly applied;

a gesture accomplished that should never have been accomplished, or withheld when it should have been given. Somewhere at the back of my mind, too, a series of questions was forming: where did love, as distinct from liking, come into it? Which came first, the love, or the constituents of love? Was it accident, or some impulse far beyond my present comprehension—and perhaps beyond anybody's comprehension—that caused one to do the "right" things, and so "make love"—or was it love itself, already operative, in some far recess of the soul, that passed its spirit messages through the oubliette of the body? I knew that these questions were there to be answered, but that at present I could do no more than formulate them in crude and incomplete terms. I had at least begun to learn that I was a seeker after a truth I knew instinctively existed, but though I had made a few steps forward I knew I was still stumbling with outstretched hands, like a man in the dark.

As a matter of fact Renée returned to Griffiths the next day. I felt ashamed that I had been such a minor episode in her life and that I had gained so much more from it than she apparently had. Perhaps indirectly it had had some effect, for although she didn't stay long with Griffiths she settled down with Cartwright, and some time later I heard they had become engaged. As for Griffiths, he really did give up his philandering as soon as he moved to his theological college, though from time to time he would look back to it with a fierce yearning. After he was ordained he married— of all people—my cousin Amy, whom he had met at my home.

*　　　*　　　*

I've never believed that length of time has a great deal to do with intimacy. There are times when a single caress, a single kiss, or even a single look, can establish it.

While I was still at school I met a girl during the annual seaside holiday. We found ourselves one morning sitting side by side on the same raft. It was a very rough day and nobody else had ventured that far out. I loved swimming against the great, heaving yellow breakers that made me lift my chin to avoid getting a smack across the forehead. So, apparently, did the girl. We sat close together on the slippery raft, that tugged at its moorings like a bucking bronco. It was so rough that a life-guard was always hovering near us, dipping

28

up and down and sometimes right out of sight, resting on his oars and staring at us glumly as if he felt cheated because we had not been swept out to sea.

In spite of the life-guard, we enjoyed the most perfect sense of privacy. We just sat there, holding hands, our legs dangling in the water, the waves every now and then flooding across our laps and right up to our chins. Once or twice, greatly daring, I slid my hand up and laid it over one of her breasts. She would lean against my hand, and the nipple would show through the thin clinging material. Once or twice, too, I kissed her, through the beads of salt water. I could smell as well as taste the sea on her lips, as well as the rubber of her tightly fitting bathing cap which framed her face in a perfect oval. But mostly we just *looked* at each other. There was something wildly beautiful about that rapt engaging of the eyes, very soft and tender, while the wind howled around us, the seagulls perched on the edge of the raft scolding us, and the water slapped angrily beneath the slats.

We never met away from the raft, and oddly enough we never arranged to swim out together. One or the other of us would always be out there waiting. Sometimes I wondered whether she had come from the beach at all. Then on the fourth day the weather changed. When I got to the beach it was crowded with holiday-makers. So was the stretch of water, now as calm as a mill-pond, between the beach and the raft. The raft itself was tilted at an alarming angle, but this time from the weight of bathers congregated on it, scrambling on and off, and shrieking with laughter. I glanced up at the sea wall above me, and fancied I detected a quick movement—but whether it was the girl or not I never found out. But at intervals over the years the memory of that raft, lost among waves like chunky grey paving-stones, of the touch of our hands, and of that rapt and tender circling of our eyes would come back to me like a healing draft.

I don't want anyone to run away with the idea that I'm extolling the virtues of a platonic relationship. I don't believe such a thing exists. There can be friendship between a man and woman without intimacy, it's true. I've had many women comrades in my life. But I would have considered it ludicrous—not to say insulting, to both of us—to have felt that the basis of our friendship wasn't also a sexual one, no matter how indirectly. Whenever a male and a female creature are together, there is a mutual awareness of sexual difference. That doesn't mean, of course, that it always has to be acted on. Some people seem to think that if one doesn't keep demonstrating it, it might somehow disappear, as if it were a commodity that had to be actively conserved. But that's nonsense, because sex is everywhere; it's a constant, like light or the air we breathe, and it runs through everything—art, science, politics, religion and, of course, love. Those who try to practise any of these without it are dangerous people indeed, the material out of which fanatics and dictators are made.

*   *   *

It must be getting on for the end of October. But this extraordinary Indian summer goes on. The sun is so hot that it's quite easy to imagine it's high summer. It burns rather than shines on to the wall, so that it seems to be breaking it up into its original components. Sometimes I get the fancy that I can see all the atoms dancing in front of me like so many agitated fleas.

It has made the wall a warm peach colour. There's the same colour on the cheek of that young nurse—the one who reminds me of Tanya. There's the same texture on her cheek too.

This morning she took my pulse. I suppose she's done it dozens of times before, but for some reason this was the first time I really noticed it. I took a rueful look at the stringy wrist sticking out of the arm of my pyjama jacket: it looked like an electric cable that's been stripped of its covering.

At first she had some difficulty in finding a pulse at all. I could feel her fingers digging through all that string. Then I felt a flutter, like that of a dying butterfly in a jam-jar. Our eyes met: the expression in hers wasn't either neutral or patronising, but somehow inquiring. After a while I could feel her own blood throbbing at the tips of her soft, warm fingers. Then both our pulses settled down to a steady, rhythmic throb, mine gaining strength from hers, until pulse answered to pulse. I found it healing and peaceful, like the warm, crumbling light on the wall. When she took her fingers away, she gave me a very odd look. I thought I read in it a kind of respect. I think I must be getting better.

*   *   *

Several weeks have passed. Now when the nurse is about— tidying up the room, making the bed and that kind of thing —I talk about practically everything that comes into my head. It has been years since that happened. At my age nearly everybody you were once intimate with is dead, and so you get into the habit of letting your thoughts wander about inside your head like an army of ants that has lost its leader. It's a great comfort to be able to let them out, even if it does mean that I have to start marshalling them into some kind of order again: that alone had taken ten years off my age. But what is really wonderful is that she listens to whatever comes out without the least sign of surprise or uneasiness. She doesn't seem to mind that my ideas come at her from all sorts of unexpected angles. She brings to each one of them the same calm, serious attention . . .

I don't know where this particular thought came from, but I suddenly found myself asking her if she took the pill.

" No," she said. " Not any more."

Usually her face is rather pale, with a calm, tranquil look, but now blood rushed into it and I found myself marvelling at the sheer efficiency of the natural mechanism: no man-made circuit could have achieved such fantastic speed. I marvelled, too, at the smooth, even tinting of her skin.

" I thought you all did," I said. " Doesn't it give you free-dom, equality, that sort of thing?"

" It used to . . . It doesn't any more—not for me, anyway."

She bustled round the room, banging the doors of my wardrobe and locker, thumping at the pillows. But gradually her face went quiet again and I thought she wasn't going to say any more. Then when she had already reached the door, she paused, and turned back to my bed. She looked straight into my face with a wide-eyed, almost severe look. It re-minded me so much of one of Tanya's expressions that my heart turned over—and, truly, the idiom is right: I could feel it make a slow, dipping movement, like performing a somersault in water.

" It *was* wonderful at first," she said, " An end to all that messiness and anxiety—you could make your own choices . . ."

" But in the end you didn't like it?"

" I liked the pill itself all right—it didn't give me any of those side-effects they talk about, or anything like that . . ."

" Then what was the matter?"

31

Her face flushed again. Her eyes flashed.

" The *men!*" she cried. " *That's* what!"

" Why, didn't they like it?"

She glared at me angrily. I gave her a shifty look back. I felt embarrassed as if I ought to apologise for the whole of my sex.

" I don't understand," I said (but I did; and my heart ached for her).

" They took it for granted," she said, "and so after a time they took *me* for granted!"

" How do you mean?" I prompted her in a dull, mechanical voice.

" I went out with a man a couple of weeks ago. We went to bed together. Then all of a sudden I remembered that I'd forgotten to take the pill (perhaps I didn't really want to remember) . I told him—you know, as nicely as I could . . ."

" And what did he say?"

" He looked at me—a sort of pitying look, as if I was half-witted or something. Then he went on . . . doing things . . . exactly as if I hadn't spoken. ' But we can't." I said, stopping him, ' not like this.' ' My dear girl,' he said—no, really, ' My dear girl,' in that bloody superior way they have—' If you can't be bothered to take the normal precautions, you can't expect *me* to be concerned!' ' Now wait a minute,' I said, ' You *are* concerned. You are lying in bed, with me—hadn't you noticed?' ' What *are* you talking about?' he said. ' Us!' I told him, ' and what we're doing. You've heard about the birds and the beasts and the flowers, haven't you? We might make ourselves a baby.' ' What's that to do with me?' the son of a bitch said, ' It's up to you now. It's not my responsibility any longer! ' "

She started to laugh, but her voice trembled. " Not *his* responsibility! " she cried. " Don't you see? I might just as well not have been there at all! Not me, the whole me . . . The pill! It *ought* to have given us freedom, like you said, but it's made us worse slaves! Now men don't have anything at all to worry about—and by God they don't! They just expect you to be available, like a packet of cigarettes in a slot machine! "

She gave a sob. She cut it off quickly and looked very angry with herself . . . but again it reminded me of Tanya and the way she used to cry when I had really hurt her. A hopeless, mourning kind of cry like that of a child whose

32

trust has been horribly betrayed. My heart tumbled over again, and before I had realised what I was doing I had held out my old stringy arms to the nurse . . . She hesitated for a moment and then she became very brisk and bright again. She plumped up the pillows as if they were punch-bags, and tucked my arms under the sheets so tightly that I felt like a mummy fresh from the embalmer's. But she gave me a friendly look, wrinkling up her nose and smiling, before she whisked across the room and out through the door.

But you see what I mean—there is something badly wrong somewhere.

My mind wanders, it circles like ripples on a pond . . . I was talking about a laying on of hands . . . Yes, touch, yes the shared orgasm that scoops out the most secret corners of one's being . . . yes, those moments of perfect union with Tanya. I was thinking that they can sustain you through months, or even years of denial . . .

There were such periods during Tanya's long illness. Griffiths came to visit us during one of them, I remember. He had become even more parsonical with the years. He had lost the sleek black hair of his youth and had a sleek scalp instead. His stomach bulged so neatly that I always imagined that if it were exposed it would look just like a larger replica of the scalp. His voice had developed an extraordinary boom. It vibrated as if the rotund bulk, and even the rotund limbs, were hollow, a continuous echo chamber of flesh and bone. The odd thing about it, though, was that under all the extravagant mannerisms and pomposities there was a real priest. It was this second self, indeed, that had brought him to see me at this particular juncture, and I could even hear it breathing behind the far from elevated conversation that followed.

" We manly men," he began, " it is hard for us, is it not?" I stared at him, uncomprehending.

" Oh don't think, my dear fellah, that I don't understand . . . or that my cloth makes it any easier for me! "

" What *are* you talking about?" He ignored my question.

" The young girls I come into contact with, in the course of my professional duties," he went on, " so trusting, so dewy-eyed, asking my advice on all manner of problems . . . It's hard, hard . . . After all, I, too, am only a man . . ."

" You mean you're still having trouble keeping your busy paws to yourself?"

" My dear fellah! " He raised the objects in question in a gesture half protest, half benediction, then stared at them thoughtfully. He wasn't really offended. There was a gleam of humour in his eyes, combined with a rueful and quite affectionate acknowledgment that I had known him for a long time.

" But *they* change, don't they?" he asked.

" Who do?"

" Why, our lady-wives, God bless 'em! "

" They get older, naturally. So do we."

" Ah, but alas! A man's desires remain ever young! . . ." He folded his hands firmly over his paunch. " I was merely about to observe that it's difficult to feel the same about them . . . in *that* way . . . as we did in the days of their pristine freshness . . . I'm not talking of spiritual . . . ah . . . affinity . . ."

" I should hope not! "

" But honestly," with a gush of confidence, "Come now, man to man, don't you find it difficult, in the circumstances, to feel the same about Tanya?"

" Not in the least."

He pursed his lips disbelievingly. He dropped his eyes, and I saw that they were focused, with a thoughtful expression, on the region of my crotch. I grinned at him. He was wondering whether I was past it!

" What I mean—no offence meant, and Tanya is the dearest, sweetest creature, but she's been ill for a long time . . . I ask myself the same question about my dear Amy—a saint, a positive saint. But, well, not to put too fine a point on it, my dear fellah—what can we see in them now? D'you know—in *that* way?"

"I remember," I said, grinning at him again. " I remember—here! " and I laid my hand on my crotch.

" Really! " Griffiths said. " Really! " His eyes nearly popped out of his head, but then he too grinned, and in that very instant a score of sensations I had shared with Tanya came back to me, each of them separate and distinct. It was astonishing, this uniqueness and I realised that hundreds more such encapsulated sensations were stored away in that queer time-space continuum we call memory, and that each of them, when called upon, would emit its own pure bell-note. Above all, I realised that all these memories were as much a nourishment as the honey in the cells of a honey-

34

comb. I was feeding on them during a long period of drought. I knew, too, that Tanya was drawing upon her own store. They would last us both as long as was necessary. We were husbanding our sensual resources. The real sense of that word husbanding suddenly came home to me so forcibly that I blurted out to Griffiths:

" You see, I really *am* her husband! "

He didn't know what to say. He made a vague movement with his hand, as if he were knocking down a whole series of incipient erections.

" Ah, um," he boomed at last, " Marriages are made in heaven, my dear chap, ah um . . ."

For some reason this made me angry. " And you," I shouted, " can fuck off! "

The nicest part of him came out then. He grinned all over his face, and gave me a good-natured slap on the shoulder with his podgy hand.

*   *   *

With the odd ideas I've been trying to describe, it's not surprising, I suppose, that I got myself into all sorts of scrapes, often of a peculiarly romantic silliness, when I was a young man. I had all sorts of day-dreams. The most common of them was that ancient one of rescuing a damsel in distress from a dungeon, or a dragon, or a brothel. The only thing is that with me day-dreams tended to become actuality. One of them turned out to be the central reality of my life.

It happened just after I'd made my first determined pass at Trudy. There was some sort of cultural reception at the British Consulate in Curitiba, though in fact it wasn't much more than a glorified bun-fight, with the guests brawling to get at the best cakes and biscuits. I remember there were little jars scattered about filled with cigarettes, and the men were filling their cases from them, while the more rapacious of the wives were blatantly emptying the contents into their handbags. A cultural attaché who had been sent down from Rio for the affair—a tall, thin man with a sallow complexion and an Assyrian beard who combined an utterly un-English appearance, a positive distaste for cultural matters of any kind, and a barely concealed dislike of foreigners, hovered in the background with a pained expression on his face. The talk he was supposed to be giving was cancelled when it was discovered he didn't speak a word of Portuguese.

Trudy had retreated to her office, where she was sitting

35

behind her typewriter, with a cup of tea and a plate of cakes beside her. She was wearing a long skirt of brick-red colour, and a particularly pretty blouse tied at the neck with a bow.

I had gone into the office to look up something in *Who's Who*, but as I turned over the pages I couldn't keep my eyes off the curve of Trudy's breasts. It's another of the mysteries I've often pondered—how that curve can create countless quite different effects—in fact I doubt if any one outline is exactly the same as another. And yet it *is* only a line, a line, moreover, that is strictly limited in the sense that all breasts are, after all, more or less breast-shaped. It must be the rapt contemplation of this linear mystery that has turned many an infant at the breast into an aspiring Picasso.

When I had finished looking up my reference, I put the book back on its shelf, walked straight over to Trudy and, as unthinking as a sleep-walker, cupped my hands over her breasts. She didn't look surprised, or pleased, or anything in particular, but she made an odd kind of nudging movement, pouting her lips at the same time as she twisted at the hips and pushed out her breasts in a gesture of dismissal. I removed my hands at once and she flashed me a conventional though friendly smile. I was slightly discomfited, but my eyes was still so enraptured by those curves that I didn't stop to think about it. The strange thing is that it is only now that I can feel what it was that was bothering me. Although that shrugging movement had been quite good-tempered there was something disembodied about it. The breasts had been firm and springy, but there had been something about them that just didn't suggest the texture of flesh . . . How strange that this should come back to me now, a message that got blocked somewhere along the nerves for some reason so that it has only now reached my brain. If it had done its travelling quicker I might have saved myself a great deal of trouble. That's one of the worst things about the so-called wisdom that comes with age: you don't just realise your past mistakes with the brain, you have to *feel* them all over again . . .

The next day I had to go inland to a place called Sao José de something or other—ridiculous that I can't remember the exact name because it's now a city as big as, say, Sheffield or Detroit as far as population's concerned. From what I know of these South American cities, though, I don't suppose it looks so very different; the same mixture of occasional splendour and pervasive squalor, but on a far larger scale. Even when I was there there were already half a dozen skyscrapers. They looked tremendously imposing from a distance or on picture-postcards, but when you got close there were all kinds of scags and sags in the fabric, and inside, among the splendid chandeliers and ultra-modernistic fittings, furniture, and statuary, there were crumbling, scrofulous patches. As likely as not, too, half of the skyscrapers won't be finished: the lifts will stop at the sixth floor and the two or three stories above that will be slowly mouldering away, while the flat roof will be a jumble of abandoned concrete blocks, bags of cement, wheelbarrows and piles of sand.

One thing I'm certain of is that there will be redness everywhere, a choking red dust for most of the year, a pervasive red paste in the rainy season. Sao José is right in the middle of a vast area of the *terra roxa*, the rich red earth which grows the best coffee in the world. You just can't get away from the redness. When you look closely at the gleaming white skyscrapers, for example, you see that in reality they are a pinkish colour. There are red smears or streaks on the inside walls, and on the sheets and in the baths and wash-basins. When the water comes out of the shiny chromium taps, it, too, has a reddish tinge. There's red inside your ears and caked round the hairs of your nostrils. When you take your shirt off there's a red band round the inside of the collar, and after you've left the area it takes weeks for your skin and your underclothes to recover their natural colour.

Sometimes I used to have the feeling that the earth was bleeding. It wouldn't be surprising. Day after day and week after week hundreds and thousands of beautiful trees were being laid low by the axe or gouged out of the red earth by bulldozers or burned down as they stood, to make way for interminable rows, league upon league of them, of coffee-bushes so neat and compact that from a distance they looked like green bosses set in a gigantic solitaire board. And that, too, will still be going on.

Above all, I'm sure that in spite of all the skyscrapers Sao José is still fundamentally a shanty-town. When I was there the shacks—of wood, or corrugated iron, or hammered-out petrol cans, or merely cardboard and sacking—outnumbered

37

the stone buildings by about a hundred to one, though you weren't immediately aware of it because they were tucked away in all sorts of corners and crevices.

It was raining cats and dogs on that evening, long ago, when an acquaintance of mine named Joaquim took me down a sea of churned-up mud that had had the temerity to call itself Avenida da Liberdade after its imposing namesake in Lisbon.

Joaquim had been a bank clerk in Curitiba, but had come to Sao José about a year before determined to make his fortune by selling second-hand trucks, which were then almost literally worth their weight in gold. He was already well on his way to doing so. He had a clever, oval Italian face (he was a third-generation descendant of Italian immigrants) and a quiet, gentle manner that belied his shrewd business sense. We had been friends in Curitiba and had corresponded since he left. He had often expressed the wish in his letters to show me the delights of the Avenida da Liberdade.

The place he took me to was tucked away at the end of a winding alley, opening off the main road. It was a long, one-storied wooden building, something like an outsize English parish hall, except for the rows of multi-coloured lights outside which gleamed on the surrounding mud so that it looked like the floor of a slaughter-house, and for the legend " Sampaio's Bar " above the doorway.

The main part of the building consisted of a long, low-ceilinged room, lit by naked electric light-bulbs, with benches along the walls, and a number of tables and chairs ranged at the far end. There was a bar and behind it an evil-smelling kitchen. A brass band, of incredibly dented instruments, blared away from a small dais in the centre of the room. A number of couples were dancing energetically but quite decorously. Waiters in dirty white aprons, balancing trays of food or drinks, threaded their way through the dancers with amazing dexterity. So many cheroots were being smoked that the air was a colonnade of thick blue coils. Everybody talked and laughed and swore at the tops of their voices and the din was indescribable.

At first sight it all seemed jolly but quite respectable. Indeed I remember feeling worried about the state of my trousers, which were caked with red mud practically to the knees, and which, as the mud dried, stuck out as if they were made of

38

canvas. But I soon saw that most of the other men were in much the same condition. The majority of them were coffee planters or prospectors of one sort or another, some of them dressed in bush-shirts, breeches and leather leggings, others in expensive linen suits. All of them had hard-bittten expressions, bright, acquisitive eyes, and complexions brick-red from sun and dust. They spent money like water. They had to, for everything was a fantastic price. I noticed that Joaquim paid the equivalent of three English pounds (which was a great deal in those days) for a bottle of Scotch whisky. When I asked for *cachaça*, the rum of Brazil, cheap and nasty by itself, but excellent with lemon and coarse white sugar, the waiter looked at me with a pained expression and explained that it was the drink of a *caboclo*: real gentlemen drank whisky. He agreed to send out for a bottle, however, from one of the lower dives, though I had to pay a fearful price for it.

There were a number of unaccompanied girls in the room. There weren't many of them, and they weren't making themselves at all conspicuous. They were sitting demurely, sometimes singly, sometimes in pairs, and at widely spaced intervals, on the wooden benches along the walls. They were all young and pretty, and dressed, not at all showily or provocatively, in good-looking dance frocks. To begin with, indeed, I thought they must be there simply for decoration—or even, perhaps, that they might be relatives of the customers, segregated along the sides of the walls while their menfolk got down to the serious business of drinking.

After a while, I began to notice that every now and then a man would beckon to one of the girls, and she would immediately get up and very quietly join him at his table. It was all done with the utmost discretion. The gesture might be no more than the raising of a forefinger or even of an eyebrow, but even I, who was very thick-headed about such things, realised that I was not witnessing a family reunion. As soon as the girl was seated the man would pour out a glass of whisky and push it across to her. It was ridiculous, but the girls were so young and fresh-looking that I felt I wanted to go over to them and read them a lecture on the evils of strong drink. Sometimes the man would also order a couple of platefuls of stewed chicken or *feijado*, and the two of them would eat and chat in a leisurely manner for several hours at a time.

But eventually they would get up and, still discreetly and un-obtrusively, join the eddies of dancers round the brass band, whose members were by now scarlet in the face and dripping with sweat—it was very hot and they were dressed in full, if extremely bedraggled, uniforms with tight, high collars.

I watched one couple get up from a table quite close to ours—a large, ginger-haired man in a grey alpaca suit and a gaudy cummerbund, and a tiny, plump, black-haired Japanese girl. They stood at the edge of the dance-floor and negligently placed their hands on each other's shoulders: the girl had to stand on tip-toe in order to do so. Then they shuffled off, and a little later I saw them come round again. For some reason I found myself waiting for them to reappear. The minutes ticked by. I thought that perhaps they were glued cheek to cheek at some spot on the other side of the band, and I stood up to look. There was no sign of them.

"Did you fancy her yourself?" Joaquim asked, puzzled by my antics.

"No, it's just that they seem to have disappeared."

Joaquim laughed, and stood up beside me. "Watch," he said, "by that curtain over there."

I could just pick out a curtained doorway at the far end of the room and to the left of the band. Tobacco smoke shrouded it so efficiently that it might have been laid there for the purpose. A moment later I saw a couple of dancers approach it. Slowly, and with no appearance of haste, they edged their way across the floor. Then they slipped silently away from the dancers and the scurrying waiters and dis-appeared through the curtain. Its trembling had barely subsided before another couple came through from the other side, hand in hand, to vanish almost at once into the swirls of blue smoke.

"But surely you realised?" Joaquim said, as we returned to our table. I shook my head. It may seem hard to credit, but it was the first time I had been in a honky-tonk—unless I had done so without realising it, which might well have happened. I was still very simple-minded about brothels. I knew in my bones that they ought not to exist, that there was more than enough love and tenderness in the world, if only it could be freed from all the shackles, to make them superfluous. I knew that they were a symptom of the slavery of men and women alike to values that had nothing at all to do with the old gods I worshipped.

Anyway, I now began to watch the discreet little eddies of activity around me with more attention. I noticed that most of the couples who had disappeared behind the curtain spent the rest of the evening together. On the rare occasions when they did part, the girl would quietly return to her seat along the wall, but she would refuse to be engaged again until a decent interval had elapsed, and usually not until her previous client had himself left the building.

" It is the custom," Joaquim explained, with a certain pride and a touch of irritation at my obtuseness. " Quite often you will see the same pair together for a whole week or more. It can be arranged, though it costs a great deal of money. Sometimes the girl goes away with the man for good—a lot of girls come here to look for lovers, or even husbands." He sighed, then added, " But that is very expensive indeed . . ."

I didn't pay much attention to him, because I was following the direction of his gaze, which was focused, with a wistful expression, on a blonde girl who had just seated herself on the bench nearly opposite our table. She must have felt his eyes upon her, for she glanced up quickly, smiled, and gathering up her handbag, threaded her way through the scurrying waiters to our table.

As she put down her bag, Joaquim placed his hand over hers. She smiled at him, and, without moving her hand, sat down beside him. They gazed into each other's eyes for some time before Joaquim introduced us. Her name was Lotte, and she came from one of the German enclaves. She spoke a few sentences in German for me, proud of her command of the language—as a matter of fact her German was better than her Portuguese. Joaquim gazed at her proudly and fondly. " Now you see," he said to me in English, " why I must work so hard to become rich . . ."

Again I didn't pay much attention. I had been dimly aware for several minutes of another girl, also sitting nearly opposite our table. Surely there was something familiar about her?

When I looked across again, she was sitting bolt upright and staring straight at me with large brilliant eyes. I stared back—and suddenly I recognised her. I was so startled that I pushed my chair back and stood up. As I did so I noticed out

41

of the corner of my eye that one of the waiters, a big man with a lugubrious expression that was heightened by a very bushy walrus moustache, looked at me sharply. In a vague sort of way the idea did cross my mind that to draw attention to myself in this way was to break the code of discretion, though it never occurred to me that it might also be dangerous.

By now the girl had reached our table. We stood beside it for several moments carefully examining each other. There was no doubt about it, it was the girl whose betrothal party I had attended in the village of the Russian Old Believers. I could hardly believe my eyes. I went on staring at her until, with an uneasy glance over her shoulder, she seated herself and pulled at my arm to make me follow suit. I offered her a drink from my bottle of *cachaça,* but she grimaced and shook her head. Neither of us spoke. We just sat there, very still, gravely studying each other's faces. Joaquim and his girl, after a brief glance at us, had resumed their intimate whispering.

I was surprised now that I hadn't recognised her earlier. It was partly the difference in clothing. The dark blue dress she was wearing was very simple, ankle-length, and sleeveless, square-cut round the neck and with no other decoration beyond a flower pushed through the top button hole. But it was much more revealing than all those Cossack-type clothes in which she had been bundled up when I last saw her. Although her arms and shoulders were beautifully rounded (and so smooth and unblemished that they took my breath away), and the flesh above the square neck of her dress had that wonderful sheen and ripple which convey the impression that it is a continuation of the breasts themselves, she didn't appear anything like as plump. I felt quite shocked when, glancing downwards, I caught a glimpse of a bare ankle and a gracefully arched foot, very smooth and white, as if she had only that moment peeled off the thick woollen stockings of her Cossack garb. Both ankle and foot looked naked and vulnerable; I drew my own feet under my chair for fear I might accidently tread on hers. It was just as strange to see her head freed of its shawl-like scarf. It was like looking at a freshly-modelled head, unveiled for the first time in a sculptor's studio. Her hair wasn't as dark as I had thought it. It couldn't be called either black or brown. It was more like the deeper colour on a tortoise shell, and it had the same warm glow.

42

But she gave the same impression of fluidity in her movements, especially round the hips, so that I again had the feeling that the upper part of her body was poised, floating upon them. Her grey eyes had the same grave, questioning look. The lips were still slightly parted, as if in surprise. The pucker of secret amusement at the corners of her mouth had gone; it was replaced by something both sad and stern. But the combination of innocence and awareness that had so struck me in the Old Believers' hut was still there. What was most noticeable, though, was an air about her, in spite of evident signs of strain, of a kind of aloofness, even serenity, as if she really had no connection at all with her present circumstances. She was like a princess in a fairy tale who has been placed under an evil spell that surrounded her with ugly shapes which can hurt but neither alter nor destroy. Most important of all, she still made me feel, in some distant recess of my being as yet inaccessible to my waking self, just as she had in the Old Believers' village, that she belonged to some ancient mystery in which I too was a partaker.

I didn't doubt for a moment that she was in this place through some accident not of her own making. I asked her what had happened. It was very simple. Her Russian fiancé had for some time been chafing under the rules and regulations of the Old Believers' community. Not long after the betrothal party I had attended he had persuaded her to accompany him to Curitiba. There they would get married, he told her, " in a proper church "; he had a job waiting; he wanted to become " a real Brazilian ".

" I didn't want to go with him," (she was speaking fluent Portuguese now) " but I did want to leave the colony. The old religion doesn't mean as much to the younger ones . . ."

She hesitated and looked carefully around her. The expression on her face wasn't exactly fear: the underlying serenity wasn't ruffled: it was, rather, a surprised realisation that such a thing as danger existed and must be taken into account— though I could not understand this at the time.

" I was very ignorant," she went on, " I have been protected, cut off from the world . . . I feel I have to travel many new roads . . ."

Her expression darkened. " But this ought not to be one of them."

43

" But how?" I cried. " How did *this* happen?"

" It would be better," she said, " if we didn't seem to be talking so seriously . . ."

" We can talk as we damn well please! " I was still at the age when one imagines that indignation and belligerency are a magic wand that will wave opposition out of existence.

" Perhaps we could dance?" she said gently, looking straight into my eyes.

" Of course."

As we got up I noticed that the waiter with the walrus moustache was collecting glasses from the next table.

We joined the slowly drifting stream of dancers. She was incredibly light in my arms. I held her with a kind of awe. When my hand touched her naked shoulder I felt awkward and inadequate, as if I ought to have been able to make my fingers transmit some special degree of solicitude and respect. At the same time there was another sensation, which I couldn't define; something momentous which drifted away from me. It wasn't until many years later that I realised it was a signal from the heart of my being which I of all people, professing my kind of secret faith, ought to have recognised.

Soon we were half-hidden in the haze of tobacco smoke, our voices drowned by the blaring of the band.

" Tell me, then—what happened?"

" There was no job in Curitiba."

" Did he marry you?"

" No. There was no money. He brought me here."

" Here? This place?"

" No, to Sao José—at first . . ."

" You mean . . .?"

" There was no work here, either . . . He only knows how to grow rice and sing in our church . . ."

" So then he *did* bring you here?" She flushed.

" Yes. I didn't know what it was . . . He said I could make some money singing Russian songs . . . I brought my balalaika with me . . ."

" Is he still here? In Sao José?"

" I don't know. He left me sitting at a table. He said he had to see the manager, about the singing . . . I haven't seen him since."

" You've got to get away! "

44

" Oh yes, of course. I've tried, several times. They wouldn't let me go."

" How can they *not* let you go? They don't have slaves any more—even in Sao José!"

" The clothes I'm wearing . . . they're very pretty . . . There are other dresses, too . . ."

" Of course, they aren't yours . . . They provided them?" She nodded.

" Well then, I'll pay for them! Then they'll let you go!"

For the first time the inner serenity seemed to falter. She hesitated and swallowed, as if her throat was paining her.

" There was . . . other money as well," she said. Her voice trembled.

" He sold you!"

She said nothing. At that moment we came opposite the doorway with the curtain. Her body gave a sudden spasm. We danced slowly past the doorway and round to the other side of the band. When we drew level with our table we broke away from the dancers and returned to our seats. Joaquim and his German girl looked at us curiously. There was no sign of the waiter with the walrus moustache.

I didn't go into any details with Joaquim. I simply told him that I wanted to take the Russian girl away with me, and that I was going to arrange it then and there with the manager. I asked him to keep an eye on her while I was gone. He jumped to his feet and laid a hand on my arm.

" No, no!" he said. " You can't—not like that! There have to be preliminaries . . . preparations . . ."

" Nonsense!"

The German girl gave me a scared look, and snatching up her handbag scurried off and made herself as inconspicuous as she could among a group of girls on the other side of the room. Joaquim was still saying something as I shook his hand off my arm and strode down the room, past the band and the bar, and out into the little vestibule beyond. On our way in I had noticed a door marked " Private ". I knocked, and without waiting for a reply, pushed it open.

I found myself in a small room with pale lime-green walls, spattered with reddish-brown smears from squashed mosquitoes. The only decoration was a trade calendar with a picture of some sort of squat, but quite unidentifiable machine: all the leaves

45

had been torn off, and the calendar was in any case three years out of date.

The only furniture in the room was a rickety, office-type desk, so kicked and scuffed that most of the stain and polish had long since been removed. On the desk was an equally rickety electric fan of archaic design, which made as much clatter as a water-wheel. The turning mechanism wasn't working properly, so that it directed a blast of hot, sticky air, smelling of sewage first in one direction and then, suddenly and without warning, in another. At the moment it was playing on the desk, ruffling the crisp black hair of the man who was seated behind it.

He was dark complexioned, broad and stocky. He was wearing a short-sleeved khaki bush-shirt, the pockets bulging with fountain pens, pencils, half-smoked cigars, a very dirty comb, and a fat, greasy wallet. His forearms were closely covered with black hairs of such astonishing length that they waved about like fringes in the blast from the electric fan. There were so many rings on his fingers that it looked as if he were wearing knuckle-dusters.

He didn't seem in the least surprised to see me. He sat, slightly sideways, picking his teeth with the pointed end of a very large gaucho knife. I was wondering how he managed to do this and to smile at the same time, when I realised that his lower jaw protruded, disclosing a row of misshapen but very white teeth, like the tubers in potatoes, or a row of small tusks; the illusion of a continuous grin was caused by the fact that his mouth was stretched sideways by his monstrous tooth-pick. When he removed it, the little tusks still showed, but it was clear that he was not in the least amused.

"Well?" he said, attacking one of his back teeth with the knife, and opening his mouth wider than ever in order to avoid cutting his lips. He was still sitting sideways, and he did not look at me.

"There's a girl here," I said. "She wants to leave. I am going to take her away."

"Why? Isn't she happy?" He spoke in a deep, guttural voice, but so softly that I had difficulty in hearing him above the noise of the electric fan. I moved closer to the desk. The hand holding the knife went still for a moment.

"No, she's not happy," I said. "It was an accident, a

46

mistake. It's not her kind of life. She doesn't want it."

"Which girl?"

"She's a Russian girl. She comes from . . ."

"Yes, I know the one you mean." He didn't seem in the least put out.

"I will pay what is necessary, of course," I blundered on.

"Most of the girls are happy here," he said.

"How much?" I began to take out my wallet. He didn't move, but one eye followed my movements.

"Yes, most of the girls are happy here, most of the time," he went on. "Why shouldn't they be? We give them good clothes, good food, good beds to sleep on. Some of them even get husbands . . ."

He removed the knife and examined a particle of food skewered on the end of it, screwing up his eyes as if he were a jeweller inspecting a gem.

"We give them good soap to wash with," he added as an afterthought.

"Then you will let her go?" I held the wallet at the ready.

"You know our laws." Then, withdrawing the knife and sitting upright, though still sideways and without looking at me:

"Senhor, this is a free and civilised country. Every man is free to do as he pleases . . ." This was uttered in tones of the most patriotic piety. If I had been wearing a hat I would have felt obliged to doff it. Then he gave a wolfish grin— "I'm not so sure about the women though!" and then, like a bullet from a gun: "How much?"

I was being paid in cash at this time and had just received a month's salary. It was at English rates, so that even allowing for the Gold Rush prices prevailing in these frontier towns there ought to have been enough to pay several times over for whatever small wardrobe they had bought the Russian girl. In addition I had some English five pound notes and several travellers' cheques in the inside compartment of the wallet—which in fact represented practically all the liquid assets I had. So, thinking myself very clever, I mentioned a sum which came to about half the contents of the wallet.

He smiled. It was a curious, slow-motion performance, because of the unusual configuration of his jaws, which pulled his lips back, then left them where they were for several seconds after the smile was really over. His sharp little teeth, glistening with saliva, looked whiter than ever. He said nothing, but resting his left elbow on the desk tilted the palm of his hand in my direction as if it were a kind of offertory plate. Again there was not the slightest indication that he was looking at me, but when I took the greater part of the notes out of my wallet and made to pass them over, his fingers snapped to, then opened several times, in an impatient, admonitory gesture. I hesitated for a moment, then very reluctantly placed the wallet on the outstretched palm. It did not move for a second or two, as if calculating the weight, then, with startling rapidity, the fingers closed over it, his whole body swung round and he began, very efficiently and dexterously, to extract the contents of the wallet.

My heart sank as I watched all the notes pulled out, folded and stuffed into one of the bulging pockets of his bush-shirt. I was busy working out what I was going to live on during the next month. The inner compartment of the wallet, however, was rather cunningly concealed under a false flap, and hoping that he wouldn't investigate further I held out my hand.

He shook his head. "Senhor," he said, very softly, "there is also the question of the money we had to pay for this girl. It was a very greedy young man she had, I regret to say." As he spoke he was extracting the English notes and travellers' cheques from the inside of the wallet. He laid them on the desk in front of him and began to examine them.

With some difficulty I controlled the impulse to snatch the wallet and the money back, at least aware that that much discretion was required.

"What are these?" he said, indicating the travellers' cheques —a form of currency then little known, and probably not at all in Sao José. I explained. He nodded, and began to stuff the travellers' cheques, together with the five-pound notes, into another of his pockets.

"They will be no use to you," I told him.

"Why?"

"I have to sign them."

"Then you will please do so." I shook my head. "No," I told him, "I will take the girl—and I will sign them for you tomorrow."

"You will please sign them now," he said in a wooden voice.

48

"Ah, but you see," I said, congratulating myself on my cunning, "That will be no use to you at all. The cheques have to be signed at the bank, in the presence of the cashier." He sat very still, looking down at them, for several minutes.

"You can come with me to the bank tomorrow morning," I prompted him.

"What hotel are you staying at?" he said, very suddenly.

"The Boa Vista."

"May I see your passport, senhor?"

I extracted it from my hip pocket and laid it on the desk in front of him. The electric fan suddenly changed direction, ruffling the pages. He picked up the passport and studied it carefully. Then he put it back on the desk. "I see," he said, quite mildly.

He picked up my wallet, turned it upside down, gave it a last shake, and handed it back to me. I took it ruefully; it felt as limp as an old slipper.

He thought for a moment, then pushed the five-pound notes into one of his pockets. He was about to do the same with the travellers' cheques when my temper suddenly got the better of me, and leaning forward I snatched them up, together with my passport, and put them in my own pocket.

"You can come to my hotel tomorrow," I said. "We will go to the bank together."

He shrugged his shoulders, and picked up the gaucho knife again. I waited for a few seconds, but as he seemed completely absorbed in his dental explorations, I turned on my heel and walked out.

When I got back to the main room I found that it had filled up since I left. The tobacco smoke whirled and billowed as if a battery of cannon had just fired a salute. I pushed my way through the crowds and reached the table where I had been sitting. Four complete strangers were occupying it. I looked frantically round the room, but there was no sign of either Joaquim or the Russian girl. Indeed there seemed not to be a familiar face in sight. More than that, everybody looked not just different but *very* different: different clothes, colours, complexions: even the smoke seemed to have changed to a different shade of blue. There was something else that had changed too: the babble of voices seemed to be louder and with quite different tonalities. I began to get a very weird feeling,

49

as if I had strayed into an entirely new time-space spiral.

I shook myself. I was tired and overwrought, I told myself: I was letting my imagination run away with me. In a place like this there was a steady flow in and out: by some freak there had been no overlap of customers this time, that was all. As for the different sound, it was simply that the band was taking a break.

I turned back to the table and began questioning the occupants. The two men were drunk and quite incapable of understanding what I was saying; the girls giggled and shrugged their shoulders; either they, too, were tipsy or I wasn't expressing myself clearly—my Portuguese tended to deteriorate when I was excited or perhaps they chose not to understand me.

I made my way back along the room and into the vestibule. There was no one about. I tried the door of the office I had left only some five minutes before, but it was locked. There was a stench of urine in the air. I wondered where it was coming from, then noticed a short passage-way to the right of the office; a well, rather, for I had only to take a couple of steps into it to find myself confronted by a rough swing-door with the words HOMENS scrawled on it. At that moment the doors opened and one of the members of the band emerged, doing up his flies. I caught him by the collar of his tunic and pushed him against the wall. He was a small, skinny man. He weighed so little, in fact, that without realising it I had lifted him several inches off the ground.

For a moment I thought he was going to have a heart attack. His eyes bulged like grapes dropped into boiling water. His skin turned the colour of old pewter. Then, as nothing worse happened to him, his eyes sank back into their sockets, his complexion resumed its normal muddy-yellow colour, and he gave me an ingratiating smile. He had a thin black moustache on his upper lip: his breath and sweat alike smelt strongly of chillies and black beans.

"Listen," I growled at him, "There was a girl in there, a Russian girl—very pretty . . ."

He gave a high-pitched giggle. "A lot of pretty girls, eh senhor?"

I gave him a little shake. "Listen, this girl—she was wearing a dark blue dress, with a flower in it."

He gave another frightened giggle. "A lot of pretty girls, eh

50

senhor?" he repeated inanely, and then, desperately, as my grip tightened: " All pretty—all the same . . ."

" No they're not," I said, giving him another shake. " This one was a Russian girl—I told you just now, she was wearing a dark blue dress . . ."

" How can I possibly remember, senhor?" he wailed.

" You've *got* to remember!" I held him harder against the wall. " Now listen carefully. I left the table—it was on the side of the room facing you. A friend of mine stayed with the girl . . ."

" So many people!" he wailed again. " I can't remember, senhor!"

" Start remembering, *now!*" I said, and pushed him so hard against the wall that he was splayed there like a squashed mosquito. He gave a long, hopeless sigh, as if he expected the next moment to be his last.

" The man she was with," I said, " This friend of mine—he had a silk handkerchief in the breast pocket of his coat— bright yellow . . ."

I saw his eyes flicker, and I knew he had remembered. But he went very still, almost as if he had stopped breathing.

" Well?" I said. His eyes turned aside. " I didn't notice," he muttered.

I suddenly panicked at the thought of all the time this was taking up, and as I pushed him against the wall again, shaking him at the same time, I must have exerted more strength than I realised, for a kind of shocked, startled look came into his eyes, and the word, " Yes!" came popping through his lips like a pip squeezed from an orange. I felt a pang of shame, and relaxed my grip.

" Well?"

" I saw this man," he said, talking very quickly now, in a hoarse whisper. " I saw you too, senhor, and the girl. After you'd gone they sat at the table for a few minutes. Then I saw Vicente go up to the table . . ."

" Vicente—who's that?"

" A waiter—well, really he's a sort of chucker-out—you know, senhor, there's sometimes trouble in a place like this . . ."

" A fellow with a big droopy moustache!"

" But yes, senhor!" he cried: he almost wept for joy at having pleased me at last.

51

" Go on! "

" Well, senhor, Vicente said something to the girl. She got up and looked at this friend of yours. Vicente took hold of her arm. She didn't want to go . . ."

" But Joaquim! What did he do?"

" Senhor! Senhor! I saw him speaking to Vicente, oh very urgently! Then when Vicente began dragging the girl away, he tried to stop him! He tried very hard!"

He gabbled this out at top speed, and in an indignant tone of voice, as if he and Joaquim were bosom friends and it was of the utmost importance to reassure me of the fact.

" And then?" I asked.

" Well, senhor," very ingratiatingly now. " I'm sorry to have to tell you that there were other waiters who . . . who . . ." He darted a frightened look at me to see how I was taking it. " Go on! " I gave him a shake, though only a little one.

" They . . . well, senhor, in a manner of speaking, they . . . well, they pushed him out . . ."

" And the girl? The girl?"

" Vicente took her away."

" Where?"

" I will tell you, senhor! I will tell you! They went through the curtain—you know . . . I don't know what happened after that. I swear it to you, senhor, I swear it by all the saints!" He infused so much terror and appeal into these words that when I let go of him he dropped or, rather, slid, down the wall and on to his feet, I patted him on his head. He gave me one more scared look, then scuttled back into the urinal.

I returned to the dance-hall and strode over to the curtain. One of the waiters saw me, put down his tray, and made a movement towards me. But by now I was in a state of blind rage, and after regarding me with a thoughtful look he let me pass.

I found myself in an annexe, also made of wood but not as solidly built as the main hall. The roof was thatched with dried *carnaúba* leaves, as big and coarse as those of tobacco; they straggled in places over the windows, as well as letting in chinks of light under the eaves: it had stopped raining, and there was a full moon, as well as stars as big as grapefruits. There was, indeed, a decidedly al fresco air about the place, almost as if it was a seaside holiday camp.

The ground plan consisted of several parallel corridors linked, as if by the rungs of a ladder, by shorter ones. The planks of the walls were untreated in any way. The tightly sealed windows of the outer corridors had evidently never been cleaned since they were inserted: a useful cross-section of the insect and vegetable life of the region over the past three or four years could have been scraped off the panes. The doors were also of unplaned and unpainted timber. They were set so close together that I felt as if I were in a cow byrne. The impression was heightened by the condition of the straw matting which had once covered the concrete floor but which had been scuffed by countless feet into a semblance of litter. The rustling noise it made under my feet chimed in with a background of sound, as continuous and, curiously enough, as soothing, as the swishing of the sea, built up of the whisperings, murmurings, moanings and creakings that came from behind the doors.

I tried the first of them. It was unlocked. The room, or, rather, cubicle beyond it was so small and plain that it served merely as a frame to the large, uncovered bed and the two naked figures upon it. There was a violent, bucking motion at the moment I flung open the door, merging a second later into an oddly static *chiaroscuro* effect: a broad swarthy back, with a head twisted to one side to regard me over its shoulder, the face bearded and brooding; while another face, small, pale and questioning, looked out from under its shaggy armpit.

For some reason I was very much aware of these peculiarly plastic effects as I rushed from cubicle to cubicle, almost as if I was leafing through the sketch-book of an artist specialising for the first time in studies of the nude. I was surrounded, it seemed, by a tumble of limbs, disposed now this way, now that, with now the bunched muscular lines of the male upper-most, and now the soft, muted curves of the female, while the hot, sticky hair of armpits and crotches disposed itself into infinite gradations of shading and shadowing.

At another and less elevated level of my mind, as in a kind of anti-masque, I found myself reflecting, as I threw open door after door to be confronted by buttocks, ranging, also in infinite gradations, from jet black to snow white, that I was being treated to a unique demonstration of Brazil's famous complexity of colour—a veritable album of racial diversity.

And so I ran along the corridors, as if I were in a dream,

throwing open one door after another, and just as in a dream or fairy-tale all the doors were unlocked save one, and that the last I came to. But the corridor was narrow enough for me to be able to set my back against the wall, raise my leg and direct a kick at the lock with all the weight of my body behind it. Indeed I kicked so hard that not only did the lock and the panel to which it was attached hurtle into the room beyond as if it had been projected from a cannon, but the whole door came off its hinges and lay tilted across the entrance.

There was a murmur of startled voices from the other rooms, as if a civil war had just broken out, or an earthquake. I had a fleeting glimpse of doors opening on either side of me and of startled faces (accompanied by other inquisitive segments of the human anatomy) peering round them, before I jumped over the shattered door and into the room beyond.

I had already seen, in the moment the door burst in, that the Russian girl was indeed there, seated on the edge of the bed and fully clothed. She had jumped to her feet, and now the impetus of my headlong rush was such that I nearly knocked her down, and had to put my arms round her to stop her falling backwards.

What I shall never forget—though it has taken all these years for the memory fully to unfold itself—is the complex mixture of expressions on her face, a mixture which makes nonsense of our apparent subjugation to chronology or circumstance. On the surface was the shock of my precipitate arrival, and behind it the anxiety of her situation. But lurking farther back, as if on an entirely different time-plane, there was a kind of affectionate, comradely amusement, as at the antics of some young animal, at the extravagantly and unwise violence of my actions—and behind that again, in the moment of my arms closing round her, that thoughtful, inward expression you see on a woman's face when she is speculating on a man's suitability, in the deepest sense, as a lover or husband.

I was, in fact, discomfited with humiliating ease. Holding the girl by the hand I marched down the corridor, while the exposed bits on either side popped back into their cubicles like cuckoos withdrawing into their clocks. The whirls of tobacco smoke revolved in the draught as we burst through the curtain, and swallowed us up. The band was playing again, though half-heartedly, and we passed quite close to it. The little man I had encountered outside the urinal was back in his place. Our eyes met. The battered trumpet he was playing let out a series of plaintive bleats as we passed.

We passed into the vestibule, and I thought it was going to be child's play. Then as we passed the office, the door suddenly opened, a hand emerged, snatched the Russian girl from my side and dragged her through the door. Before I had time to recover my wits it had slammed to and the key was being turned in the lock from the inside. At the same time, and before I had a chance to fling myself at the door, the waiter with the walrus moustache and three others emerged very quietly from the little passage leading to the urinal. They were carrying long gaucho knives, and it was evident that they were not intended for picking teeth. Still, I told myself, the idea was no more than to speed the parting guest, and after a rapid assessment of the odds I decided that for the time being discretion really would be the better part of valour—and backed towards the entrance. The door was already open: a black sky gashed with those big, brilliant stars lay beyond—but so, I saw, did another group of villainous-looking chuckers-out, also armed with long knives. There was a bump inside my stomach, as if a donkey had given it a kick. I'd heard all the usual tales about life being cheap in South America. I knew that murder was as common as house-breaking, and treated about as seriously. On two occasions in Curitiba known murderers had been pointed out to me: both of them impeccable young men from Sao Paolo, whose families had bought off the police and the magistrates. It was a very different matter now that I found myself likely to be at the receiving end. I just couldn't believe it. I remember saying to myself in amazement: "They're really serious! They *mean* it! They want to kill me!" And I experienced a kind of hurt feeling that anyone should really want to blot me and all my precious thoughts, interests and activities out of existence. "But they can't!" I said to myself, "There isn't another one of me—how can they want to end it?" I could have burst into tears.

All this flashed through my mind in a matter of seconds. Then my reflexes took over and I found myself racing back into the dance-hall. In times of danger I suppose one does become like a child again, taking in everything that affects one, like

55

a sponge soaking up water, instantaneously—I had somehow caught the slight uneasiness that had passed between my would-be murderers, and I knew they wouldn't want to create a disturbance inside the hall itself; that they would have pocketed their knives; and that they would follow after me at as unobtrusive a pace as possible.

I knew, too, that I had to make the most of the few seconds' start that this would allow me. The crowd had thinned out in the few minutes since I had left and for that reason perhaps the band had chosen to take another break. No one showed any surprise at the speed with which I plunged through the smoke and over to the curtained doorway: if anyone did notice he probably thought I'd just discovered that my wallet was missing—or perhaps that I was suddenly visited by a particularly fierce spasm of concupiscence.

I raced down the first of the corridors. Obviously there must have been an exit somewhere in the annexe. But I didn't find one at the end of the corridor. I dashed down the next—still nothing. Half way along the third corridor I began to feel sick with fright. I could see nothing but a blank wall ahead of me, and I could now hear a purposeful padding of feet not far behind. At the end of the corridor I turned in desperation to the nearest door and flung it open.

I found myself looking into the face of my little bandsman. He was in the act of taking off his trousers. On the bed behind him lay a naked negress of monumental proportions. Her eyes rolled in astonishment at my sudden intrusion. As for the little bandsman, he stared at me unbelievingly, his mouth open, his eyes protruding. Then he completed the operation of removing his trousers and threw them to the ground in as eloquent a gesture of resignation as I've ever seen. At the sight of him standing there, naked from the waist down, his very thin but very hairy legs surmounted by his bandsman's tunic, still buttoned up to the throat, I gave a yell of half-hysterical laughter.

It quickly faded as I heard the pad-pad of feet drawing closer. The little bandsman summed up the situation in a flash. He looked at me sharply, then gave me a crooked grin, which nevertheless had a touch of complicity in it, as if our previous encounter had established some sort of bond. He jerked his thumb over his shoulder. I followed the direction in which it was pointing and my spirits gave a leap. To the right of the bed a portion of the wall had been stove in at some time, probably by the kick of a mule tethered outside. Several of the planks had been broken through and others badly splintered. The only attempt at repair had been the tacking up of a length of sacking. I patted my unexpected ally on the shoulder and hurled myself at the damaged wall. My head was hard in those days and I broke through as easily as if I had been diving through a paper hoop.

I landed on all fours in the slimy red mud of a small yard. Fate seemed to have made up its mind to make this a night of bizarre happenings, for I found myself next to a girl squatting on her haunches and relieving herself—not a very unusual occurrence, I may add, in a place where the open air, even of a muddy yard, was preferable to the noisome lavatories. The girl was, naturally, surprised by my sudden advent, but not particularly incommoded. She finished her business, rose to her feet and swished the long skirt of her dress—a bright orange which went very well with her black, frizzy hair and large black eyes—into position. I, too, scrambled to my feet. I was unhurt except for a grazed forehead and rather a painful bruise on my left knee-cap. There was a scrambling, followed by a series of crashes and cursings from behind me. Through the shattered planks I saw that my pursuers had tripped over my little bandsman, as he was trying to pull on his trousers.

The girl, too, summed up the situation in a flash. She caught hold of my hand and pulled me across a few yards of mud and through an open doorway. A very large negro in a faded blue singlet that had split across the chest loomed up out of the shadows. The girl said something to him; he gave a hoarse chuckle, slammed the door to, locked it, and with a beatific grin on his face, leaned his back against it. A moment later I heard my pursuers scrambling through the wall of the building I had left and across the yard. The girl turned to me.

"Up there," she said, pointing to a dark and rickety stairway, "And mind you choose me!"

I didn't wait to ask her what she meant, but started up the staircase. There was a banging on the door behind me; I glanced over my shoulder. The girl had gone, but a flash of white teeth told me that the doorkeeper was still deriving amusement from the situation.

At the top of the staircase I found a door. I pushed it open and went in. I was in what was quite a smart room for this part of the world. There were armchairs, a settee, a standard lamp with a faded and torn shade of green silk, an upright piano also faced with green silk, and a parrot as big as a turkey seated on a perch too small for it. The tray intended to catch its droppings was also too small, and this rather spoiled the appearance of the carpet—but a carpet of any kind was a rare enough phenomenon in Sao José.

A tall woman, who might have been anything from fifty to seventy, confronted me. She had piled-up ginger hair, a sleeve-less low-cut dress which revealed a good deal of sagging freckled skin and a black velvet band with a crucifix attached round her throat. She looked a little surprised to find me appearing from the back entrance, but recovered quickly, and clapping her hands, called out in a high, nasal twang:

" *Meninas a sala!*"

At first I was nonplussed at finding myself in yet another brothel, though it wasn't really surprising, considering that the whole district was taken over by them. This, at any rate, was obviously a very superior place, run in the best Lisbon style.

There was a faint swishing noise as of dresses being smoothed down and stockings straightened, and a moment later the *meninas* sailed into the room through the double doors at the further end. I was surrounded by them—tall girls, short girls, fat girls, thin girls; girls white, black, brown, yellow and every shade in between; girls half-dressed and girls fully clothed; girls with watery blue eyes, rouged cheeks, and frizzy gold hair decked with pink bows; silent, surly girls with incipient black moustaches and wearing bush-shirts, jodhpurs and riding boots, complete to the huge spurs of the district; tall, dreamy girls with black kiss-curls plastered against their cheeks and necklaces reaching to their navels; and imitation schoolgirls (or perhaps they were real ones) in gym-slips that revealed a lot of very mature thigh. They stood around me, each in the pose that suited the character she assumed—languid, helpless, truculent, or timid—their eyes fixed on me to catch the slightest flicker in my own that might betray my natural preference.

At first I was so bewildered that I didn't recognise the girl who had let me in, and I had to make a careful scrutiny, to the

Madame's evident disgust. Then I spotted her: she had some-how found time to tidy up her hair, apply a fresh coating of lipstick and put an orange flower in her hair. She studiously ignored my glance, and I had to go up to her and touch her on the shoulder. Immediately the rest of the girls broke up their poses and, chattering animatedly—and so fast that I couldn't decide whether they were exchanging uncomplimentary remarks about my person and the choice I had made, or simply resuming a conversation that had been interrupted by my arrival—swept out of the room as quickly as they had entered it.

Madame produced a little notebook, bound in limp leather, and a silver pencil with a long tassle attached to it.

"How long?" she asked, regarding me severely, her ginger eyebrows arched.

I shifted awkwardly from foot to foot.

"He says for the night," the girl interrupted. A flicker of respect entered Madame's eyes as she entered the information in her notebook. She gave me a gracious nod, sank with a sigh on to the settee, kicked off her high heeled shoes and began (of all things in that climate) knitting. The girl took me by the hand and led me to her own room.

This, too, was a cut above the usual for this part of the world. The plank walls were white-washed: a gaudy picture of the Virgin and Child, an even more gaudy frame, hung above the bed. Scattered here and there on the other walls were cut-outs from magazines and newspapers, including a picture of a busy street intersection in Sao Paulo, a large, rather blurred portrait of an American film star, and an advertisement for a baby food, showing a very fat and dribbling baby. There was a rickety chest-of-drawers along one wall. Several dresses pinned up in sheets of newspaper hung from a row of hooks on the door. There was a small washstand with a cracked jug and basin, and beside it (an unusual refinement) a bidet on an iron tripod. A crocheted counterpane covered the bed; on top of it lay a large "kewpie" doll, the bow in its hair threadbare, and most of the paint on its face worn off, revealing the lead coloured undercoat, so that it looked as if it was in the last stages of heart disease.

"The old cow down there mustn't know what's going on," the girl said, as soon as she had closed the door. "She disapproves of disturbances. Ah, what barbarity! As if a good fight hurt

59

anybody from time to time!" She threw herself backward on to the bed and kicked her legs in the air, as if she were riding a bicycle upside down. Then she sat upright again, her cheeks flushed, her eyes sparkling. "What fun it is!" she cried. Then, patting my arm, "One gets so bored, you know."

I looked puzzled. "Oh, there has been one little fight already!" she explained. "While you were in the *sala* waiting for me. Oh it was so *funny!* You see, Umberto opened the door —very suddenly. Two of them fell in. Umberto slammed the door—wham! He stamped on the heads of the two scoundrels inside. Then he opened the door again, and as the rest of them made a rush threw the two unfortunate ones at them. They went over—wheee!—like a row of bottles! Umberto is very strong, of course . . ."

She turned to me, putting her hand confidentially on my arm. "He is *mine!*" she said proudly.

"What . . . what . . . do I do, though?" I asked, and thinking that out of courtesy I ought to add some explanation, I mumbled, "I don't really feel like, er . . ."

"I should think not!" she cried, "What *filth!*" slapping me across the cheek, and then immediately patting my knee in a comradely, reassuring way.

"Those . . . those *macacos* outside, they'll still be hanging about. You'll be safe here, though . . . Don't worry, Madame won't know what's going on. She'd order you out if she knew. ' I keep a respectable house.' " (She gave an accurate imitation of Madame's nasal twang.) "She comes all the way from Lisbon, that's why she speaks so funny."

"But there must have been a lot of noise outside just now," I said, "when Umberto . . ."

"Ah, but you see," she interrupted, "Umberto has such— how shall I put it?—such *delicacy* in his movements. *He* would not have made much noise—and outside, of course, there are always noises."

This was true enough. As I stopped to listen for a moment I could hear, above the blaring of music from a score of nearby dance-halls, burst of angry shouting, shrieks, bangs, curses. I had got used to them, as one gets used to the loud chiming of clocks inside a house.

"Come! We will have a drink now," the girl said, getting up from the bed. She produced a bottle from a cupboard and

60

filled two glasses. We sat on the edge of the bed to drink them.

"It seems quiet outside now," I said after a time. "Perhaps I ought to be going. I have things to do . . ."

"But aren't you enjoying my company, amigo?" she cried, in a disappointed voice.

"Oh, yes!" I hastened to assure her. I wondered whether I ought to tell her about the Russian girl next door, but decided against it. She asked no questions: she took the fracas in which I had been involved as a matter of course.

"In any case," she told me, "this is mostly an all-night house."

I thought that this might be a tactful hint, so I took out my wallet. This time she slapped my face so hard that my head felt as if it was composed of a whole set of tuning forks.

"It is clear that *you* have no delicacy!" she screamed at me. "Donkey! Can't you see that this is different?"

I mumbled some sort of apology and put the wallet away, remembering as I did so that it was in any case sadly depleted.

My apologies must have touched the right note, for she rubbed the cheek she had just slapped, and gave it a quick, sisterly kiss.

"After all," she said, "you're still only a boy!"

I felt a little piqued at this, and was about to try and demonstrate to her that she was mistaken when there was another twang from inside my head, reminding me just in time and I emptied my glass instead.

"Good boy!" she said. "Now we'll wait till Umberto has finished, and then we'll go to sleep."

"You mean . . . they'll come again?"

"Oh yes! They won't give in as easily as all that! That would be *too* dull!"

"You mean this sort of thing has happened before?"

"But of course! We have to have *some* relaxation, you know." Her face clouded. "Not very often, though; Madame is so stuffy . . . Umberto finds it so tame that he'd go if it weren't for *me*." She got up from the bed and took a quick look at herself in the mirror before sitting down again.

"Then, of course, he *hates* those dogs next door!" She thought for a moment, then added with satisfaction. "And they hate us!"

We sat on the side of the bed for another five minutes or so. The girl became abstracted, listening intently. Then there was a rush of feet, the opening of a door, shrieks, yells, thumps, bangs, all together and as sudden as a clap of thunder. The girl jumped down from the bed, her eyes shining with excitement. I followed suit, and made for the door. In a flash she darted in front of me, locked the door and stood with her back against it.

"What are you thinking of?" she cried. "Do you *want* to get yourself killed?"

"But I must go and help Umberto!"

She laughed in a manner I did not find at all complimentary. Then as I took another step towards the door, she gave a quick glance into my face, immediately read the pig-headedness in it, and just as quickly threw her arms round my neck, pressed her body against mine and adopted a gentle, crooning, slightly husky voice.

"My poor boy! You don't understand. They are *very* bad men!"

As I opened my mouth to protest, she planted her lips over mine with the impact and accuracy of a bolt finding a bull's eye. The astonishing thing about this kiss was the immediacy of its erotic effect, in spite of the obviousness of its purpose in distracting me from what was happening outside. When it had lasted long enough to reduce the back of my legs to jelly (while her arms round my neck never for a moment relaxed their grip) she removed her lips, and in the same crooning voice whispered:

"A nice boy—and, ah, such a *man* too!"—and began to guide me back to the bed. I collapsed on it with a gasp. "You see," she went on, "Umberto *understands* these sort of people!" Then, as (still shivering from the expertness of her kiss) I put out my arms, she pushed them aside and said briskly:

"Besides, you would be spoiling Umberto's enjoyment. He's the solitary type, really."

The uproar outside stopped as abruptly as it had begun. The girl sat up, and leaned forward, listening intently. There were faint lines of anxiety on her forehead: they smoothed out, one by one, as a series of small noises reached us—sighs, groans, whisperings, a dragging sound, a bubbling cough, a door closing softly, a key turning and the scraping of bolts and last of all a low chuckle. The sounds didn't mean much

62

to me, but were apparently full of familiar significance to the girl, for when they had died down she turned on her side and snuggled down in the bed with a smug, contented look on her face, as if in the presence of a routine as harmless and comforting as winding the clock and putting the cat out. As an afterthought, she put out her hand behind her back, found a portion of my anatomy, patted it, and almost immediately fell into a deep sleep.

There were two other minor interruptions during the night, one of them, which took place just after the cocks began to crow, was attended by a good deal of forensic display, conducted first by one voice then another. Both approaches met with the same response—a warning clearing of the throat from Umberto, who was presumably sleeping downstairs, followed, after a decent interval, by a sound that managed at one and the same time to be muted and a bellow, and then (when that failed to have the desired effect) by the drawing of the bolts, the hurtling of a large body, various thuds, groans and grunts —and then silence once more.

On each occasion I sat up in bed, one hand grasping the corner of the sheet, ready to make a dash for it if it proved necessary. But the girl merely made little protesting noises in her sleep, which seemed to be telling me that there was no longer anything to worry about, and though I hadn't expected to go to sleep myself, the next thing I knew the girl was shaking my shoulder and holding a cup of steaming black coffee under my nose.

When I had finished it, she conducted me to the front door. I looked round me warily.

" Oh, they won't do anything here! " she said. " As you see, our front door opens on to the main road. In any case it would not be wise in broad daylight . . . And of course Umberto will have taught them a lesson! "

" What is your name? "

" Oh, they call me Maria. "

I tried to thank her, but she merely gave a perfunctory nod, and leaning against the door-jamb, raised the knuckles of her left hand to the corner of her mouth, and yawned. I turned and walked away. After a few yards I looked back. She was still leaning against the door. On either side of her, other doors were open and other girls were standing in exactly the same attitude. Sometimes they waved to each other or called out a languid greeting. I half expected to see them stoop to gather up the morning milk and the newspaper. The morning was going to be fine. The sun was already sucking up moisture and turning the mud into a fine red powder. An occasional cock was still crowing. A dog barked in the distance. The smell of coffee was everywhere. It was a peaceful, domestic scene: human beings sleepily taking up the bits and pieces of their lives for another day, just as they might be doing in Surbiton or Welwyn Garden City.

I went straight back to my hotel. To my surprise I found Umberto waiting outside. His face, arms, throat and the portions of his muscular torso protruding from the faded blue singlet were criss-crossed with bits of sticking plaster. But there was a contented grin on his face.

He accompanied me into the vestibule of the hotel, and spent a good deal of time peering into corners, under tables, and even behind the reception desk, while the clerk regarded him warily. At length he appeared to be satisfied—though by no means pleased—that none of my pursuers were lying in wait for me. He thought for a moment, then pointing to some of the more accessible plasters, gave one of his throaty chuckles, clapped me on the shoulder, practically knocking me to the ground, then strode off, still chuckling.

I went up to my room, had a cold shower, and changed my clothes. Then I set off for the police station. It was an action that revealed how utterly English and provincial I still was.

I blush at the memory of that tall, gangling young man (there was already a good deal of rugged bone, but I hadn't yet put on much real bulk) and his automatic expectation that there must always be " authorities " who would see that justice was done . . . A secret faith, an inner self should be in a state of continuous development: it should extend, not limit, the range of one's knowledge and awareness, and my behaviour made it only too clear how much I still had to learn.

There were some lessons waiting for me at that police station. I had no sooner entered than the flap of the counter was raised and I was hustled behind it and into an office beyond. It was almost identical to the one I had been in the night before, and the man sitting behind the desk might have been the brother of the dance-hall manager (perhaps he was), apart from the fact that there was a long black cheroot in his mouth instead of a gaúcho knife and that he was wearing a uniform. Not that the uniform made all that much difference, because the shirt, trousers, and floppy peaked cap were of that olive-dun colour which blends with the predominant skin colour so completely that it seems a continuation of it.

Inside the police captain's office matters proceeded at the same spanking pace. A number of documents were thrust under his nose and he rubber-stamped them one after the other. In less than a minute I was seized again and propelled towards another door. Not a word had been addressed to me, and I had been silent for the simple reason that the speed with which everything had happened had had the usual effect of making me forget every word of Portuguese I had ever learned. All kind of things were tumbling through my mind, but in English, and I couldn't translate them. When I was half-way through the door, however, I did manage to dredge up two words. "What charge?" I shouted, digging in my heels so that I remained stationary for a moment between my two attendants.

"You haven't paid your hotel bill!" the police captain snapped back, and then, removing his cheroot from his mouth, he gave me a slow, wide grin—at the same time holding aloft by finger and thumb a piece of paper which I did indeed recognise as coming from the account-book of the hotel where I was staying. It was then that I remembered that as I had been leaving the hotel, the clerk on duty had told me, with a decidedly shifty expression on his face, that my bill was in my pigeon-hole. I had paid no attention because I had already arranged with the proprietor—or so I had assumed—that I should settle up not at the end of the week but when my visit was over.

I don't know whether it was the realisation that I had been well and truly had, on all sides, or the fact that I still couldn't get my Portuguese to work, but suddenly I flew into a rage—so suddenly that for a while I set the whole process in reverse, like a film being shown backwards. I threw off the two constables who were holding me, gave the captain a shove just as he was rising from his chair, so that he landed on the floor, marched into the outer room, threw up the flap, brought it back down on the hand of the policeman who had been standing behind it, reached the door, and was running down the bungalow-like steps of the building—when something hit me on the side of the head.

Like most people, I have known that pang of reality I did not wish to face seize hold of me in the very instant of waking, like a mouse pounced on by a cat which has been waiting patiently by his hole all night. But I have never known such a diabolical matching of inner despair and outer circumstances as when I came to in that ghastly gaol in Sao José.

The first thing I was aware of was a banging on top of my skull so intense that for a moment I thought I was being bludgeoned all over again by half a dozen truncheons or revolver-butts, or whatever it was that had laid me out as I ran down the steps. When I groaned it stretched the skin of my scalp: I could feel the dried blood cracking and a whole new series of painful sensations started up. I became aware that my right cheek was resting on something that was at one and the same time gritty and tacky, and in the same instant my sense of smell came awake, so distinctly that it might have been a separate self recovering consciousness. It registered, first of all, that bruised, musty smell you get from earth that has degenerated into dirt. Crowding close behind it, like an obscene animal, was the sweetish, nauseating stench of stale urine. Instinctively I took a deep breath until, realising that there was no cleansing air to take in, but only the multiple stink like some heavy layer of gas, I began to retch. My eyes felt as if they were being dragged over hot cinders as they began to take in, as if in some astonishing slow-motion close-up, a thin trickle of yellow bile issuing from my lips. I watched it, still in slow motion, spread out until it joined a small pool beyond, and realised, as my stomach lurched and trembled, that I must have already spewed half my guts out. I concentrated on trying to jerk myself away from the mess. After what seemed a super-human effort I succeeded in moving a fraction. The small movement, besides increasing the resonance in my head (which now felt as if someone was banging away inside it at a brass gong) brought other sensations within my range of consciousness. I could hear a murmur and a stir around me. Somewhere near by there was a rattling of bars accompanied by a monotonous shouting. A foot suddenly loomed up beside my ear. I became aware of a whole row of legs, clad in ragged and dirty cotton trousers, shuffling past my head. I succeeded in swivelling my eyes slightly. I could just make out a shadowy figure at the head of the queue pressed against the corner of the wall, jerking horribly. I thought I must be in the grip of one of those worst of nightmares, in which one's most cherished beliefs and affections have been turned inside out, in a kind of mocking obscenity. I opened my mouth and tried to scream, but no sound came. I closed my eyes, fiercely screwing up the eyelids, and again lapsed into unconsciousness.

When I next came to I was half sitting, half lying against the knees of a policeman, who was crouched down beside me pouring water over my head from a billy-can. The water was running down the inside of my shirt, and I put out my hand in protest. The policeman held the can against my lips. The water was warm and tasted of rust, but I drank greedily. Apart from the banging inside my head I felt so much better that I was able to struggle to my feet and stagger over to a bench against the nearest wall. The ragged, yellow-faced occupants eyed me with that paradoxical mixture of curiosity and indifference which, I was soon to learn, is peculiar to prisoners. The policeman followed me to the bench, keys jangling from his belt. He leaned over and began to part the blood-clotted hair at the back of my head. I gave a jerk as his fingers found a lump the size of a tennis ball.

" You'll do," he said, not unkindly, and left the cell, clanging the grill behind him. It was only then that I really remembered what had happened to me, and while he was still busy with his keys, I got up and staggered over to the grill.

" There must be some mistake," I said.

" Yes?" he replied in a bored voice, in which was conveyed the obvious implication: " That's what they all say."

" Yes. You must have found out from the hotel by now? My bill . . ."

He finished locking the doors, nodded in a perfectly amiable fashion and strode off, whistling between his teeth. I caught hold of the bars and gave them a feeble shake.

" I demand to see the British Consul! " I said, in what was intended to be a wrathful roar, but came out as a kind of croak. I remember thinking what a stupid remark it was anyway—doubly so in this case because there was no British consul within six hundred miles.

I clung to the gate, feeling giddy again. The man who had been sitting next to me on the bench came over and led me back to my place. There was a kind of undulating movement as the others squeezed up and I observed a technique with which I was to become familiar—it consisted of a splaying of the legs and a spreading out of the hams by the occupants of the bench in order to preserve each others' place: it was an unwritten law that those who occupied the bench first thing in the morning should have a right to it for the rest of the day, but it was asking for trouble to leave too obvious a gap.

The man who helped me back to my seat was especially adept at this spreading technique. He must once have been a very fat man indeed. He was still bulky, though pouches of half-filled skin now hung from his upper arms, the back of his neck and shoulders, and another pouch hung over the top of his trousers, particularly noticeable because the singlet which was his only other article of apparel had shrunk well above the navel, and in addition the hem was fretted and scalloped, as if it had been chewed by caterpillars.

I fell into a doze from which I was aroused by a terrific din, similar to one which I dimly remembered having heard while I lay half conscious on the floor of the cell. I opened my eyes. Two young men, encouraged perhaps by my own feeble efforts a few minutes before, had caught hold of the bars of the iron gates and were shaking them furiously to and fro, at the same time yelling at the tops of their voices, over and over again:

" We are innocent! We demand to see the Governor! We must be released immediately! Our father is a state functionary! He is acquainted with the cousin of a Senator! We are people of consequence! "

This went on without a moment's pause for about half an hour. A policeman then appeared outside the doors of the cell with a truncheon in his hand—and struck at the fingers clasping the bars with such speed and dexterity that he managed to get a blow on each pair of knuckles.

The young men let out a yell and jumped back. Whimpering softly, and tucking their hands under their armpits, for all the world as if they were just leaving the headmaster's study after receiving six of the best, made their way to a corner and sank to the ground, leaning against each other in an attitude of the utmost dejection. They were so alike that they might have been twins. They both had greasy black locks stuck to their foreheads, long aquiline faces with receding chins, black eyes, restless but lifeless, and an odd kind of pallor, shiny and slightly blueish, almost as if they had been gassed. The likeness between them was enhanced by the fact that they were wearing almost identical suits made of a very coarse blue serge and now much crumpled and stained. They were also wearing shirts and stiff collars: both of these now looked more like the rags used by motor mechanics, and the shirts had frayed and parted round their collar-bones, so that the collars had worked free, ringing their skinny necks like halters; even so such get-ups were a rare enough phenomenon in Sao José. The occupants of my bench, although they had nodded approvingly at the policeman's intervention, presumably being as bored as he by the monotonous outcry, were now casting looks of mingled commiseration and respect in the young men's direction.

" You, senhor," the fat man said, turning towards me, " will, of course, recognise these young men for gentlemen."

" What are they here for?" I asked.

" They are salesmen—*travelling* salesmen," the man on my left interrupted (an extraordinarily shrivelled up little creature, with a shaven head displaying the evident signs of ring-worm or some other infection of the scalp) in tones of the deepest respect. " Excellent goods, which only the best sort of people buy . . ."

" Unfortunately," the fat man added, spreading out his hands in a deprecating gesture, " there was some doubt as to where they obtained their last consignment of goods . . ."

" But they are well-placed young men," my other neighbour intervened, " men of family and education . . ."

" How long have they been here?" I asked.

" Oh, only six weeks, but you see they are not used to such conditions; at home, no doubt, they mix with quite a different sort of person . . ."

" Six weeks . . . What was their sentence?"

" Sentence?" the little man asked, with a frown. " They have not been *sentenced*! Surely, senhor, you don't think . . ."

" This is only the charge cell!" the fat man spoke indignantly. " We are, of course, all innocent! . . ."

" Oh yes, we are all innocent!" the little man chimed in, and all the occupants of the bench took up the word " innocent " in unison.

" But six weeks without a hearing!" I cried.

69

"Oh, but that is nothing!" the fat man said, laughing, indulgently, "none of us has been here less than three months, senhor, and many a good deal longer than that!"

I must have turned green again, for the little man suddenly fished in the pockets of his filthy denims, pulled out a drooping cigarette-end, and, as if it were some life-saving drug, pushed it expertly between my lips. Somebody else produced a match and lit the cigarette end for me. I drew gratefully on it, rolling the smoke round and round my cheeks, as if I was tasting some rare wine. A dozen pairs of eyes watched me greedily, lifting their heads like pointers when I opened my lips and emitted the smoke.

After a few puffs I handed the butt to its owner. He refused to take it, though his eyes were moist with longing. "But no, senhor!" he said, with a courteous little bow. "You finish it!"

It was like smoking tarred rope, but surprisingly the smoke cleared my head and I was able to look round the cell properly for the first time.

It was about twenty feet square, lit by a small grilled window close under the ceiling. There were about thirty occupants, some of them sitting on wooden benches (there were two of these in addition to the one I was on), others on the floor. The floor was inches deep in filth, especially round the three uncovered toilet buckets, which were placed at intervals, each of them filled to the brim with brownish-yellow liquid.

As my stomach gave an ominous heave, I snatched my eyes away—and they alighted on the corner near which I had been lying when I first regained consciousness. Suddenly I remembered the queue of shuffling feet near my head, and my nightmare imaginings. I could see that the corner was not even: there seemed to be a dark hollow, as if made by a rat. But no one was standing there now. It *must* have been a nightmare, I told myself—except that my companions, who had noticed the direction of my gaze, began to nod and nudge each other with knowing smiles and chuckles.

"The young Englishman," one of them said. "It is evident that he is *much* better!"

There were several hearty guffaws at this. The thin little man patted me on the arm.

"Don't worry," he said, "it's only an hour to wait for dinner!" But this only made the matter more mysterious.

I closed my eyes to shut out the gaping black hole and the horrors it conjured up. When I opened them again everybody had lapsed into a listless silence. Those on the benches were either lying back against the wall, their vacant eyes turned upward towards the ceiling, or leaning forward, elbows propped on knees, heads supported on their hands. Those on the floor either squatted on their haunches or lay full length. The two young men sat back to back, knees raised, like a pair of book-ends.

In the stillness I could hear the distinct sound of each man's breathing. The mosquitoes were as audible as sirens. Somewhere a group of police were playing with dice. I could hear their raucous shouts and laughter, and even, every now and then, the striking of a match, while the rattle of the dice was so distinct that one could envisage, and almost identify, the thick china of the container. Farther away a woman was screaming, and a cell door clanged. There was a faint rustling noise, accompanied by heavy breathing, beside me. The little man on my left, his hand plunged into his trouser pocket, the knuckles nearly breaking through the paper-thin material, was painstakingly masturbating. The stillness became even more intense. Everybody seemed to hold his breath, until with a grunt the little man reached his climax.

It was the signal for the outbreak of an irritable, though still muted stirring. Somebody swore and slapped at a mosquito. Several people began to cough and spit. The two young men got up and went over to the iron grill, leaning against it hopefully, but apparently too listless to start another round of complaint. Their suits looked more squalid than ever; the seats of the trousers were stiff and shiny with coagulated filth. Somebody produced a bundle of limp and yellowing pages, torn from an illustrated magazine six months out of date, and passed them round among his neighbours. The recipients held their pages gingerly by the corners, scrutinising them slowly from top to bottom, over and over again.

Suddenly everybody jerked upright, listening intently. Somewhere in the distance I could hear a clanging and rumbling. A stir of expectancy ran round the cell. Those who had been lolling against the wall sat bolt upright; others joined the two young men peering through the bars of the cell doors.

The clanging and rumbling drew closer. They were ac-

71

companied by the rattling of keys, the clanging of cell doors, and a rising murmur of eager voices. The fat man got up from the bench and went over to the corner of the cell. He began probing with his fingers into the hole in the wall. Bits of bread fell out, some of them wet and soggy, those lower down as dry as toast. I watched in horrified fascination, my heart sinking.

The fat man returned. He clapped me on the shoulder. " Not long now, young man!" he said. The skinny little man grinned ingratiatingly and leaned against me.

"*You* shall have first go!" he murmured. For some reason the others found this excruciatingly funny. They threw back their heads and yelled with laughter.

The rumbling now sounded like thunder; a moment later a huge black cauldron, mounted on wheels, thickly encrusted with some substance that looked like dried glue, stopped outside the cell. A pungent steam (which, in fact, smelt not unlike boiling glue) rose from the bubbling, heaving contents.

Beside the cauldron stood another man carrying two large panniers, suspended from a wooden yoke across his shoulders, and filled with hunks of bread. He was wearing baker's overalls and a cloth wound round his head, both indescribably filthy. He also had some sort of skin disease which had raised large eruptions on his hands and face, similar in appearance to the heads of those hedgerow plants which as children we used, most appropriately, to call " scabs ". These eruptions looked as if they were dusted with flour, though perhaps it was boracic powder, or a by-product of the disease itself. Whatever the explanation, I experienced an ominous quivering of the stomach as I took the piece of bread he handed me.

For some reason the gates of the cell weren't unlocked, and even the bowls of soup, ladled out of the cauldron by the two policemen, who plunged their bare arms deep inside, were passed through the bars. As the bowls were too wide to go through without tilting, a part of their contents was inevitably spilled, to contribute a further slippery layer as it was trodden over the floor of the cell. There was in addition a good deal of pushing and jostling at the bars, resulting in a further spilling of the contents of the bowls.

These were made of an aluminium alloy so thin and light

72

that you felt that you had to hang on tight in order to prevent them floating away. The spoons, an odd brownish-grey in colour, were made of an equally insubstantial material, which you could bend like putty.

I sat down on the bench and regarded my meal. The bread, still warm from the baker's oven, was blueish-grey in colour and doughy in texture. The soup was thin and sticky, with bits of chopped macaroni, like so many white maggots, floating in it. I could not bring myself to touch either, though most of my cell-mates were eating eagerly, tearing off bits of the bread and dipping them in their soup.

As soon as the cauldron was trundled away the occupants of my bench began to display an excitement which seemed to have nothing to do with hunger. What was worse, I myself appeared to stand in some special relation to it. I was the recipient of a number of conspiratorial looks, nudges, and slaps on the shoulder. I began to tremble. Again I had the sensation of being part of a horrible travesty of something I held particularly dear, as if some ritual or visitation which in the past had seemed to me to hold the very essence of truth was about to be presented to me in a peculiarly corrupt and distorted form from which I might never recover.

I was dimly aware that the skinny little man was scooping at the hole in the corner of the cell with his spoon, which he had bent double in order to give it greater solidity. Out of the corner of my eye I saw, too, that the fat man was collecting a piece of bread from each of the occupants of my bench (I was now the only one still sitting down). As he took each piece he carefully pushed it into the palm of his other hand, then, closing his fingers over it, began to squeeze as if he were softening a piece of Plasticine.

Finally he came over to me, and pointed to the hunk of bread which still lay untouched on the bench beside me. Thinking that perhaps he was collecting contributions for someone who was particularly in need of food, I tore off a piece and handed it to him. He looked surprised, then murmured:

" If the senhor permits?" and stooping down expertly removed the soft bread from the centre of the hunk, leaving the crust behind. He nodded and smiled encouragingly at me, now joining both hands together, he worked away at the soft bread they contained, with an intent expression on his face.

73

The others crowded round him, watching him with the same absorbed expression. Then, very slowly, his hands still reverently joined, the fat man walked over to the corner of the cell, closely attended by the others. He began to press the kneaded bread into the hole, with infinite care, like a dentist filling a tooth.

When he had finished he came back to me, gave me a courteous little bow, and pointed towards the corner. I stared up at him, uncomprehending. There was a murmur from the others, part excited, part anxious.

" You see, senhor, we have kept our promise!" the little man said, squeezing my arm. " I told you you would be the first!"

Then, when I still did not respond, and with a quick glance in the direction of the fat man's handiwork: " But you must hurry, senhor—otherwise it will not be so good . . ."

There was another pause, during which I continued to stare at my cell-mates. It was broken by a murmur in which anxiety was mingled with exasperation. The fat man, clucking his tongue impatiently, bent down, placed his hands under my armpits, lifted me to my feet, and then, before I had a chance to resist, hustled me over to the corner of the cell. He pointed at the hole, crammed with bread which was already beginning to lose its moisture round the edges, and made a number of gestures whose import was quite unmistakable, though I stood there with my mouth hanging open like the village idiot. As a matter of fact I knew perfectly well what he was getting at, but my mind and my body were alike numbed by revulsion. When the fat man explained to me, in considerable detail, the exact nature of the privilege I was being offered I could still do no more than shake my head, and when I tried to answer him I found that I had once more forgotten my Portuguese. He tried again, repeating his pantomime in slow motion, touching my shoulder before each gesture, very patiently, as if he were dealing with a child or a moron.

At length the little man, with a yelp of anguish, tore open the front of his trousers, exposed an erect penis, long and thin as a pencil, and, holding it at the ready, charged at the hole in the wall, then standing courteously aside after a few thrusts, by way of demonstration, he waved me forward with his free hand. At this I backed away, grinning idiotically, waving my hands, and managing at last to bring out a few sentences of

74

broken Portuguese, which endeavoured at one and the same time to decline the honour and to express appreciation of the spirit in which it was offered.

There was a sympathetic murmur from the onlookers. " The Englishman—he has shame," one of them exclaimed. " Poor boy! He is impotent," another said, and a third added, " It is venereal disease, an advanced case!" The fat man, putting his arm round my shoulder, escorted me back to the bench with the greatest solicitude. In the meantime the skinny little man was busy making the most of his opportunities. The others crowded round him cheering, shouting ribald encouragement, urging him to hurry, or cursing him for having jumped the queue.

While this was going on, and in order to hide my embarrassment, I had picked up my bowl of soup. My hands, however, were shaking and the watery concoction trickled out of the spoon before it reached my mouth. A wave of nausea seized me, and I pushed the bowl aside. Immediately the little man, who had by now returned to the bench beside me, pounced on the bowl with a yell of delight. Bearing it carefully and reverently, he hurried back to the corner. When the others saw what he was carrying, there was a shout of excitement and the head of the queue drew back to make way for him. Scooping out the bits of warm macaroni from the still steaming bowl he slapped them into the hole. A moment later there was a howl of rage as it became evident that in doing so he had once again placed himself in a position of advantage.

Recalling it all now I'm not sure that I don't find it more comic than horrifying. I have reached an age when almost everything seems comic. It has to be something very serious indeed—the death of a child, say (those I loved are already all dead) to strike me as truly tragic. Even my own dissolution, though I vigorously object to it, seems to me as often as not as a kind of primitive joke. The older I get the more tolerant I become—of myself as well as of everybody else. At this rate I soon shan't have any principles left at all.

But in those days I was still a bit of a prig. I was terrified of inconsistency and hypocrisy. I had advanced a few steps along the road of my own kind of faith. I had discovered a few of its truths. I jumped to the conclusion in consequence that I was the only one who understood it properly, that I was the sole

75

guardian of its purity. I began by regarding the disgusting daily scramble in the corner of the cell as a grinning, mocking temptation, with myself as a kind of Sir Galahad holding aloft the uncorrupted doctrine. Then, when I discovered a few days later that the heavings and gruntings were beginning to arouse an itch of concupiscence in my own body, I was horrified and dismayed. " I am a fraud!" I told myself, " So *that's* all there was to it—I am really one of them! They are my brothers!" I said it with self-loathing and disgust. That's where I was wrong. They *were* my brothers.

Not that the time I spent in that gaol wasn't grisly enough. There really was a coarsening of the sensibilities; you felt it creeping over you like an infection. By the end of the first week I had become quite hardened to the frantic activities that accompanied the arrival of the bread and soup (those were the only articles in our diet). They were no worse than other more furtive practices that were hourly taking place around me. After a while it aroused no more disgust in me than the sight of a fly buzzing round a dung-heap, or cattle bellowing at a salt-lick. I was even able to eat the foul bread and soup. Indeed I began to look forward to its arrival with a sort of passion— and to realise, if still only dimly, that my cell-mates crowded round the hole in the wall were merely acting out the same passion in a different form. After all, they had been there longer than I, they had had to contend with an infinitely vaster stretch of the grey, stinking, enveloping monotony.

Those prisoners you read about who enrich their spiritual lives behind bars usually have behind them the support of a definite conviction, just or unjust, for a definite crime or a definite commitment to some great political or religious cause. In that cell in Sao José we were nothing: we had not even the reality of having been brought to trial: we were in limbo. The suspension between grace and damnation, so to speak, seemed to pull the mind into scrambled threads until it became one huge wad of cotton-wool. Conversation became no more than the utterance of a few basic wants or rejections, or at the best a desultory chattering, like that of monkeys in a zoo. I was aware of no great thoughts when I fell silent, only random dreamings which led nowhere. What powers of concentration I retained were concerned with such problems as whether to sit on the left ham or the right, whether to ask for a page of the

76

dismembered magazine, or whether to use the sanitary bucket now or later.

The stink of that bucket became the very embodiment of the monotony, and ever after the slightest whiff of a similar nature has had the effect of momentarily turning me into a half moribund carcase—even now, when I'm pretty close to that anyway.

The nights were the worst. Then the stink seemed to gather an extra concentration and to stalk about the cell like an evil ghost that has nearly succeeded in materialising itself, leaning over us as we lay huddled on our coats or scraps of sacking or newspaper, and breathing in our faces. It wasn't so bad up to about three o'clock in the morning, because there were shrieks, and yells, and bangings all over the prison, accompanied by drunken laughter and singing when the prison officers and trusties were having a party, and there was plenty of noise, too, from outside. But from three to six, when we were given a mug of watery coffee and a hunk of stale bread, it was so silent all around us that our stirrings inside the cell were like those of maggots in a grave.

Those are the worst hours in the hospital too—and sometimes when I am awake then I imagine I am back inside the cell; but soon I am bound to hear a stirring or a bustling somewhere in the distance, and when the dawn comes I know I shall see the sun or its shadows on the wall of my room, and ordinary dying seems almost lively and decent by comparison.

In spite of myself, though, I got something out of the experience. I learned something about monotony. I learned that just being alive isn't enough. I learned that there are two rhythms working side by side in our bodies. There's the working of the organism: the heart beating, the blood flowing, the lungs rising and falling, the bowels opening and closing: and *that's* a running-down process, in which more cells are decaying than are being renewed. I realised, in fact, that when you're really bored you are actually experiencing the slow dying of the body. And the nerves scream in protest: they're not satisfied with the slow, even tick-tock of dying: they want the other rhythms, the rhythms of living, movement of a different and much more irregular kind, riding roughshod over the grim underlying—and utterly monotonous—motions of decay. They demand climax and renewal. When the monotony was at its worst and the submerged tick-tock at its loudest, I found that whatever defiance I still retained expressed itself in an itch of desire . . .

Cartwright once told me that madmen shut up in institutions often indulge in continuous, frantic masturbation. I can understand it: they have come closer than anybody to feeling that nothing exists apart from the relentless tick-tock of their own organic decomposition. In their terror and rage they reassert the rhythms of life. We ought not only to pity them but to admire them—and indeed be grateful to them, because they are reminding us that there is one part of the body that has nothing whatever to do with the process of dying.

And the same was true of my cell-mates in Sao José, if only I could have fully understood it. What they were doing in the corner of the cell wasn't pretty, but it was better than any of the varieties of slow dying—from sitting in a cell or a hospital ward staring at nothingness to making money on the stock exchange and keeping up with the Jones's.

The sect to which they belonged was, it is true, too primitive for my liking. I had no wish to join in. I think I would have gone mad myself first, or perhaps have succumbed completely to the living death of monotony. Now that I have no principles left I'm not so sure that I wouldn't have done better to join them . . .

As it was I sank lower than at any other time in my life. To begin with I kept badgering the prison officers about the date of my trial, and even contemplated joining the two young men in their vociferous onslaughts on the iron grill. But I got nothing out of them beyond a perfunctory, " Tomorrow, perhaps, senhor," or a blank silence, or a grin. The grins were the hardest to bear. They weren't derisive or hostile or cruel: on the contrary, they were quite sympathetic, indulgent even, the kind of amused smiles a parent bestows on a child when he asks for the moon. I dreaded these smiles so much that after a while I stopped asking questions. I almost lost interest in the whole business. The grey fungus of monotony spread over me, inch by inch.

I got to the stage when the to-ings and fro-ings in the passage outside the cell became vague and remote, like the flickerings of an ancient film. But one day, to my surprise, I found myself lifting my head with some faint though undefined stirring, at the

78

shrill sound of a girl's voice, raised in vehement protest. A moment later the girl herself drew level to the door of the cell, accompanied by one of the prison officers.

"Don't lie to me!" she was yelling, "I am *not* one of Enrico's girls, and everybody knows it! It is Paolo I have been sent to—it is a birthday present from his father!"

"But senhora," the officer replied in a wheedling voice, "Enrico has specially asked . . ."

I didn't catch the rest of the sentence or the girl's reply.

There was nothing in the least unusual about the incident. Enrico was a double-murderer doing life. A man of great charms, he often stopped outside the cell to pass the time of day. As the oldest inhabitant of the gaol (he had already served fifteen years) and the most popular of the prisoners with officers and inmates alike, he had secured for himself many privileges, including the free run of the prison during the day time, invitations to most of the officers' parties—and, as he seemed to be well supplied with money, as many girls as he wanted. A different one, indeed, visited him nearly every day, and I had long since ceased to pay any attention to them as they passed our cell.

I didn't pay a great deal of attention this time either. All the same, it struck me that there was something familiar about this girl's voice, and as she passed I thought, though without much conviction, that it was Maria, with whom I had passed the night after my disastrous attempt to rescue the Russian girl.

As far as I could tell, she had not as much as cast a glance in the direction of the cell I was in. I shrugged my shoulders, and dismissed the incident from my mind.

Then, a few days later (how many I don't know) there was a slamming of doors, followed by footsteps and the murmur of voices in the distance. There was something about these sounds entirely different from anything that I'd heard before, something purposeful and decisive. In prison your ears become attuned to these small differences—just as they are in childhood. Everybody else in the cell was aware of it. Even the most listless lifted their eyes or turned their heads. The two young men, who had been sitting back to back, jumped to their feet, looked at each other wildly, and tried to straighten their bedraggled ties.

I got up too, my heart unaccountably thumping. I went over

79

to the grill and peered through. To my utter astonishment I saw Trudy, of all people, calmly walking down the corridor. The chief gaoler and his assistant were trotting at her heels, and bringing up the rear, with a slightly incredulous expression on his face, was Joaquim.

But nobody had eyes for anyone but Trudy. She was magnificent. She was dressed in a spotless and beautifully pressed linen skirt and a delicious strawberry coloured blouse that clung to her bust more strikingly than ever; her back was straight, and her cheeks were flushed, partly in anger and partly in excitement. All the occupants of the cell got to their feet. Everybody gave a polite little bow. The two prison officers for their part were so busy bowing and scraping that Trudy appeared to tower above them: with their drab uniforms and sallow faces they were like toads in the presence of a kingfisher—or of a princess in a fairy tale. With an imperious gesture Trudy indicated the locked gates. There was none of the usual slow nonchalance about the opening this time: " click! snap!" I was out; and " clang!" the gates had closed behind me. Trudy flashed me a smile, challenging and slightly defiant, as if she was saying: " You see? I've done it! *I* can have unusual adventures too!"

The smile faltered fractionally as she took in my filthy condition, but a moment later her extraordinarily clean, pink fingers closed on my arm in a defiant squeeze. There was a murmur of mingled wonder, envy and approval from behind the bars. Trudy inclined her head graciously and firmly turned me away. I waved my free hand, and there was another murmur, full this time of heartfelt goodwill. I felt quite a pang as I was ushered along the corridor. As we turned the corner there was a frantic rattling at the bars of the cell.

" Voss' Excellencia!" the young men were shouting. " We are here unjustly! Help us! You are a lady of influence! Intercede for us, we beg of you! Our second cousin knows a senator! We are people of consequence, vossa excellencia!"

When we reached the office I stared round me in amazement. I recognised it as the same room from which I had been hustled —how long ago was it? Months? Years?—but at first I thought it must have been re-decorated. Then I saw the stains and squashed mosquitoes, in exactly the same places, and realised that what had surprised me was the light. The room was full of light. It jutted into the outside world; the outside world flowed into it. My eyes filled with tears.

The police chief noticed it and made one last effort to regain the initiative. Seating himself behind his desk he put on a pair of dark glasses and directed the lenses at me.

" The senhora," he said sternly, " has paid your hotel bill. That is a step in the right direction, of course—*but* . . ."

He got no further. " I will now have your receipt, if you please," Trudy interrupted in an icy voice, directing a gaze at him against which the dark glasses were no protection at all. He lowered his head and crumpled into a dun-coloured heap. Laboriously he signed the piece of paper in front of him, and handed it to Trudy. She took it by the edge, examined it with insulting thoroughness, nodded curtly and put it in her bag. There was silence for a moment. The police officer looked round him uneasily, then at Trudy. She gave him a long stare, tapping one foot impatiently on the floor. With an exclamation of apology the police officer jumped to his feet, came round from behind his desk, and opened the door, bowing respectfully as Trudy sailed out, her arm in mine, followed by Joaquim, with the same incredulous expression on his face.

Ivan's old Ford was parked outside the police station, but there was no sign of Ivan himself. Joaquim got into the driver's seat. My luggage from the hotel was piled on the seat beside him. Trudy and I climbed into the back. Her hand still lay on my arm. I stared fascinated at those astonishingly pink fingers and nails. After we had been driving for about five minutes I began to tremble violently. A spasm crossed Trudy's face, as if somebody had twisted her arm. She pulled my head down on to her shoulder. It slid on to her breast: I felt it give a quick heave; then it went very still as if she were taking great care with her breathing.

A few minutes later I sat up with a jerk. So far I had been in a complete daze, with no real idea of what was happening to me. Now I suddenly realised that we had driven out of Sao José and were already some miles along the bumpy track that passed for the high road to Curitiba.

" Stop! " I said to Joaquim. " We've got to go back. I have to find the Russian girl!"

" It's all right," Trudy interrupted, in a soothing voice. " We know all about it." Then, when I stared at her wild-eyed, she

81

added with a touch of smugness. " Everything has been arranged! "

" How did you find out about me?" I asked. " Was it . . .?"

" Yes, it was the girl from the Portuguese House "—she spoke as if she might be referring to some official cultural centre— " She noticed you when she visited the prison for her . . . ah, her assignment."

" She came to me," Joaquim explained. " Apparently she had seen us together—luckily for you! "

" But didn't you wonder what had happened to me before that?"

" I called at your hotel the day after the affair at Sampaio's —and they told me that you had already left for Curitiba. There was no reason for me to disbelieve them."

" How long ago was that?"

" Nearly six weeks."

" Six weeks . . ."

It seemed both shorter and longer than that. While I was living them the six weeks had been measured out second by second, so that they seemed an eternity. Now they were beginning to disappear, swallowed up in my normal life with the rapidity of a cobweb consumed by fire. It seemed a pity that so much concentration of time had been wasted in that way. And so quick a transposition into another life seemed a betrayal of those I had left behind.

" Then when Maria came to me," Joaquim continued, " I went to Curitiba. I know what things are like in Sao José. I had to see your nearest consul—he was the only man who might be able to help you."

Trudy lowered her eyes, with a smug expression on her face.

" The senhorita—she was magnificent! " Joaquim said.

The British Consul in Curitiba was, in fact, a lazy and ineffectual little man. But Trudy, it appeared, had soon reduced him not only to the condition in which we had left the prison officer, but also to an unaccustomed efficiency. She had stood over him while he pulled the necessary strings and obtained the necessary documents. " Then I went to Ivan," Trudy explained.

" Why Ivan?"

" I knew he was a friend of yours—and he had a car. Besides, he's a Russian—and Joaquim had told me about this . . . this Russian person you had become so quixotic about . . ."

"Yes! The Russian girl! What are we going to do about her?"

I spoke with a good deal of agitation. Trudy withdrew her arm.

"I told you. I've arranged it all with Ivan."

"Where is Ivan now?"

"You will see in a few minutes."

To change the subject I said: "But what happened when you got to Sao José? It's one thing to pull strings in Curitiba—but quite another to make them jerk in this God-forsaken hole!"

"I took the papers to the mayor myself," Trudy said, "then to the Prefect of Police . . ." She paused, then added, her eyes shining, "They both wanted to marry me!"

"She was *truly* magnificent!" Joaquim repeated with great fervour.

By now we had turned off the main road and were bouncing along a track so narrow that the fronds of the dwarf palm trees that lined it on either side slapped our faces, then dragged themselves along the inside of the car as if reluctant to leave it. A hundred yards further along and we came to a small clearing, dotted with orange trees, their fruits a rich reddish-ochre, though no larger than ping-pong balls. At the back of the clearing stood a small wooden shack, tilted sideways and with several of its planks awry. It was almost swallowed up in the embrace of a banana-tree, whose huge ragged leaves dangled over it like the wide sleeves of a monk's habit.

In front of the hut stood Ivan, arms folded, neat and self-contained, a caustic smile on his pale face. His voice was, as always, flat and unemphatic, though the words with which he greeted me were warm and friendly. I was again struck by the odd contrast between his appearance and his actions. It was not appearance only: there really was some corrosive inside him which knitted up his body and controlled the expression on his face. And yet by some extraordinary and absolutely steadfast exercise of the will the outward manifestations of his inner bitterness were always good. Six weeks in a Brazilian gaol had already widened my concept of human goodness. It is only now, though, lying on a hospital bed, that I have begun to understand that the will is not always inferior, even in matters of faith, to that spontaneity to which, in my romantic years, I so unhesitatingly gave the priority.

83

We entered the hut. It was empty apart from ourselves: Trudy had rented it for a couple of days, sending the occupants to Curitiba for the first, and almost certainly the last, holiday in their lives. She had cleaned it, hung up new hammocks, and even nailed tin cans with bunches of flowers in them to the walls. This last touch was more than I could bear, and turning to Trudy I took her in my arms and kissed her. It was the first time I had done so in so full-hearted a way. It was a kiss which I remember to this day; but I was startled to find how clumsy it was, with noses and eyelashes in the way and the pressure of my arms failing somehow to co-ordinate with that of my lips, as if it was the first kiss that either of us had ever exchanged. To begin with Trudy's lips went rigid, as if they were lined with bone; then suddenly they relaxed—but a second later they began to tremble, and the stiffness kept coming and going so that I couldn't tell whether she was trying to draw my lips closer or seeking to repel them. What seemed strangest of all was that although the warmth of her lips quickly turned gratitude into desire, it also filled me with a sort of restless anxiety which I could not for the life of me define.

It was Trudy who broke off the kiss, with a quick, puzzled look at me. She gave herself a little shake.

" I'm glad you like what I've done," she said, in a thoughtful, almost rueful voice.

" What are we *doing* here?" I asked.

" We had to make it look as though we were leaving Sao José," Trudy explained.

" Yes, of course. But what are we going to do about the Russian girl?"

" We shall get her out tonight," Ivan said, very quietly.

" Ivan will," Trudy broke in, in a tone of voice which contained a certain amount of reserve, as if she were suggesting that Ivan was far more likely to comport himself decently and sensibly than I was. Perhaps she saw the thoughtful expression on my face, or perhaps she had already gained an inkling of the streak of obstinacy in my nature, for she added:

" Ivan's not known there—in Sao José, or in . . . in that place."

" You mean you don't want me to go?"

" Naturally not—you *would* be recognised. You will stay here with the car—we can't take that, because that might be

84

recognised too. I've got horses—they are in the outhouse over there. You'll be waiting for us at the end of the track . . . *with the engine running!"*

She spoke these last words, breathlessly, almost in a whisper, as if they were a kind of drug, offering unheard-of revelations, which one might venture to take, once, by way of daring experiment.

"What about Joaquim?" I asked. "Isn't he better known than any of us in Sao José?"

"That's why it's safer for him. Nobody will be surprised to see him there. In any case we shall wait until it's dark—and he will be staying with the horses."

"And you? Do you mean to say *you* will be going with them?" Trudy was so suburban and wholesome looking that I still found it difficult to associate her with Sao José and its doings. But her eyes were bright; she looked like a schoolgirl about to visit a public bar for the first time in her life.

"Oh, yes," she whispered, and blushed. "I shall be . . . playing my part."

"While I stay here?"

"Yes—now don't be awkward, I have worked it all out!"

"We'll see about that!" I muttered. Only Ivan heard me. He looked from one to the other of us: the corner of his mouth twitched.

I was beginning to feel myself by now, except that I was becoming increasingly aware of a taut, gritty feeling on my skin—and of the acrid smell rising from my filthy clothes. Trudy must have caught another whiff too. Her nostrils quivered, as if she had been about to wrinkle her nose, but had remembered in time that " this was reality, this was Life! "

"There's a stream at the back of the hut," she said. " A bit muddy, but there's a good current, so it should be healthy."

I took one of my suitcases from the car, and went round to the back of the hut. The stream lay between steep banks lined with over-arching giant ferns. I took off my clothes, one by one, holding them between finger and thumb and dropping them in a heap, as if they were discarded bandages. I was about to leave them where they were, but on a sudden impulse I scooped a hole in the loose earth and fern-mould, and shovelled the filthy rags into it with a stick. I found some stones and made a little cairn over the place. I hated the thought of the dogs or the half-wild little pigs grubbing up something that had been so much a part of me.

I looked down at my naked body. I had lost a good deal of weight and my hip-bones jutted. The accumulations of dirt had turned my skin the yellowish-brown of the country; dried sweat had deposited salty-white tide-marks, so that it looked like an envelope that had been re-directed half way round the world. Looking at it reminded me of Trudy's glowing pinkness and the perfection of her rosy finger-nails.

I took a piece of soap from my case and waded into the stream. My skin blended with the water, which looked and felt like warm tea. But Trudy had been right about the current. It pumped through the very centre of the stream, throwing up bubbles, broad and flat at the top like miniature domes, glinting in the sun. These struck me with such force, breaking as they did so and throwing up a little scatter of spray, that I felt as if I were being aerated. The current seemed to be flowing through me, and removing the inner as well as the outer mud of my prison experiences.

It was an easy matter to clean away the dirt on my skin, but I was surprised and glad to find how quickly the dreadful torpor that had begun to settle on me in the cell could be dislodged. I was young and resilient, of course. But in fact I had just learned something that I have always found of tremendous value—and never more so than here, lying on this hospital bed. It was simply that opposites are incredibly close together: despair that seems impermeable, a permanent condition of one's being, can turn into joy in an instant, with so minute a time-lag that it is impossible to say that there has been a change; it must have been there all the time. It *is* there all the time. As children we know it: as adults we forget it, or come to believe that we are separated from it by rock as thick as a mountain. But for each of us, the life we should be leading is never more than a skin's breadth away . . . I can hear mine throbbing away at my ear-drums at this very moment . . .

Perhaps this idea came to me then because, when eventually I climbed out of the stream, my body looked so white and new. It's an odd thing, though, I also felt a pang of guilt at the sight of all that clean flesh. I was glad I had got rid of my prison clothes, but at the same time I half wished I had slunk off into

86

the woods like an animal, with the smells still about me, and my skin still toughened and varnished by dirt and sweat.

When I opened my case and put on the clean clothes, still smelling of soda, I could hardly believe they belonged to me. They made me feel disembodied. I was quite surprised when, returning to the hut, Trudy flashed me a look of recognition—and of approval. She too had changed—into jodhpurs, and another blouse of a different material but the same strawberry-pink shade which blended so perfectly with her complexion . . . She had a very clear skin which flushed easily, the blood coming and going in different parts of her body like neon lighting—and always that delicate shade of pink. Ivan had also changed into riding-breeches. He was wearing a jacket, one of its pockets unaccountably bulging. It became cooler as the sun suddenly disintegrated into long streaks and filaments of orange and black against a pale blue sky, slightly green at the edges. Gradually the green deepened, until it was the colour and consistency of the baize on a billiard-table; then, suddenly, it began to spread, turned an even darker green, and as it touched the farthest horizon, plunged into a uniform blackness.

Trudy had brought provisions with her, and we ate while she explained her great plan to me in more detail.

"We shall go in about midnight," she said. "Joaquim will stay with the horses, a few yards back from the entrance to the *Saudades de Lisboa* . . ."

"The *what?*"

"That's what Maria's place, next door to 'Sampaio's Bar', is called," Joaquim explained.

"Very appropriate too . . . But how does it come into the picture?"

"You'll see in a minute," Trudy went on. "You see, Ivan will go into this bar place—what do you call it? . . . 'Sampaio's Bar' —yes. Well, he will look out for the Russian girl, in the . . . ah in the usual way . . ."

"Do we know she is still there?"

"Yes, of course. Your . . . little friend Maria knows some of the girls there—she's being most helpful, by the way. Ivan will take the Russian girl into this Annexe place, in the . . . well, in the usual way—and straight out through the back door . . ."

"Just a minute, there isn't . . ."

" Yes there is," Joaquim interrupted. " For some reason you missed it when you were there. It's in the last of the corridors . . ."

" And Umberto has got hold of a key for us," Trudy continued. " He will be waiting for Ivan and the girl outside the door. He will take them across the yard, and through the back door of the *Saudades de Lisboa*—the one Maria took you through. Ivan and the girl will go through the *Saudades* and out at the front door."

So far this all seemed quite reasonable. It was certainly sensible to take the Russian girl through the *Saudades,* rather than risk the dark yard and the winding alley leading on to the main road. There were usually so many people passing to and fro in front of the *Saudad*es that it would surely be difficult for any pursuers to attempt anything there—especially if there were really efficient get-away arrangements.

" But where do *you* come into all this?" I asked Trudy. She hesitated a moment. " You see we must make sure that Umberto can get Ivan and this Russian girl through the *Saudades* without the—what do you call them?—the Madame?—knowing anything about it." She paused. " She doesn't . . ."

" Yes, I know. She doesn't approve of ' goings-on '."

" So I'm going to make sure! "

" *You?* But how? "

" I shall engage this Madame person in conversation! " Trudy said gravely.

" What *are* you talking about? How can you? What . . ."

" I shall pretend to be someone with . . . well, a special interest in these sort of things—you know, curious, about the prospects and that sort of thing."

I stared at her, and then at the others, in horrified disbelief.

" Surely you can't be serious, any of you? " I said.

Ivan obviously wasn't. His lips were twitching as if at some bitter joke, but he stared right through me when I looked at him in appeal. As for Joaquim, he was quite besotted with Trudy: after her performance in the gaol he was convinced she could do no wrong.

" You must be mad! All of you! " I cried.

" It's an excellent plan! " Trudy replied sharply. " I've worked it all out! "

" But Trudy—*you*, in a place like that—you of all people! "

I couldn't have chosen my words more unwisely.

"Why me 'of all people'?" she cried. "Go on, tell me! Tell me!" She caught hold of my arm and gave it an angry shake.

"Haven't I got what it takes? Is *that* what you mean?"

I looked at her. With her face flushed and angry tears in her eyes, she looked in fact more desirable than I had ever seen her.

"It's not that," I said. "But you're not the type. You don't know anything about these things. The Madame wouldn't believe you for a moment."

"She will! She will!" Her lips trembled. I half expected her to stamp her foot. Then, very quietly, she added. "You'll see! Oh, you'll see!"

"It will be a fine thing, won't it," I pointed out, "if Ivan gets the Russian girl out—and then finds that *you* are in!"

She looked a little thoughtful at this, but Ivan broke into one of his rare laughs—an extraordinarily reverberant sound to come from so neat and dapper a frame.

I continued to do my best to dissuade Trudy, but she would not listen. She had become still and distant. Two lumps, like small biceps, formed on either side of her upper jaw. They took away from the softness of her face, making it look square and sullen.

I tried again to bring Ivan in on my side, but he seemed bored by the whole business.

"Don't you *want* to get this Russian girl out?" I asked.

"I *shall* get her out," he said icily. "The frills do not concern me."

Eventually Trudy announced that it was time to go. She herself saddled the three horses and led them round to the front of the hut. They were small, shaggy, and with so many blotches, bumps and callouses that they looked as if they had been nibbled at by a whole army of rodents.

Trudy mounted the smallest of the animals. It was so dispirited that it did not even raise its head. Joaquim clambered on to the animal next to it—and then Ivan mounted the remaining horse, very slowly, as if reluctant to make contact with so inferior a beast.

"We'll leave you to pack the things," Trudy said. "Then— don't forget to bring the car to the end of the track. As soon

89

as you hear us coming back, start the engine. We'll just let the horses loose—they'll find their own way back."

" And what will the Russian girl be riding?"

" Pillion," Trudy replied, softly, " behind Ivan."

In the brightness of her eyes I could almost see a picture forming. She dug her heels into her mount's flanks, and tugged at the reins in order to produce a dramatic wheeling movement, looking a little crestfallen when it turned out to be no more than a spasmodic trot.

" We may not be gone more than a couple of hours," she said. " Mind you have the car ready."

Her manner was a little subdued, but she brightened up when her horse, as she turned it again, really did perform a kind of lurching arc, owing to the fact that it had stumbled over an ant-hill. At this Trudy's head jerked back in triumph. She rode very correctly, her back straight, chin up, as if she were at some English country gymkhana. By contrast, Ivan slouched in the saddle, holding the reins loosely, his head hung at exactly the same angle as his mount's, so that the pair of them looked as if they were engaged in some interminable retreat from Moscow.

The three of them set off. The darkness swallowed them up, but I could hear an irregular clip-clop, punctuated by a sliding, scrambling noise as one or other of the horses missed its footing. A few moments later, a softer, more muffled beat told me that they had reached the main road to Sao José.

I waited until the sounds had disappeared, then went back inside the hut. My head was throbbing, and I had a hot, prickling sensation along my cheek-bones. I sat down on a stool and found that I was shaking so much that I could hardly stay on it. In fact I had caught some kind of gaol fever which I didn't throw off properly for at least a month. The rest of that night, in consequence, seemed to take place under arc-lights; everything was dazzling, larger than life. I can recall it all most vividly, but I'm not sure whether what I recall is fact or fever.

I began by imagining Trudy at that English country gym-khana. I could picture the animal, plump and glossy between her thighs, and her own firm flesh, with the blood that suffused it so eloquently. I saw it as in a three-dimensional film, to which tactile sensation had somehow been added. There seemed to be

90

acres of flesh—and this led me to think, with mounting alarm and, to my dismay, an almost intolerable itch of desire, of Trudy at the *Saudades de Lisboa*. Or, rather, Trudy's body. All kinds of lurid fantasies flashed through my mind. I saw her held down and stripped, while Madame gloatingly assessed her finer points, prodding, poking, probing, kneading, while the others crowded round admiring. The image blended with memories of Rembrandt's "School of Anatomy", and of the Edinburgh medical students leaning over the body of the beautiful prostitute murdered by Burke and Hare. Then a moment later I was imagining Trudy's magnificent living torso being broken into, while her eyes dilated in outrage—shocking, pathetic, yet somehow ludicrous.

At this, I got up, and rushed round the hut collecting our odds and ends, as if there wasn't a moment to lose. I had the sense, though, to snatch up an old straw hat which was hanging behind the door; with this on my head, the brim pulled well down over my eyes, I might pass for any other prospector out on a jaunt.

I ran out of the hut, loaded the things into the car, and drove down the narrow track, hesitated at the junction with the main road, where Trudy had told me to wait—then headed for Sao José as fast as the engine would take me.

Those old Fords were marvellously adapted to rough conditions. This one was terrifying to drive; it bucked and shied like a frightened colt and the steering wheel felt as if it was going to spin out of my grip at any moment. When the car lurched into a pot-hole—and some of them were so big that she actually fell, like a lift whose cable had been cut—it felt as if she was falling apart. Indeed, at the best of times the parts seemed merely flung together, and they made as much noise as a row of tin cans tied to a string. But nothing actually broke, and her bonnet would come nosing out of the pit as if she were some indestructible old lizard, still dragging her reticulated sections behind her—while under all the coughings and splutterings there was a steady, comforting throb. When, in fact, it came on to rain I made a point of driving through the deepest ruts, so that the car would gather a good camouflage of mud.

The road in front of the *Saudades de Lisboa* was crowded and no one paid any attention to me. I turned the car and then parked, facing in the direction from which I had just come, a few yards beyond the house and just round a curve, in a position from which the car was out of sight of the entrance, though I myself could see the entrance in the driving-mirror. I could also see the noses of the horses sticking out from the little alley. Presumably Joaquim thought they would be less conspicuous there, though it seemed an awkward arrangement to me. I didn't get out of the car. In my muzzy condition I didn't have any clear plan, apart from a vague idea of getting them away more quickly than their flea-bitten nags could possibly manage, and a general instinct that something would go wrong. In addition there were the feverish imaginings about Trudy. At first the fact that I was sitting in the car a few yards away was sufficient to still them, but after a few minutes they started up again, more alarmingly than ever. I struggled to hold them in check, but I could stand it no longer. I got out of the car, quietly closing the door behind me, walked back to the *Saudades de Lisboa*, pushed open the front door and climbed the stairs.

The double doors of the *sala* were closed. I put my ear to one of the panels: it was a pale olive-green, still showing traces of a florid Mamoeline design, despite the grease deposited by innumerable processions of finger-tips.

It was obvious that there were a number of people on the other side. I could hear a variety of rustlings and whisperings, accompanied by a periodic clinking noise, and a more sustained background murmur. I was unable to identify the sounds, except that I thought I recognised Madame's voice. But what puzzled me was the peculiarly muted, almost monotonous nature of the sounds. My imaginings became wilder: was this the result of lassitude succeeding some unspeakable orgy involving Trudy's opulent but so disengaged torso? Then as I caught the clinking noise again a more horrifying suspicion flashed through my mind—it came from surgical instruments; it was an anatomical investigation that was taking place; and the steady murmur was that of the demonstrator!

I pushed open the doors and marched in. The murmur of voices stopped abruptly. On the other hand, the tinkling noise was louder. It came from dainty cups and saucers held in hands that had been momentarily agitated by my sudden appearance. A bevy of girls, in their best long dresses, their make-up muted or removed, demurely seated on low stools or chairs,

92

were grouped in attitudes that suggested a Victorian school-room, round the straight-backed settee, on which were seated Trudy and the Madame, apparently deep in a conversation of the most genteel nature—except, perhaps, that the podgy hand which rested on Trudy's knee conveyed a certain suggestion of speculation.

It removed itself to raise a rickety lorgnette which focused itself in my direction. A dozen pair of eyes followed.

"What, pray," Madame demanded, "is the meaning of this intrusion?" (and in Portuguese the words sounded even more intimidating).

"Do you not realise, young man, that we are closed "—and then as a hasty afterthought, "for the moment?"

"Can you not see," she continued, as I stood there goggling, "that we are entertaining?" She drew herself upright, propping herself against a pair of stays. I could see the flesh wobbling over the tops like sheep trying to scramble over a fence. She, too, had put on her best gown. It was a kind of gold lamé, the folds still sprinkled with the powder of disintegrated moth-balls. It was impossible to tell whether it was the same powder or hastily applied talcum which lay in the creases of her gingerish-yellow bosom, or—reduced by sweat to a thin paste —in between the quaking jellies of her breasts. Beside her Trudy looked incredibly firm and rounded; at the same time her flesh had a luminous, yeasty quality; it seemed to float, like that of a Rubenesque goddess seated on a cloud.

Madame continued to regard me for several seconds through her lorgnette. For a moment I thought she might recognise me from my previous visit, but six weeks in gaol had given me a shabby beard, while the fever, which I could feel niggling away inside my bones, like a host of burrowing insects, gave me an odd look. The girls stared at me just as haughtily still holding their tea-cups, and I could have sworn that I saw their little fingers rear like so many caterpillars.

At last Madame spoke again. "We must send for Umberto!" she pronounced in a voice of doom.

"No, no—it's only my brother!" Trudy said quickly. She was quite calm, her breast rising and falling as evenly as that of the sleeping beauty at Madame Tussaud's, though there was a slight flush on her cheek-bones. Her expression was at one and the same time demure, watchful, defiant, and triumphant.

" Ah! " Madame said. She looked sharply from one to the other of us.

" You are both English, it is true," she said doubtfully, with another hard stare at us, which obviously drew disparaging comparisons between my appearance and that of Trudy.

" The family have sent me," I said quickly.

" Ah! " This time the exclamation carried much more conviction.

" Our father—he is an English lord," I said. A faint smile flickered at the corners of Trudy's mouth.

" Yes? " Madame said, with a respectful, slightly disappointed, but still calculating look at Trudy. " *She* is a lady—that is quite clear! "

She thought for a moment, then moving to the far end of the settee patted the small space left between herself and Trudy. I lowered myself into it. On my left I was conscious of folds and layers of flesh, like warm foam-rubber, which took several seconds to readjust themselves. On my right I felt the firm pressure of Trudy's thighs. The combination was oddly exciting.

" Yes," I said, addressing Madame. " We have always had trouble with her."

The slight smile touched Trudy's lips again: the flush on her cheek-bones deepened.

" Ah, yes! " Madame replied, patting my knee, while casting another appraising look at Trudy's. " I have known other cases . . ."

She paused. " That was in Lisbon, though. I didn't think English families . . ." she added, rather thoughtfully.

" We travel a great deal," I said. " A diplomatic family, you know—not at all typical . . ."

" Daddy is in Rio de Janeiro now," Trudy interposed, in a small voice.

" Visiting the President," I added, suppressing a desire to laugh.

The small eyes rested on me; the little mouth pursed up, thrusting the lips forward in a ridiculously perfect rose-bud.

Trudy came to the rescue once more.

" They are old friends," she said. " Mummy and Daddy are often guests on the *Paqueta*—you know, the President's yacht."

94

Madame was satisfied: Trudy's calm voice carried complete conviction; the circumstantial detail clinched it.

"I expect," she said, turning to me, "It began as a concern for fallen girls?" I nodded.

"Yes," she said. "It usually begins that way. That has been my experience."

She gave a deprecating little cough.

"I have known cases," she said, "which benefited from a little first-hand experience . . . It satisfies curiosity, you understand—gets them over the rebellious streak, makes them docile, ready for the right kind of match?"

"The family have been thinking of a finishing school in Switzerland—run by nuns, of course!"

"Ah, the poor child! You have no idea what they do to a spirited girl in those places! . . . I quite agree with your family, of course, that something must be done . . . But you've no idea how much a real *loura inglesa* is prized in these parts—especially if she's a lady into the bargain! Men go mad, quite mad. I've known them empty their pockets—a thousand, five thousand, ten thousand cruzeiros!" She darted a quick glance at me to see if I was impressed. "Even *twenty* thousand!" she added, staring me straight in the eye. She paused, then when I said nothing:

"I am talking of a girl without a protector" . . . She laid a hand on my knee and squeezed it. "If a protector comes into it, of course, there's always his cut as well . . . ten per cent, say . . ." She squeezed my knee again.

"Even more perhaps, if it's a blood relation . . . such as a brother!" And she squeezed my knee so hard that I half expected the knee cap to pop out of its joint.

But at that moment Umberto, from somewhere in the lower regions of the house, bellowed a snatch from a popular ballad, paused, then repeated the phrase. I guessed, from the slight stiffening of Trudy's thigh, that this must be a pre-arranged signal to let her know that Ivan had successfully extricated the Russian girl, and was presumably waiting down below.

I allowed a few minutes to elapse, then, removing Madame's hand from my knee, I got to my feet, making a peremptory elder-brotherly gesture to Trudy to follow suit. Turning to Madame I whispered in her ear: "I shall remember. We have property in the area. We shall be here again in the autumn . . ."

The eyes sparkled for the first time. "Ah yes," she said.

" You may very well come riding this way, may you not?— You and your sister . . ." Then, wistfully, " Of course a whole week-end would be better . . . for both of us . . . And it would satisfy Missy's curiosity "—the jaws snapped, " for good!"

I took Trudy by the arm. The girls, abandoning their sylvan poses, scrambled to their feet, and crowded round her, finger-ing the material of her blouse, stroking her arm, uttering little cries of admiration. Trudy, very gravely, went from one to the other, shaking hands. Each of them dropped her a curtsy. At the door Madame clasped her to her bosom; she planted a kiss on each of her cheeks, her eyes registering the warmth and smoothness of the contact as she did so.

" My dear child, I shall not say good-bye," she said, " *Ate logo!* That is all—*ate logo!* Your brother, I am sure, will bring you to visit me again . . ."

" We will find our own way down," I said, " it will be more discreet."

As I was closing the double doors Madame called out to Trudy: " And next time, my dear, I shall have *real English tea* for you!"

I closed the doors and we started down the stairs. Half way down the stairs Trudy gripped my arm. " You see?" she said, in a husky whisper, " You see? I've done it!"

" Yes—and now we must hurry! The others will be wait-ing . . ."

But she seemed to have forgotten this aspect of the matter altogether.

" Don't you realise what has happened?" she said, pulling at my arm and causing me to slow down. " Don't you realise? *I have been in a brothel!* Just think of it! A real brothel!" She broke into a delighted laugh. " What *would* they say at home!"

I pulled at her arm and got her moving again.

" And I'll tell you another thing," she said breathlessly, as we ran down the stairs. " That woman in there—she *liked* me! She thought I was—well, all right! *Now* do you see?"

Maria, Umberto, Ivan and the Russian girl were waiting in the darkened hall. Ivan looked at Trudy's shining eyes with a sardonic smile. His attitude seemed to be one of ironic flippancy, as if, out of politeness, he was taking part in a charade that bored him almost beyond endurance. But at the same time he

96

seemed to be holding himself in, as if he were nursing a peculiarly bitter secret. There was something taut and highly charged about him, like a high tension wire. He wasn't in the least surprised to see me.

The Russian girl was standing beside him. She was very still, a veiled, almost remote expression on her face. But one could sense the tension in her too: her eyes seemed to be resolutely emptied of expression, as if she did not dare admit hope into them. I felt dissatisfied and oddly depressed that I could not find something special to say to her. For some reason the fact that we met again in circumstances of drama and urgency filled me with a sense of guilt, as if I had committed some unpardonable vulgarity.

As for Maria, she was thoroughly enjoying herself. She ran up to me, threw her arms round my neck and gave me a comradely kiss. " That's a *good* boy! " she said. She startled Trudy by giving her a nudge in the ribs with her elbow, and bursting into a peal of laughter which she quickly smothered with her hand. Then she rushed at Umberto, who was shaking his head and muttering, " I don't like it! It's been too easy! I don't like it! " and began darting kisses at whatever parts of his torso she could reach by standing on her toes, or squeezing his massive biceps, as if in gratitude for some new and exquisite pleasure.

" We must go! " Ivan said in a harsh whisper. Umberto opened the door and looked out. " No one, " he said, " No one— it isn't natural! "

It was indeed quite unnaturally quiet outside. By chance we had struck one of the rare interludes in the coming and going along the Avenida. There was no sign of Joaquim and the horses.

" The car's just round the bend, " I said, leading the way. Everything was quiet, and I was feeling rather foolish about my earlier intuition of disaster, and, to tell the truth, a little apprehensive as to how Trudy, on reflection, would react to my interference with her grand strategy, when I suddenly heard a startled grunt behind me, followed by a thud. I turned round to see Umberto lying on the ground with a long *gaúcho* knife sticking out of his huge back.

There was a kind of click inside my mind, like that made by the shutter of an old-fashioned camera, and everything seemed

97

to go unreal again. The five of us staring down at Umberto, his face almost buried in the red mud, and the group of dark, menacing figures emerging from doorways and slowly encircling us, seemed to belong to a masque rather than to real life: the knife, still quivering like a tuning-fork, was an ingenious stage-effect, and even poor Maria's piercing scream as she flung herself on Umberto and tried with both hands to wrench the knife out seemed strangely stylised. As if I were looking down from a gallery I saw Ivan seize the Russian girl's arm, while his free hand went inside the pocket of his coat. A moment later the hand was withdrawn: it was holding something squat and black: there was a crack, not much louder than the splitting of a piece of firewood, a spurt of orange flame, as theatrical seeming as the knife in Umberto's back, and the man nearest Ivan slid to the ground, in soundless slow-motion. It was only when I caught a glint of little tusk-like teeth and I recognised the man lying practically at my feet as the proprietor of Sampaio's Bar, that I came back into my body, and was aware of Trudy whimpering beside me. At this my fist shot out almost automatically, knocking down the man in front of me. The rest of them hesitated, and we broke into a run. We reached the car and began piling in. After their momentary hesitation our attackers were closing in again. Very calmly Ivan raised his hand and fired again. This time there was a yell that pierced my eardrums: a man was scrambling about on one knee, clasping the other with interlaced fingers. Ivan pushed the Russian girl into the back seat of the car and clambered in beside her. I took the wheel, with Trudy beside me. The car started at once: in the driver's mirror I saw Ivan turn round, lean out of the side of the car and fire again. Then as we gathered speed a tremendous hubbub broke out behind us: the street had suddenly filled; doors and windows were flung open, and a crowd had formed round the still figures huddled in the roadway. I thought I caught a glimpse of Madame with her arm round Maria's shoulder, leading her back into the *Saudades de Lisboa*. As we rounded the bend I caught a glimpse, too, of Joaquim, standing with the horses. He must have decided it would be safer to wait there than in the alleyway. He gave a start as he recognised the car, recovered himself and, guessing that something must have happened (he must have heard the shouting if not the pistol shots), waved to us to go on. At that moment there was

98

a rumble of thunder overhead, and drops of rain as big as pennies began to fall.

I headed in the direction of Curitiba as hard as the old Ford would take us. At first I thought our get-away would be brought to a stop before it had properly started, for a full-scale tropical storm had developed, and the road was soon in a terrifying condition, with large stretches deeply flooded and the edges of the pot-holes crumbling until they were sizeable craters, while miniature avalanches of mud, gravel and boulders came cascading down the steep banks on either side. But somehow we got through, and after a while the storm eased a little. Ivan and I took it in turns at the wheel, and we stopped for neither food nor sleep. Towards the end the fever I had caught in the gaol took a real grip: I was trembling and sweating and chattering away like a magpie. I remember that I kept imagining that I could smell the sanitary buckets in the gaol, and that the only way to get away from them was to drive faster— and oddly enough I have never driven better in my life.

It took us nearly eight hours to get back to Curitiba, but even so we got there long before the news of our escapade. The storm had destroyed the telegraph lines from Sao José, which were unreliable at the best of times. The road would be impassable for a month, and there was no railway. In any case, in those days a few odd killings in the red-light district of a remote pioneer township did not provoke the authorities to any great urgency.

Obviously, though, events would catch up with us sooner or later, and it was necessary for all of us to get out of the country as soon as possible. Once again Trudy was superb. Ivan and the Russian girl were, of course, the first priorities, and Trudy had already organised everything for them before she left Curitiba on her rescue mission, including passports and visas (how she did this in the case of the Russian girl I never discovered) and passages to England from Buenos Aires.

She had argued, quite rightly, that Buenos Aires would be a safer port of embarkation than a Brazilian one, and we were only a few miles from the Argentinian frontier. Ivan and the Russian girl crossed over the day after we returned to Curitiba. Afterwards I learned that they had been married by the ship's captain during the passage to England. For a few years afterwards I received an occasional laconic note from Ivan, sometimes with a scribbled message from the Russian girl at the bottom, but then I lost touch with both of them.

I had not been able to say good-bye before they left, because I had been delirious with gaol fever. Trudy nursed me through it and somehow managed to get everything ready for our own departure. Before the week was out we too were on our way to Buenos Aires, where I quickly recovered. Trudy, though, had lapsed into a curious frame of mind, perhaps as a result of re-action. She became very quiet and reserved. She had discarded the more fetching of her blouses, wearing only those which were severe in cut and buttoned up to the throat. Some of these, however, still left her arms bare above the elbow. Her forearms always fascinated me: they were smooth and rounded, and somehow they always looked especially naked. I could not keep my fingers off them. She submitted with an expression on her face that was both defiant and somehow slightly sneering. Then one morning she appeared in a blouse I hadn't seen before, with loose sleeves that buttoned at the wrists. She seemed, too, to be at pains to smother the lines of her figure. She didn't actually wear a corset, but she kept her brassière so tightly strapped that when I put my arm round her my hand en-countered what can only be described as a corsage—and that so hard and spiky that it might have been an article of medi-eval armour. It could not alter the beautiful line but it certainly froze it into still-life.

She always allowed my hand to remain where it was for several seconds before pushing it away sharply, even roughly. On these occasions her jaw jutted slightly, as if she were grinding her teeth. At the same time there would also be a smug, self-satisfied expression on her face, as if she were saying, " Now *I've* seen life too, so be damned to you! "

At other times it would seem to me that she was begging me to rescue her from some network of impenetrable defences she was busy erecting round herself. I found all this baffling, and sometimes infuriating, and yet poignant in a piercing, almost unbearable way. The sense of her physical presence, shrouded, muted, and embattled, filled me with a fury of desire, but it was a desire shot through with pity, anxiety, and other emotions that I could not define but which frightened and disturbed me. That picture by Rembrandt continued to haunt me: in my nightmares I would find myself confronted by a beautiful female statue upon which I was expected to operate, only to discover I was all fingers and thumbs or that the essential instruments were missing.

Nevertheless, by the time Trudy set sail for England there was, to use the quaint terms current in those days, an "understanding" between us, and I had more or less promised to follow her as soon as I had sorted out my business affairs.

* * *

Well, that has been a surprise. I had no idea I was capable of such sustained excursions into the past. Theories, yes, and protestations of faith supported perhaps by occasional flashes of memory—but not such a re-creation—no, more than that, a re-living of a whole section of my life.

The odd thing about it, too, is that until now it was not a section I greatly cared to recall. I had always looked upon it as too exposed and arid—a table-land for the frantic drumming of youth. In recent years I have, on the whole, preferred the contemplative hollows, where the vegetation, or so I supposed, was so much more luxuriant.

Am I, then, beginning to doubt the beliefs on which I have tried to base my life? Or is it that I have reached back to a particularly hectic part of my life because my faith has, in fact, deepened? So that for the first time in my life I give the context in which that faith operates its proper due, and appreciate at last the sacramental nature of fortuitous circumstance?

What I know for certain is that my unexpected re-entry into that forgotten landscape has rejuvenated me. I feel a gush of energy from that young heart to this old one.

Yesterday I got out of bed and managed to walk over to the window. It was a dismal enough scene, in a drab November light, that lay before me. But I felt a tremendous surge of joy and love for the square of institutionalised lawn, sprinkled with mist like crystals, the few trees with bare branches like rusty wire, the expanse of wet tarmac with its parked cars and ambulances, and the dust bins round the entrance to the kitchens, and the scurrying figures of white-coated doctors and attendants, and the nurses hugging their dark cloaks about them.

One of them looked up at my window, and I felt myself beaming at her idiotically, though from that distance (I am

101

three floors up) my face could have been no more than a knobbly white blur. But a few minutes later the door behind me opened and the young nurse who reminds me so much of Tanya came in. She stood for a few moments, regarding me gravely, then came and stood beside me. I was afraid that she would make one of those scolding or patronising remarks that nurses commonly address to the aged. But she merely said, in an even, matter-of-fact voice, " You can put your arm round my shoulder, if you like," almost as if she were inviting a simple intimacy. I was, to tell the truth, glad enough of her support: I felt dizzy, and my limbs were quivering like those of a daddy-long-legs. But my hand resting on her shoulder (the cloak was still wet with mist) throbbed with love, present love and the memory of all the love I have given and received in the past. Before we reached the bed, too, I began to laugh. She was laughing too as I fell back and pulled the covers back over myself. She didn't attempt to help, or pat the pillows, or fuss in the usual way. She just sat on the side of the bed and we laughed together like conspirators.

*   *   *

The room is in semi-darkness most of the day now. A little grey light filters through the windows and under the door, swirls round a while, then leaks away again, like water out of a shallow lock. There are no longer flickerings on the wall for me to watch. But I get over to the window at least once a day. Sometimes it's after dark, but I don't mind: I can watch the lights of the houses in the distance and imagine the hands that switched them on. I can imagine, too, the hands that draw the curtains to blot the light out, apart from a tiny sliver of gold. I like that best of all: I don't envisage anything in detail, any more than you do when you remember a phrase of music or catch the scent of honeysuckle: there's just the feel of men, women, children; lovers, fathers, mothers; eating, drinking, sleeping, laughing, making love. Quarrelling, fighting, and hating too: it doesn't matter: they fill me with the same ache of poignancy and love.

Sometimes I see the lights of an electric train in the distance, like a string of iridescent bubbles, and I can feel the bodies of the standing passengers jostling together, and the hams of

102

the seated ones wobbling in unison, while the newspapers crackle and the briefcases balance on bony knees and steam mists up spectacles and rises with a peat-like smell from wet mackintoshes and umbrellas.

Sometimes I have to be content with the headlights of a car that drives up to the hospital, and then I conjure up the hands on the steering wheels, the legs brushing against the gear levers, and the sideways twist of the body as the driver gets out of the car, then stands upright, then slams the doors, then walks briskly away . . .

The reason why some of these explorations of mine have to take place at night is that they would be strictly against the doctors' orders—or, rather, would be if they knew anything about them. The doctors are puzzled by me as it is, not because I'm getting better but because I'm not getting worse, as presumably I should be with this second operation in the offing. This, their attitude seems to imply, is not only against the regulations, but downright discourteous on my part. If they knew I was getting out of bed as well I should have no reputation left at all.

So my jaunts are confined to the periods when they and their myrmidons are out of the way, and when the young nurse is on duty—and sometimes, of course, that means night duty. Quite often, as a matter of fact, she has to come when she's off duty. But in one way or another, at some time during the day or the night, she sees to it that I have my half hour or so at the window. Not that either of us admits that I need any help. She does not come as nurse to patient. We behave as two people who share a secret time together which has become infinitely precious to us.

Sometimes when we get to the window she brings up a couple of chairs and we sit, side by side. Usually, though, we stand, me with my arm round her shoulder. I like it best like that. Especially when it's dark, because sometimes the headlights of a car, or a light suddenly switched on in one of the rooms facing this wing, encircles us with a kind of golden nimbus. I have tilted the mirror of the dressing-table so that I can look in it when this happens—and then I can see our two figures, blurred and wavering like ghosts. At first the faint light accentuates the differences between us, flowing soft and lambent round her slender young figure, but high-lighting the fluffy whiteness of

103

my hair and beard. But gradually it flows round us with equal emphasis, enclosing us in a single flickering contour, so that there is only the ghostly suggestion of a tall man with his arm round the shoulders of a girl, like an emblem in a stained-glass window.

As we stand there I describe what I see, and she listens, very still and intent, sometimes giving a little gasp, as if she were suppressing the sound of her breathing for fear it should cause her to miss something.

I tell her what I see with my inner as well as my outer eye. How the light of one of the lamps placed round the asphalt falls along the cheekbones of a passer-by in such a way that I am sure I know how old they are and whether they are sad or smiling—and how it reveals, like an X-ray picture, the young boy or girl still lurking beneath the lineaments of age. I describe heads, cheeks, shoulders, legs, ankles, feet. I speak of the heat and fume of human reality emanating from hairy nostrils, warts, decaying teeth, unwashed flesh.

"That doctor getting out of his car now," I say, "You can see that his arches have fallen, and he's scratching himself where his coat is too tight under the armpits!" Or, "Look at that girl sniffing the air before she goes into the hospital to visit somebody. You can tell by the way she tilts her nose that she prefers the mist to the hospital smell and wants to run back into it!" Or, "That woman, waddling at the hips, she's pushing her stomach out to tell us that her poor womb is tired, and that she's sad for it . . ."

The nurse seldom speaks, though every now and then she gives one of her shoulders a little jerk, as if to say: "Go on! Go on!" Once, though, she suddenly clasped my hand and said:

"I don't think it will ever be ugly again! Any of it!"

All this time my arm round her shoulder lies quite still and peaceful. I am aware of her supple young body beneath it, of the resilience of her bones and sinews, aware and grateful; but the contact, though unequivocally that of flesh to flesh, is utterly free; there are no secret pressures given or received; it is as if we formed a circuit, by means of which my new found pity, love, and awe for human flesh, young or old, innocent or corrupt, poured outwards, to return filtered and purified, not only to me but to her also. I have for a brief while become her fleshly conductor or mediator to that central mystery of the flesh—compassion. And so I have learned that my kind of belief has its final reserves of revelation just as much as any other.

*   *   *

As I've said before this isn't an autobiography. I haven't the slightest wish to set down what happened to me " then, and then, and then . . ." In the course of a long life a lot of events have attached themselves to me. In that sense moss really does gather on rolling stones. But it's the stone that I'm mostly concerned with. Not that I think the moss isn't important too: it's the colouring on the globe, which dips in and out of sight according to the tilt of its axis and the laws of its own trajectory. Some people say we collect the events we deserve, but that's only true within limits: it doesn't give anything like enough scope for the operations of pure accident. It would be much nearer to the truth to say that it's the events we remember that we deserve.

What I remember now is my first glimpse of Trudy in England. She was living with her parents . . . in Surbiton. I arrived at the station there on an early train, and for some reason very few people were about. In fact my memory always creates a picture of the platform as a kind of stage, lifted against a lowering grey sky, and absolutely deserted except for Trudy—and a dog.

It was a warm, muggy day and Trudy was dressed in much the same way as when I had first known her in Curitiba, except that she had a light linen jacket over the inevitable blouse. The latter, indeed, was flimsier than any she had dared to wear in Brazil, where they are so much more strait-laced about that kind of thing. The lovely curves of her breasts were, in consequence, very much in evidence: the firm flesh above them looked as if it had been moulded, the cleavage as if it had been chiselled. The effect was somehow reminiscent of those eye-catching, too-good-to-be-true advertisements for swimsuits and undergarments you see nowadays along the sides of the escalators on the London Underground, and which make you want to run back, up or down, so that you can have a closer look.

At the same time she seemed diminished, almost as if underneath the swelling clothes and blooming skin the body had died. There was a stiffness about her face, as if she had not long left the dentist and the effects of the injection hadn't yet worn off. Her eyes had the perfect clarity of health, the whites a kind of translucent enamel, their whiteness matching that of the small, even teeth; but the pupils seemed static, almost fixed, with an uneasy flickering in them like whisps of straw that have just caught fire.

As I looked at her I experienced a terrible pang—the first of many; so many that looking back on it now my relationship with her seems one continuous pang. I get it even now as I write about her. It's as if she produced some abrasion inside my chest that never healed. Time after time I've tried to work out exactly what that odd sensation, as sharp as the pain of bronchitis, really meant. Was it guilt, doubt, unsatisfied desire, love? I think there was love in it. The other elements too, no doubt, but certainly love—yet love which was somehow *tabu* as far as I was concerned.

It takes a long time to learn that neither desire nor love is always enough by itself. When I was young I believed that I only had to trust to my body and all would be well. I knew even then, of course, that the body was a far surer and subtler guide than the mind. It had its own priorities and preferences, and there were many things which the mind imagined it wanted that the body simply would not permit. But I didn't realise then that the body, too, could make mistakes, that it, too, needed educating. Nor did I realise that inside the body there was also a daemon—and *that* never made mistakes. *That* knew, without a shadow of doubt, what should be done, what the whole course of one's life ought to be; and if one deviated from it by as little as a hair's breadth, it would never let one rest, afflicting one with as many aches and pains as Prospero inflicted upon Caliban.

Its instrument, of course, is that same centre which I invoked at the beginning of this journal—that organ which is the geiger-counter, the computer which sorts out a network of sensations far too complex for the human mind to encompass, and reports back to the daemon, who can distinguish in a flash between essential rightness or wrongness. There are times, though, when its findings (which are made entirely for its own sake) don't get back to the organism as a whole, and so there is

106

distress of body and mind. Sometimes it's a distress which lasts a lifetime. You have to be very lucky indeed to be put in touch with that daemon—and perhaps it's only luck. Certainly the daemon doesn't care tuppence for your mistakes, of mind or body, or whether you have fallen in love suitably or unsuitably. It exists in and for itself; as far as you are concerned it's the innermost and unknowable mystery . . .

Where *did* this idea come from, though? I haven't introduced a daemon before. I suppose you might say that it's the same with all religions. Every one of them becomes more and more complicated the more you think about it—and more and more confusing when you try to formulate it. Apparently it's never possible to talk just about one God; you have to divide him out among trinities and so on. Perhaps I'm merely trying to show that my particular faith is just as open to elaboration as any other. For the most part, though, it's best to stick to that organ which is the true intermediary: it has become flesh, and it has the gift of tongues.

I don't mean to say that Trudy was not pleased to see me. On the contrary—but pleased is not quite the right word. Grateful is closer to it, but that in some purely private sense that didn't involve me, and attended by something fretful and anxious that caused my heart to thump in a peculiar way, as if an extra burden had suddenly been thrown on it.

I was disturbed, too, by the way she threw her arms round my neck. Trudy had never been free and flowing in her movements; there had always been something slow and measured about them but that had corresponded perfectly with her statuesque kind of beauty. About this embrace there was an unexpected clumsiness, which I somehow found both jarring and poignant.

She was somewhat hampered, it is true, by the fact that one of her hands was still caught up in the loop of the dog-lead.

" I've brought Mick to meet you," she said, in a bruised sort of voice, then added, with a sudden jerky emphasis, " He's *my* dog! "

She gave the lead an impatient shake, and the dog reluctantly scrambled to its feet, raising doleful eyes that slid sideways when I looked into them. He was one of those woolly spaniels whose bodies, if they go a pound overweight, appear to swell outwards and in the process to lose all connection with the rest of their bodies, so that the coat looks as if it's been thrown on as an afterthought. Mick's coat, in fact, when I stooped down to pat him, seemed to slide about under my fingers like an ill-fitting toupé. It was one, moreover, which caused me to shudder. It was not that it was actually dirty; obviously it had been freshly washed and brushed, but the thick curly clumps of hair still looked and felt matted.

It reminded me of the rugs which country women used to make out of rags when I was a boy, and place in front of the kitchen range: no matter how often they were shaken out they looked as if they harboured the coal-dust of ages. Poor Mick's coat, it is true, did have a kind of rusty-black sheen to it, but one that was reminiscent of the plumage of a dead crow. When I fondled one of his ears he gave a yelp, and I half expected to see that the ear had come away in my hand. When I felt his nose, it was hard and grainy, like pumice stone. He must have sensed my concern, for he put out a hot tongue and licked the back of my hand; the saliva dried like a film of glue; the poor beast's breath stank.

The heaviness of Trudy's features increased minute by minute, until by the time we reached her parents' home her face was set into a sullen mask. By now I was in such an odd state of mind, full of a kind of mourning love for Trudy, combined with an inexplicable sadness that made me want at one and the same time to weep buckets and go berserk, that I approached the house as if I expected machine-guns to open up from the windows.

As a matter of fact it wasn't at all a forbidding house. It was solid and square, but of agreeable, early Victorian design. The front was festooned with flowering wisteria, and it was surrounded by trees and lawns, all at their most vivid green, and by unnaturally vivid flower-beds. As it happened sunlight was also falling on it in such a way that it had a brittle golden look like sticks of barley-sugar.

Inside, too, it was light, airy, spacious. The room Trudy took me into was long, and well-proportioned, stretching the whole length of the house, with french-windows at the far end looking out on to more lawns and flower-beds. The furniture and décor were unobjectionable, charming even in that flood of light, especially the numerous vases and bowls, filled with skilfully disarranged flowers. The flowers, though, had no scent, not

108

even the big tea-roses—or perhaps it was that the aromas of various kinds of polish obscured it. These constituted a bouquet in themselves. The smell of beeswax rose from the parquet flooring; a quite different one, violet or lavender, from the gleaming surfaces of the furniture; another from the silver; and yet another from the glass of cabinets and mirrors. I've never known a house in which I've been so acutely aware of all these functional differences. It was the same, too, as I afterwards discovered, in the cloakrooms, bathrooms, and lavatories. Tile, porcelain, glass, paint-work, each had its distinctive perfume.

It was the cleanest house I have ever been in. And when Trudy's mother pushed open the french-windows and entered, with a trug over one arm filled with long-stemmed roses, each with a pearl of what looked like glycerine on it, she, too, looked impossibly crisp and clean, even though she was wearing over her flowered dress a gardening apron of coarse hessian which actually had garden dirt on it.

Mrs Bingham was a small woman, almost old enough to be Trudy's grandmother: in fact she *was* a grandmother, for her two other daughters were both married with children of their own, and the younger of them was a good ten years Trudy's senior. She had white, fluffy hair, but from a distance her complexion looked pink and girlish; close to there were innumerable wrinkles so that her skin looked like cracked enamel, and the tiny veins on the whites of her very blue eyes produced exactly the same effect.

A moment later there was the crunch of new tyres on gravel, and glancing through the window at the other end of the room I saw a large black car: bundles of light bounced off the gleaming bonnet, as brilliant as thunderbolts. Then came the thud of solid metal closing against solid metal, and a moment later Trudy's father came into the room. He, too, was small and neat (it was always a mystery to me where Trudy acquired her magnificent proportions). He had a round face, unlined except for a deep cleft on either side of the down-turned mouth, and a round, almost completely bald dome. He was dressed, after the fashion of business-men in those days, in a black coat, white shirt with stiff white collar, and pin-stripe trousers. He wore pince-nez, and the sunlight darted to and fro from their gold rims to the toes of his patent leather shoes. The hand he cautiously held out to me was small, white and dry.

I suppose he and his wife had also said something to me, in their soft, muffled voices. Indeed not long after I began to have quite violent altercations with both of them—violent, that is, as far as I was concerned—but I can't now remember a word that was spoken, except at our final interview. I see only the neat little figures, surrounded by sunlight and vases of flowers with Trudy standing somewhere in a corner like a draped statue, and me mouthing and gesticulating like an ogre, while the dog cowered under the table, every now and then nibbling at the curls on his coat.

But though it now appears in my mind's eye as a sunlit mime —or, rather, floodlit, because I always had the feeling that the sun itself was artificial, a particularly expensive creature-comfort, like central heating—I can vividly recall the feel of that house, and the sensations I experienced in it.

For one thing I was always voraciously hungry. Trudy's parents both had dainty appetites, and Trudy, although she could tuck in heartily enough away from home, automatically adjusted hers to theirs.

The way they served the food somehow made it seem even more exiguous. The meat-dish, for example, was in appearance more like a salver used for communion wafers. Papa would stand behind it flourishing carving-knife and fork in preternatural brightness, periodically sharpening the former on an equally gleaming steel, with precise, deft little movements as if he were performing a conjuring trick.

With Mama too the quickness of the hand deceived the eye: a flash of silver, a tinkle of china, and the vegetables had popped onto one's plate, and the plate had been whisked under one's nose. At the end of it I felt as if the pair of them had been conducting some peculiarly intricate operation on my salivary glands. The corners of my mouth were dripping, like those of a wolf-hound (perhaps that's why Mick took such a liking to me) and when I removed the snow-white, starch-moulded table napkin from my lips I half expected to find it soaked in blood. The food itself seemed to disappear as if my tongue, too, was that of a wolf-hound—a couple of quick licks and the platter was clean, with me still panting and my tongue hanging out.

It's true that the meals really were insubstantial—little white round potatoes which slid down the throat like pills; neat little heaps of greens which melted in the mouth like snow-flakes; and slices of meat so thin that they curled at the edges—and which, when one had chased them with a fork and rolled them all together, constituted a core of protein no bigger than a marble. But quite apart from that my appetite in that house seemed to grow to enormous dimensions.

Trudy did her best for me. At the end of every course she would firmly pass my plate back for a second helping. Her father would pause, a pained expression on his face, regard the joint or bird for a moment, his lips moving—either in calculation (the remains were always eaten cold the next day) or in silent prayer—before the carving-knife descended, reluctantly but delicately as a scalpel, while Trudy's mother kept darting startled glances at me, as if she expected me to sit up on my chair and beg.

I was so hungry in that house that in between meals I used to prowl about with a savage feeling inside me, biting my nails (as I didn't have a tail to lash) or chain-smoking. I tried raiding the larder and refrigerator, of course, but although both were of lofty proportions, spotlessly clean and quite beautiful of their kind, with gleaming chrome, enamel, marble, neon-lighting and so on, they appeared to be used exclusively for such articles of diet as milk, ice-cream, and chocolate mousse of a particularly fluffy and aerated kind. There was a deep-freeze section to the refrigerator it is true, packed with all sorts of tantalising goodies. On one occasion I did extract a rissole from it and tried to thaw it out and then cook it over the flame of my petrol lighter (the electric fires had been removed for the summer), but the results were not satisfactory: the rissole tasted, I imagine, much as did that prehistoric mammoth when it was hacked out of the ice of Siberia. As for the half-eaten joint, that I never could find: perhaps it was locked away in some secret place. I was, in any case, somewhat hampered in my search because Trudy's mother kept popping up at the most unlikely times and in the most unlikely places (on one occasion I could have sworn she was standing among the milk bottles when I opened the refrigerator door), her little rose-bud mouth open, her blue eyes protruding in an expression too startled to have got round to simple disapproval.

Here again Trudy did her best by smuggling scraps of food

into my bedroom whenever she had the chance. She would watch me, fascinated, as I wolfed them down, then, as the last morsel disappeared and, still swallowing, I made a grab at her beautiful shoulders, she would dart for the door, with an odd little half-smile on her lips.

I am not as a rule, I think, an uncouth man, in spite of my large build and (as I got older) shaggy appearance. But in that house I seemed under a positive compulsion to behave oafishly. For the first time in my life I threw my clothes on the floor when I went to bed, so that when I appeared at the breakfast table they looked as if I had slept in them. I didn't shave regularly, and when I did I left a scum of soap and bristles round the basin, and when I wiped the razor-blade on the little pink towel with a gold fringe that was provided for the purpose, I scalloped it with cuts.

The bathroom, in fact, with its porcelain and chrome, its wall to wall carpeting and fleecy white mats, its bath-towels as soft as foam rubber and as big as tents drove me to fury. On the rare occasions I had a bath I exulted in leaving a tide-mark round the capacious bath, and dirty wet prints everywhere. I cut my toe nails and left the clippings where they fell. I let my hair get tangled, then combed it fiercely, depositing coils of greasy hair and flakes of dandruff on the floor—for by now I was as badly out of condition as Mick himself.

My bedroom infuriated me most of all. I wanted to tear down the pink net curtains and the crimson hangings and smash the lattice windows, hurling glass and twisted lead on to the crazy-paving below. I wanted to defecate on the maroon pile carpet. I bounced up and down on the bed, but there were no springs to break, only a yeasty substance that sucked one in like a bog. The sheets, though—stiff, cold, smelling of lavender and with a blue floral pattern at the edges—I kneaded and pounded with my hot, restless body, until they were creased and stained with dirt, sweat and semen.

I was in such a constant state of sexual stimulation that the wild thought crossed my mind that cantharides was being mixed up with the croutons we had in our soup, or with the castor sugar we sprinkled on our fruit salad—though when I countered one of Mrs Bingham's darting glances with one of my own, it hardly seemed likely: the expression on her face allowed no scope for such skulduggery: it had passed beyond

112

disapproval, pain or shock to something approaching collapse into chaos.

Mr Bingham had reached much the same stage. He was more defiantly neat, clean, polished, and springy than ever, but he kept cutting himself shaving. Snowy bits of cotton-wool decorated his chin, which he thrust forward in order to reduce the chafing from the wings of his ferociously stiff collar: but his little wattles took on a raw and inflamed look and as all these discomforts accumulated, he began to stare about him in a decidedly wild manner. I really felt quite sorry for them both, but I just could not control my behaviour.

When I wasn't being downright uncouth, I was idiotically jocular. On one occasion I went so far as to slip my arm round Mrs. Bingham's sparrow-like body, meaning to tickle her ribs. But to my horror my hand, as if endowed with a will of its own, jumped higher, and gave her little walnut of a breast a hearty pinch. She went limp, and at first I thought (with even greater horror) that she was responding—but she had merely gone off into a faint. I laid her on the couch and sprinkled her with water from one of the rose-bowls. When she recovered she leaped up and scurried out of the room. Trudy, meanwhile, had not lifted a finger to help. She was laughing too much—silently, but more wholeheartedly, I think, than she had ever done before. Somehow this made me more lascivious than ever, and I caught hold of her and rushed her upstairs and into her bedroom, in one continuous movement.

I tore off her clothes, shuddering violently as each expanse of flesh, incredibly white and smooth, came into view. She stood quite still, only her eyes moving as they followed the movements of my fingers. When she was naked I propelled her towards the bed. As she sank back there was a faint sighing noise, though I don't know whether it came from her or from the foam-rubber mattress.

The bed, I suppose, was of the usual dimensions, but somehow it seemed abnormally high; and Trudy's body, too, seemed larger than it really was, a soft, warm mound of beautiful flesh. I felt a pygmy as I climbed on to it, and I kept on all my clothes, even my jacket, in order to give myself some feeling of substance.

Trudy lay quite still; her flesh showed no signs of agitation; even her nipples remained soft and spread out. But there was no

113

resistance. She was a virgin, but I sank into her without any difficulty, and as I did so she did not even start.

I experienced no triumphant upsurge, but only a gradual flooding, which left me with a feeling of disgust at the same time that it provoked, almost immediately, a further frenzy of desire. I flung myself on her time and time again, as if I wanted to devour her rather than make love to her, though at the same time I practised every art I knew. At the end of it I was weeping with a blend of unsatisfied hunger and an odd kind of protective yearning. She stirred then for the first time, putting her arms round my neck and drawing my head between her breasts. But whether she had experienced any physical sensation I never knew. Her body looked as tranquilly statuesque as it had before, apart from a few pink blotches caused by the chafing of my tweed jacket.

After that I went to Trudy's bedroom every night. I tried to be reasonably discreet about it, allowing plenty of time for Mr and Mrs Bingham to settle down after their Ovaltine and their nightly read under the frilly bedside lamps; but I was always tripping over things as I tiptoed along the corridor, and once in bed with Trudy I seemed under some compulsion to make as much noise as possible in my love-making. The Binghams took to putting on their radio (sunk into the pink quilting of their bed) whenever they heard my clumsy progress along the corridor. They also took sleeping-pills with their Ovaltine.

At the end of the week they were as attenuated as paper cut-outs. I felt sorrier than ever for them, but something inside me wouldn't spare them. On the following Wednesday I deliberately picked a quarrel with them—or, rather, I shouted and bawled and banged away with my fist while Mr and Mrs Bingham did little more than go alternately pink and white.

The excuse I seized upon was a wish Trudy had expressed to take singing lessons, and which her parents had discouraged. It was obvious that Trudy had a voice which was eminently worth training, though at that time it was rather colourless, and she didn't take it at all seriously. At any rate, it gave me the opening I wanted.

" What's this about stopping Trudy going to singing lessons?" I demanded during the ritual family gathering for " elevenses " —for some reason Mr Bingham was home from work that morning.

"Does Trudy *want* singing lessons?" Mrs Bingham asked, mildly surprised.

"I advised her against it, dear," Mr Bingham interposed. "So chancy, you know—and such an odd lot of people . . ."

"Don't you think Trudy should be allowed to make up her own mind about that?" I said. I had not intended it, but my voice shook with an inexplicable bitterness. Very quietly Mr Bingham replied:

"She will do that in any case. I was merely offering her my advice, based on a considerable experience of the world."

As he said this he drew himself up to the full extent of his decidedly inconsiderable height. It was ludicrous, but it also had dignity. I had a sneaking feeling of respect for him, attended by an overwhelming desire to shock and hurt.

"You want to keep her in your own mouldy little cheese-hole!" I shouted, and gave the coffee table a whack with my fist that set the white bone-china cups dancing in their wafer-like saucers.

"You want to crush her individuality! Stifle her initiative! Deny her creative self!"

Aware of the banality (if not hypocrisy) of these utterances I accompanied them by further blows on the table. The cups danced and rattled more alarmingly than ever. Coffee slopped into the saucers. A startled cry from Mrs Bingham proclaimed that it was also spurting from saucer to table. Mr Bingham drew a folded handkerchief from an inside pocket and made ready to dab wherever it might be necessary. As my tirade continued it became increasingly necessary. The three of us hovered over that coffee table—it was the long, low sort—as if we were playing an elaborate kind of xylophone—pause, gasp, startled glances, roar from me. Binghams on their toes, swaying from the hips, handkerchief poised. End of roar and bang on table. Rattle, tinkle, slop. "Ah, there! Oh!" Dash, lift, mop. Pause, gasp, startled glances, roar . . .

Trudy watched the performance from the end of the couch, head turning from one to the other of us, her hands in her lap, a demure half-smile on her lips.

I brought the performance to an end with a fine piece of bravura: "I shall take her out of this house!"—roar, thump, rattle, plop—"for ever!"—bellow, crash, tinkle, slop, scurry, mop and dab.

115

" Shall we go?" Trudy said, absolutely matter-of-fact. To my astonishment I saw our cases, with coats and hats draped over them, waiting by the door.

She got up and went across to her parents. " Good-bye, Mummy. Good-bye, Daddy." They were so startled that they proffered their pink little cheeks without a murmur. But after I had collected the bags, and Trudy and I were already half-way to the door, they came pattering after us.

" Yes?" Trudy said, half turning.

" I trust . . ." Mrs Bingham began.

" I take it . . ." her husband continued.

" I mean . . ." Mrs Bingham interrupted. " You two will be . . ." (she swallowed) " getting married?"

" It will be . . . *necessary!*" Mr Bingham added fervently, with a meaning glance at the ceiling (we were directly below Trudy's bedroom).

" No, of course not!" I bellowed. " I shall be putting her on the beat—with the rest of my stable!"

" Beat? Stable?" the Binghams twittered at each other, completely mystified. Trudy patted their shoulders. " Yes," she said, " we shall be getting married."

As I opened the front door I saw that they were already back at the coffee table. Mrs Bingham was holding a cup and saucer up to the light and peering at the underside; Mr Bingham, on hands and knees, was polishing the table with the other side of his folded handkerchief.

Mick was in the porch, a chalky looking bone between his paws. A sheet of newspaper was arranged beneath him: he had not ventured to disarrange its folds, though he had found spirit enough to gnaw one of the edges, depositing chewed-up scraps on the spotlessly clean tiles; the newspaper, indeed, looked considerably more appetising than the bone.

Half way down the path we became aware of the odd pitter-pattering he made when he walked—as if he were continually passing marbles: his paws were hard and black, and his nails needed cutting. He stopped each time we looked back, his head on one side. He didn't attempt to follow us through the gate. He stood looking at us through the bars, his eyes doleful, his paws spread out as if they were supporting an intolerable weight. He didn't make a sound, but suddenly his jaws fell open and he began to pant. I stopped and looked at

116

him for a moment. There was a very faint stirring at the tip of his tail. I opened the gate a few inches: very cautiously, watching me carefully as he did so, he sidled through the opening. When I closed the gate he made a clumsy, bucking movement, like a carthorse trying to turn a somersault, then just as suddenly settled down to his usual sedate trot, a few inches behind our heels; the end of his tail was making a circular movement, like a slow-motion egg-whisk.

*　　*　　*

I installed Trudy (and Mick) in a bed-sitter off Earl's Court Road. I didn't move in with her. I had been seized, unlikely though it may seem, with a sudden access of puritanism. I am indulgent as the next man towards the vagaries of human behaviour (especially my own): all the same I find it difficult to make any real identification between my actions at that period and my real self. I was a rudder without either pin or steersman, it seems to me.

There was nothing particularly inconsistent, I think, about my wanting to marry Trudy in a church. Most of these temples, it is true, seem dead and empty to me, but the ancient words of the services have a habit of stirring the old echoes which lurk in the dark corners and rise like a mist from the site itself. It was surely odd, though, in view of all that had gone before, that from the moment I put Trudy in her bed-sitter until the marriage night itself, I never laid a finger on her. I surrounded her with gifts instead—bouquets of flowers, bottles of perfume, gloves, scarves, trinkets—as if, I sometimes thought, I were laying trophies on a bier rather than on a bed. She seemed surprised by my behaviour, even a little piqued, but she said nothing, and I couldn't be sure whether the pique also implied disappointment.

What was odder, perhaps, was that I should have sought out Griffiths to perform the ceremony. He took quite a bit of persuading. His mannerisms were as irritating as ever, but there was a deeper concern behind them.

" Are you really sure, dear boy," he began, " that you want this, ah, union, to be consecrated in a house of God?"

" Yours was, wasn't it?"

" That's different. Amy and I came together in body and

117

spirit—the one animating the other. Yeast and unleavened bread, you know . . ."

" Which was the yeast?"

" Pardon?"

" Oh, come off it! You'll be telling me next that it was Amy's beautiful spirit you fell in love with!"

" The flesh can make the spirit rise "—he gave a sudden snigger—" and *vice versa!*"

" In any case," I said, getting angry. " Why should you assume that there's less spirit between me and Trudy than between you and Amy?"

He shook his head, the dewlaps wobbling over his clerical collar.

" It's a case of the cart and the horse, dear boy."

It was my turn to say " Pardon?"

" With me and Amy, God bless her, the spirit comes first . . . oh yes, you may not believe it, but even people like me can learn . . . I've got nothing—I mean God's got nothing against the joys of the flesh (provided they *are* joys). But He must come first—' for the Lord thy God is a jealous God ', etcetera, etcetera . . ."

" Are you suggesting that *I* don't worship anything?"

" No, but your God isn't mine, dear boy. You find God in the flesh—I find the flesh through Him. That's what I meant about putting the cart before the horse."

" I seem to remember a time when you didn't bother about the cart, or even admit that it existed—you were too damn busy mounting the horse!"

" Yes, that's what I really meant," he said, with one of those sudden flashes of honesty he was subject to: in spite of himself, and often to his surprise and distaste, his vocation was taking charge of him . . .

" Yes," he continued, " that is the point—is it right for you and me to come together in this particular, ah, conjunction? Should we feel—well, really decent about it? . . . Besides, there's Trudy and *you* . . ."

" What are you getting at?"

" I don't know, really . . . But there's something . . . something I'm not happy about . . ."

Eventually he got over his scruples and agreed to conduct the ceremony. It was a quiet wedding, with few guests. Trudy's

118

parents were there, restored to their glossy neatness, but looking if anything even more bewildered by this unexpectedly conventional turn of events. Some of my relations were there too (my parents were both dead) and a dozen or so mutual friends.

But the church didn't seem at all empty. There were too many flowers. I don't know why it was: perhaps Griffiths or Amy had had a sudden access of generosity, or perhaps a lot of the flowers were left over from some other function.

They were very large flowers: dahlias, carnations, and chrysanthemums with blooms as big as mops. They seemed not only to fill all the empty spaces, but to overflow them. I felt I had to fight my way through them to get to the altar. By the time the service was over I felt borne down and suffocated by flowers.

Nearly all of them were of a brilliant whiteness. But a lot of other things struck me as having the same quality. Trudy's wedding-dress, for example—long and flowing in an indeterminate kind of way, so that her tall figure seemed to glide, as if just emerging out of ectoplasm; Griffiths' snowy robes, so thick with starch, so shiny with heavy irons, so sharp edged of fold that he looked as if he were encased in alabaster; the choirboys' surplices, with their lace edges scalloped as daintily as if they had been pressed by thumbs out of the droppings of the tall wax candles. And the altar-cloth, fantastically laundered and apparently of vast extent, as if it belonged by right to the huge trestle-table of the reception. As the service went on, indeed, the whiteness seemed to grow more intense. The altar in particular seemed to expand, rising higher and higher, like a snowdrift. I began to wish I had brought my dark glasses with me.

Griffiths' red face rose out of all this billowy whiteness. I suppose I must have gone through all the correct actions and responses, for suddenly I realised he was delivering the usual closing homily. But not in the usual discreet murmur, intended only for the ears of the newly-weds, but in a booming voice which penetrated to every corner of the church. For some reason, too, he had chosen to concentrate on the text: " Bring forth and multiply ". His discourse, moreover, was larded with phrases so lush and sensual that they would have been downright indecent if they had not been couched in a Shakespearian style, and delivered in a parsonical sing-song. There was great play with " virgin soil opened by the plough ", for the " loving re-

119

ception of the good, ah, seed ", together with imagery connected with figs, peaches, quinces, grapes, and a lavish assortment of over-ripe skins, gourds, and pods.

He was obsessed with the idea of seed. He just couldn't keep off the subject, and there were times when I wondered whether he hadn't accidentally strayed into the Harvest Festival service. Certainly there was a plethora of references to seed-time and harvest, rains that swell the grain, good seed and bad, seeds that fall on stony ground—and even to the wasted seed of Onan. He conjured up a landscape smothered in seeds, knee-deep in them, as if they were sand-dunes.

To listen to him anyone would have thought that the world outside the church was a desert, the peopling of which was the sole responsibility of Trudy and myself. But what was strangest of all was that Griffiths' manner wasn't all lasciviousness. For some reason a passionate urgency, an anxiety even, entered every now and then into his exhortations.

In the vestry afterwards, though, he was more like his old self. When he shook my hand he squeezed my fingers speculatively. His eyes glistened, then grew thoughtful, as he kissed Trudy on the cheek, keeping his lips there a long time, withdrawing them with a smack.

Amy was there, of course, in an enormous floppy white hat. She kissed Trudy on the other cheek, retreating from it quickly as if it had stung her. Me she kissed full on the lips, with such force that her front teeth ground against my own.

As far as I was concerned, though, it was the altar that remained most firmly fixed in my mind's eye. During the course of the service it had seemed to me to be growing taller. In retrospect it grew taller still. Then it became identified with Trudy's bed (I never thought of it, somehow, as a joint possession) and with Griffiths' sermonising at the wedding. There are times when I think of the whole of my married life with Trudy as a continuous climbing up, first on to a high, altar-like bed, then on to her beautiful body.

It was a highly mobile altar-bed, I may add, because although for the first few years of our marriage we stayed within a reasonable radius of the West End—partly so that Trudy could go on with her singing lessons—we were constantly changing houses. I just had to be on the move—two years at the most in one place, then off again, a new house

120

in a new locality, the bed in a new setting and different lighting, and me climbing on to it. Often it would be a different bed too. I made quite a speciality of buying beds. I bought long beds and short beds, square beds and round beds, and beds so close to the floor that you could roll straight out of them on to the carpet. At one stage, indeed, I experimented with a plain mattress, without any support underneath it at all. It seemed to make no difference: the sensation of scaling a height, ever more laboriously, increased, whatever I did.

Trudy's body stretched on the bed also seemed to grow larger. The singing lessons, which she had begun to take seriously, did in fact have a kind of deepening, ripening effect, but this made her body even more opulently beautiful, and in fact although with the years she became somewhat more statuesque, she never became fat or bulky. I found her as desirable as ever, but my desire became increasingly desperate . . . Yes, Griffiths was right—I seemed to be carrying her, stretched on that altar-bed, from one place to another, in a continuous pouring out of myself. I felt at times like a cloud, swelling again as soon as it was discharged, pouring down its rain upon first one hill-top then another. And all to no purpose: the earth soaked up the rain, but remained barren.

Had Griffiths, by some extraordinary intuition, bestowed on him perhaps by virtue of the vocation which, whether he liked it or not, had chosen to make use of him, guessed at this? I find the thought infinitely depressing. It is a sore point with me, even now, that my marriage with Trudy was childless. It is a sore point, indeed, that in the whole of my long life I begot only one child—but that I can't bear to write about at the moment . . . In a black mood, such as the one that has crept over me while I've been writing this, I am haunted by the fear that there may not be a sterility at the heart of my being. I wonder if that may not be the source of my secret faith—or at any rate have determined the direction it has taken—a grandiose flood of words and theories to mask an inner emptiness? Perhaps, though, the same could be said of all beliefs, both new and old. Our deficiencies and failures may distort but cannot invalidate the truths that are revealed to us —and what passionately held belief does not contain its quota of truth?

These nagging doubts are something which I must resist at all costs. It is too late for them, and this is certainly neither the time nor the place for them. Now above all there must be firmness of conviction. Without it a man's life must fall into dissolution and become confused with that of his body: without it everything is purposeless . . .

* * *

The mood has passed. Even in my condition the past can jerk one back into life and hope. Even I have a present. It is not merely that memory creates a sense of continuing wholeness. The events that revive memory are evidence of a whole series of intersections which exist outside us. They reveal themselves through our senses, but they are also like the music of the spheres.

This morning something happened. The door of my room was pushed open and a new face peered round it. It was the face of a very young man, with large freckles, wide eyes, a lopsided nose and a lopsided grin, and surmounted by a mop of red hair, the coif of which had been unsuccessfully plastered down.

" I say, may I come in?" he said, then very cautiously sidled through the door, closing it gently behind him.

" I shouldn't really be here," he explained. " I'm the new junior houseman—lowest form of animal life!" He grinned deprecatingly, but looked down proudly at his gleaming white, though already much crumpled coat, with the brand-new stethoscope protruding from the pocket.

He switched his gaze to me, and said shyly:

" I'm Cartwright—junior—or, rather, junior-junior!"

I realised then why his face had seemed so familiar: the same red hair and freckles, the same lopsided nose as his grandfather —but a wide-eyed, ingenuous version, with none of the sharp, ferrety expression.

" My mother told me you were in here," he went on. " Thought I'd look you up . . . it's my first day, you know . . ."

He said these last words rather wistfully, with a quick look in my direction. I can't have lost grip entirely yet, because I knew at once what was expected of me.

" I've got rather a pain today," I said, screwing up my eyes and clapping my hand over the region of my heart.

122

His eyes flickered with a mixture of relief, joy, self-importance, and alarm. He advanced upon the bed, nearly tripping over my slippers (which I had put out in readiness for one of my expeditions to the window) as he did so, he put on his spectacles, opened the jacket of my pyjamas and laid a hand, somewhat gingerly, on my chest. The hand was cold, and I jumped—and this, no doubt, communicated an appreciable flutter to my heart. At any rate he whipped out his stethoscope, inserted the tubes, with some initial difficulty, into his ears— they had gingery fluff in them, I noticed, just like his grandfather's at the same age—and applied the bell more or less on the right spot.

My chest was undulating like the belly of a pregnant woman, though there was nothing new about that: my skin has always seemed to form an unusually flimsy shutter.

Young Cartwright listened for a long time. Then he stood upright.

"Do you mind if I examine you a bit more?" he asked. "First-rate practice, you know."

"Go ahead," I told him. "I'm delighted to have my carcase employed in the interests of science."

He blushed, in that sudden way red-heads have, so that as the blood ebbed the freckles stood out like islands exposed by a receding tide.

"Well, hardly *science!*" he said. He went to the door, opened it, peered cautiously round it, then closed the door quietly behind him and returned to my bed.

"I think it'll be all right," he said. "There's half an hour before my next lecture . . . You're not likely to have anyone barging in at this hour, are you?"

"It would be most unusual—it's the deadest part of the day."

"Good!"

He rolled up the sleeves of his white coat and began his examination. He was very thorough and intent, his lips moving as if he were reciting the order of procedure to himself. His touch, though tentative and apologetic, was gentle and carried the promise of authority.

At the end of it he straightened his back and frowned.

"I can't find anything really wrong with you," he said.

"Well, there's no need to sound so regretful about it!"

123

"No! No! I mean your organs all seem to me quite sound—well, a bit, er, slowed down, you know . . . But really, quite good, considering . . ."

"Considering my advanced years?"

He blushed again. "Well, yes . . . I . . . I don't understand it . . ."

"There was the operation, of course," I said, hoping to encourage him and to reassure him that I didn't mind the subject being discussed. "The first operation," I added, "I know there has to be another . . ."

But he was staring at me with a very odd expression. "Operation?" he said finally, in a jerky kind of voice. He pulled down the bed-clothes, and took another quick look at my torso.

"*Operation?*" he repeated, and stood staring at me, licking his lips.

I began to feel irritated, but suddenly the door opened and the young nurse walked in.

"I just looked in for a minute," she began, then caught sight of young Cartwright. "Oh!" she said.

"Oh!" he replied, and blushed. Her eyes took in his rolled-up sleeves, the stethoscope hanging round his neck, my discarded pyjama jacket and the upper half of my body, still uncovered, protruding from the bed-clothes. She squared her shoulders, opened her mouth to say something, but something in Cartwright's expression caused her to close it again. To help matters along I gave a realistic groan.

"He had a pain," young Cartwright mumbled, throwing me a grateful look.

"We know each other," I said. "His grandfather was an old friend . . ." I gave another groan.

"I see," the nurse said icily. She regarded Cartwright for a moment or two.

"I think you're wanted in the lecture-room," she said. Then after another pause, "Is it all right if I cover up the patient now . . . *doctor?*"

A whole series of blushes swept across his face, as if someone was pumping the blood in and out: the skin below his hairline began to look raw, as if from sunburn.

"Yes . . . Yes . . . Of course, nurse," he mumbled, backing towards the door. "Yes, yes, thank you, nurse . . ." He darted

124

out of the room, though as he went he threw over his shoulder a last look at her, half fearful and half thoughtful.

She closed the door behind him. "You didn't have a pain, did you?" she said, holding out my pyjama jacket. I shook my head.

"H'm," she said, "I see . . ." She thought for a moment, then added. "That one seems quite nice, don't you think?"

This advent of young Cartwright isn't as startling a coincidence as all that. I remember his grandfather telling me once that this particular grandson was the only one who showed any likelihood of following even remotely in his own footsteps. He had hardly done that—old Cartwright became a very distinguished scientist indeed, a Nobel Prize winner and all the rest of it, in that mysterious region where biology and physics were just beginning to meet. But his grandson had at least taken a roughly parallel track.

As a matter of fact old Cartwright had brought him up since childhood—his father had been killed in the war—and had doted on him, I remember, to a ridiculous degree: the only human being he had ever loved, it was said. With his son he had always been on the worst of terms . . .

It is an odd thing, but I have suddenly had a most vivid picture of this son—lying in his cradle. Perhaps it is the baby-like blushes of this young man's face that have brought back the memory. It is another instance of the criss-cross connections in the patterning of life which have always filled me with wonder. Incidents, colours, sensations, the sound of a voice—in the last resort we can only apprehend them as we apprehend the images and metaphors of a poem. A life is neither a chronological nor a logical progression. It works like a poem, good, bad or indifferent, but always with some lines better than others, whether they come at the beginning, middle or end, and always with rhymes, or images, or rhythms, or sounds, or vibrations that echo to and fro, and chime in your ear when you least expect them . . .

*　　*　　*

This glimpse of the young man's father in his cradle took place at one of his grandfather's famous parties.

Cartwright was a very *clever* man. Much of his life was lived

125

at the level of formulae and mathematical symbols shared by a mere handful of his colleagues. But he was also remarkably well-read, particularly in the more curious branches of knowledge, and he could converse knowledgeably and devastatingly on a dozen different subjects. At the same time his private life was extraordinarily adolescent. In this respect he had changed hardly at all since our undergraduate days together. It was only the scale and scope of his activities that had become more sophisticated—and remarkably *avant garde* for a period long before the advent of the permissive society.

I had some idea what to expect when I saw that his invitation card bore the words: " FANCY DRESS—VERY ".

I passed the card over to Trudy. " Knowing Cartwright, that could mean anything," I explained. " Would you like to go?"

" Why not?" She looked at me with her cool half-smile, but her eyes brightened.

" Fancy dress? I must give that some thought . . ."

" At least it doesn't say ' Strip Poker '. That's one of his specialities—in the best of taste, of course—beautiful couches, soft lights, music . . ."

She peered at the card again (she was slightly short-sighted) as if she half hoped that these words too might be included somewhere in small print. She looked thoughtful: I knew she was working out a costume that would combine decorum with the greatest possible degree of provocation.

She had changed a good deal in this respect. She still liked wearing blouses, but they had become increasingly flimsy and low-cut. She loved exposing her body. She would stand for hours admiring it in the long mirror in our bedroom. She liked to wander round the house naked, suddenly appearing in different rooms. She would pause at the edge of a window until she was sure no one was outside, then dart across, with a little gasp of excitement. She was very skilful at this, and I don't think anybody ever saw her—except me. But she always chose the busiest times of the day for these forays. She particularly enjoyed going into the hall when the postman arrived. She would stand upright, smoothing her hands on her breasts and thighs as his shape loomed up through the frosted glass of the front door. She would catch her breath as the flap of the letter-box opened and the letters came tumbling through. If the postman rang the bell because he had a parcel to deliver, she would jump back, turn to me with a little laugh, her eyes shining, and then run upstairs while I opened the door.

When I had closed it again, of course, I would follow her upstairs. These were the only occasions when any colour showed in her cheeks. If the air was cold her skin would have tightened and her whole body would have grown taut. Her breasts would distend and harden: the nipples and the circles round them seemed enormous. At least she enjoyed exposing herself to me too.

Although we were living in much the same area of London Trudy had not met Cartwright before, but we had been to a number of " fast " parties—fast, that is, for those days. Recently, too, she had persuaded me to take her to various shows in Soho and in some of the obscure pubs of the East End. These shows weren't as numerous or as resourceful as they are nowadays, but they existed, and Cartwright gave me the addresses. On several occasions, too, she insisted that I take her to Paris in order to attend the Bal Tabarin and similar entertainments—they were less glossy and flood-lit than they are now, but a good deal more suggestive. Not that I paid much attention: for the most part they bored me—but I enjoyed watching Trudy enjoy them. I think I must have hoped that they would have a melting effect. At other times I would worry in case I was assisting in her corruption. But although she was certainly addicted to them, it was like an addiction to water: it made no difference to her inside.

Cartwright always contrived to surprise one at these parties of his. It was a point of pride to him. On this occasion the door was opened by a girl wearing nothing but three flowers, strategically placed but by no means in full bloom. Another girl, similarly attired except that in place of the flower at the apex of the triangle she wore an exiguous waitress's apron, served the drinks.

None of the guests, however, had interpreted Cartwright's invitation as literally as this. There were a number of full-bellied dons in loin-cloths, weight-lifter's tights, or hula-hula skirts, which left them bare from the waist up. Several of their wives wore sporting attenuated two-pieces of various kinds, and one fat one, with short, mottled thighs, posed as Lady Godiva, but with a wig of long hair which mercifully shrouded the rest of her anatomy.

127

The most outrageously clad (or rather unclad) were Cartwright's students. But with the exception of one bemused looking girl wearing a net of unusually wide mesh and carrying a trident (I never worked out what she was supposed to represent) who was apparently Cartwright's current teen-age mistress, they stood about in groups chattering and giggling, as sexually unexciting, though also as endearing, as a school of porpoises.

I've noticed that girls in their teens go through an exhibitionist stage. Sometimes it coincides with the horsey stage. I had a secretary once, a beautiful girl with black hair, creamy complexion, even white teeth, small oval face with a neat little chin that made one long to cup it paternally in one's hand. When she wasn't at the office she was usually wearing jodhpurs, and when she wasn't wearing jodhpurs she was usually wearing nothing at all, lying on a bearskin rug being photographed, her innocent face beaming artlessly into the camera. She couldn't for the life of her understand why I thought it necessary to accompany her to the squalid little photographer she'd somehow got hold of, and who was itching to arrange her in poses of a far less " classical " nature than the ones she had chosen for herself. She would bring the prints to my office and spread them out on my desk, leaning over my shoulder and eagerly pointing out the merits and demerits of each and, her breath smelling of peppermint, demanding: " Now, which do *you* think is the best?" I kept a straight face and never once really associated the photographs with the subject. Innocence is indeed its own protection.

Trudy's fancy dress on this occasion consisted of a rose-coloured Indian sari, edged with gold. No one could look less oriental than Trudy: nevertheless she looked superb, and I could hardly take my eyes off her bare midriff.

Neither could Cartwright. His hands either. When we first arrived he sidled up to Trudy, his skinny bare legs and shoulders, both covered with a mat of ginger hair, protruding from a moth-eaten tiger skin, inefficiently cured and as stiff as a board, his ferret-like head thrust forward, and slid an arm round her waist. She shivered, but looked down at him with her usual cool expression. Then, patting my arm and vaguely waving with his free hand in the direction of various disengaged dons' wives, Cartwright led Trudy away, murmuring something about wanting to introduce her to his long-suffering wife the Renée I had known briefly in our undergraduate days and whom he had married while he was still a research student.

The dons' wives greeted me with gleaming smiles, part appraising, part challenging, but in part, it must be admitted, startled—for I was wearing a battered wide-brimmed felt hat and a vast, but by no means sweet-smelling poncho, which covered, but hardly enhanced my rangy frame. It was, if they had but known it, authentic *gaucho* dress, which I had acquired in Rio Grande do Sul during my Brazilian travels, but it certainly didn't live up to the Hollywood versions. Besides, my spurs, although, again, the genuine article, very long and spiky, with rowels as big as saucers, constituted a hazard to their bare legs. Perhaps, too, it was not wise of me to explain that the *rebenque* or riding crop I carried, slung from one wrist, was made from the penis of a bull, though that too was an authentic touch.

At any rate, the conversation was desultory, and after a few minutes I wandered, just as desultorily, from room to room. A good deal of drink had already been consumed, and there were signs that the hard core of Cartwright's guests were beginning to pair off, preparatory, as custom demanded, to slipping away to the various rooms which their host had comfortably appointed for the purpose—a somewhat hazardous proceeding, however, because Cartwright was rumoured to have ingeniously inserted peep-holes in some of the doors and ceilings for the entertainment of those of his guests who, from inclination or necessity, preferred to play a more passive role.

After a while it suddenly struck me that neither Trudy nor Cartwright was to be seen. I had never had the slightest cause to suspect Trudy's fidelity (we still used such old-fashioned terms in those days, even those of us who went to parties like Cartwright's), and this was the first pang of uneasiness I had ever felt in this respect. The memory of Cartwright's hand round Trudy's waist now made me start so violently that my spurs rattled like castanets. I had a mental picture of him tilting her back on to one of those huge beds of his, or her sari spread out beneath her like gild-flecked rose petals, while the moth-eaten tiger skin subsided stiffly to the floor . . .

Morosely I began to stalk from room to room, my *rebenque* clasped in my hand, my spurs jangling ridiculously behind me, and tripping up several of the more short-sighted guests.

Dimly aware that something like this had happened to me before in very different circumstances, I climbed the stairs and proceeded from one bedroom to another, opening the doors of those that were not locked, applying my eye to the key-holes of those that were—and in the process discovering that the rumours about the peep-holes were fully justified. Eventually I reached the top floor of the house, and opened the first door I came to.

A dim blue light was burning at the end of it, giving the room a hushed atmosphere, though the noises of the party could still be distinctly heard. I noticed then that there was a crib along the far wall, its sides lined with blue silk. Two women were standing beside it, motionless and absorbed. One of them I recognised at once as Renée, and as I got closer I saw to my surprise that the other was Trudy.

I tried to tiptoe across what was obviously a nursery, but those confounded spurs tripped me up and I arrived somewhat precipitately at the side of the crib. The two women looked up briefly and indifferently, then returned to their rapt contemplation.

Renée's habitual expression was not so much one of anxiety as of a wary, slightly troubled alertness, as if she was the participant in some game whose rules she didn't know and which were, in any case, constantly being changed—but in which she was determined to remain. Now it was softened into a kind of sad tenderness.

Trudy's expression, too, was one I had not seen before. She was looking down at the crib as intently as Renée, but her gaze was disdainful, almost sarcastic; changing after a few seconds to one that I can only describe as exultant. Then she turned quickly on her heel and made for the door.

Before she reached it Cartwright, head forward, the tiger's paws and tail flying, came bounding into the room. His girl-friend followed, trailing her trident disconsolately behind her. But it was obvious that it was Trudy he was seeking. As soon as he caught sight of her, he gave a wolfish grin, darted forward, and with a slow lingering movement, put an arm round her naked waist.

This time she firmly detached his hand and thrust it away, with an impatient, not to say imperious, gesture, as if she

130

were throwing off a bramble or a trailing plant. A look of scandalised incredulity crossed Cartwright's face.

Trudy, very calm and upright, walked to the door, frowning at him as she passed in a way which clearly forbade him to follow. Cartwright hopped about from foot to foot, in a state of considerable agitation. Realising that his student was still hanging about in the doorway, he made shooing movements with his hands, using the paws of the tiger to reinforce his point.

" Go away!" he barked. " Find someone your own age!"

The girl's eyes filled with tears, but she meekly obeyed. Cartwright turned to his wife. " You're not enjoying yourself enough!" he told her irritably. " Skulking up here, of all places! . . . Though now I come to think of it, there's room for a couch, or even another bed, along that wall there— we're getting a bit cramped . . . Anyway, why don't you find somebody?"

Then, when Renée shook her head— " Wait! I haven't introduced you to Maurice yet, have I? He's in his second year— husky type, you'd like him. Limited repertoire—needs widening . . ."

The habitual half guarded, half anxious look came back into Renée's eyes. Nevertheless she shook her head again.

" Well, what about . . .?" Cartwright said, with a meaning look in my direction. " Might be interesting to see if he's developed, eh?" with a look that was almost pleading.

Renée and I shook our heads simultaneously, though quite amicably. At the same time Renée gave a little laugh to signify the quite out of the ordinary futility of her husband's suggestion. I wasn't in the least offended. I knew exactly what Renée meant. I had become a man obsessed—and therefore as cut off from the outside world as if I was suffering from leprosy or had been castrated.

It is a condition which a woman recognises immediately. A man will seldom admit its possibility. The more unattainable a woman becomes, the more he likes to imagine that he alone has the unique formula that will free her. When a woman is obsessed by a man, not the least of her difficulties must be the constant brushing aside of all the other men who come crowding round like flies . . . Oddly enough, love works quite differently. On the whole men keep a more respectful distance when they see a woman is genuinely in love. Women, on the other

131

hand, find a man at his most attractive when he's in love with somebody else; they expand before him like flowers, catching some of the sunshine; they see him with the warmth of their own benevolence.

At that moment there was a particularly loud burst of noise from somewhere down below: yells, cheers, clapping, and then a woman's voice shrieking: "No! No! No, not here!"

A worried look sprang into Cartwright's eyes, and muttering something unintelligible he hurried out of the room. I nearly burst out laughing. I knew exactly what was in his mind. The woman's voice had sounded a little like Trudy's. I knew it wasn't, and I knew, too, that Trudy could look after herself. But Cartwright didn't. I derived a peculiar satisfaction from the thought of all the imaginings, as painful as they were lascivious, that would be racing through his brain at this moment.

Another burst of shrieking and laughter reached us. The baby stirred. Renée took hold of my arm and firmly led me out of the room, closing the door behind us. Muttering something I didn't catch, she set off in search of her husband. I lingered on the stairs and then, on a sudden impulse, tiptoed back into the nursery. The tiptoeing was superfluous, as the blaring of a gramophone was now added to the other sounds, and the door was by no means proof against them. The baby stirred again, and sighed. There was a frown on his forehead like that of an old man. I leaned down into the crib and kissed his cheek. It was unbelievably soft and warm. Suddenly a coppery red flush, like that of beech leaves in autumn, spread across the cheek—just as I saw it this morning on the face of the young doctor. It extended right under the line of red ringlets which lay flat on the baby's forehead, as fine as maidenhair fern. His breath smelt of milk.

About midnight the nature of the party changed. This, too, was according to tradition. Cartwright could switch his mood with astonishing abruptness. One moment he would be prancing round like a ferret in the mating season, the next he would be seated in the living-room demanding intellectual stimulus with an appetite apparently every bit as voracious. There was no intimation as to when the change would take place. In this persona, moreover, Cartwright was most intolerant of those who absented themselves from or arrived late at the second part of the proceedings, making loud and pungent comments of an intimate not to say anatomical nature if he caught sight of a couple sneaking in or trying to sneak away unobserved. It was, no doubt, the tension thus created which, besides making the initial stages of Cartwright's parties peculiarly hectic, gave them as a whole their unique and memorable quality.

Once seated in the middle of the large room, with his guests gathered around him in various stages of undress, which they would hastily seek to adjust—and the fact that this was a fancy-dress party contributed a particularly grotesque air to the seminar—he would hold forth on a wide variety of topics. Sometimes these were of a highly specialised and abstruse kind, though Cartwright expected his guests, whether they could understand or not, to listen with complete attention—and fortunately there were usually a few of Cartwright's fellow-specialists present to make the appropriate noises, and to be permitted from time to time to interject a comment, in order to provide Cartwright with further fuel.

One compartment of Cartwright's capacious brain, however, was of the jackdaw type, stuffed with innumerable snippets of the most fascinating and recondite information, and when he chose to draw upon it his listeners, without exception, would be spell-bound for hours.

This was what happened on this occasion, though the only item of Cartwright's discourse I can remember was a curious one about elephants (creatures for whom I have always had a special affection) which moved me at the time and has remained in my mind ever since.

" I was talking to Mathers last week," he suddenly announced. " As you know Mathers is a game-warden in Kenya; he's had no formal training, but his studies of animal behaviour are highly valued among those with any sense—and rightly so (with a glare at a distinguished zoologist who was present).

" By a combination," he went on, " of sheer patience and an extraordinary instinct for the way animals *feel*, he has managed to be on the right spot at the right time to witness things that most of *our* zoologists couldn't even imagine "—with another glare at the zoologist, with whom Cartwright, it was well known, was engaged in a ferocious feud at the time.

" Well, this chap Mathers had been following a herd of elephants for several days (no mean feat in itself). He'd noticed that one of the cow elephants was acting strangely. Every now

133

and then she'd stop in her tracks, and stand quite still, in a kind of shocked attitude, twitching her ears and raising her trunk in a groping way, almost, Mathers said, as if she were praying for support. At first this only happened for a few seconds at a time, and then she'd trot off quite smartly. At this stage the rest of the herd seemed to pay no attention to her antics.

" Then, on the second day, the pauses became more frequent. Her mate (one of the biggest bulls, Mathers said, that he'd ever seen) or her calf now took to coming up to her and nudging her, at which she'd rouse herself and trot forward again. The rest of the herd still gave no overt signs of being aware that anything was wrong, but Mathers swears that they were putting on an act, studiously turning aside, pretending to be absorbed in their foraging and so on, as if they didn't *want* to notice anything—and he says that he now began to detect a general atmosphere of restlessness and anxiety.

" By the morning of the third day it was evident that the animal was in a very bad way, and just before dusk she collapsed. The rest of the herd immediately crowded round her —just as if they had expected this to happen—and started prodding at her with their trunks. When she did not respond, beyond a few half-hearted heaves, they began collecting leaves and bundles of grass and thrusting them into her mouth. Her jaws moved a little, and she made several efforts to get to her feet. When these failed, the herd stood quite still for several minutes, gazing down at her. Then suddenly they turned and trooped away—all but the bull-elephant and the calf. These two began to circle round her. Then the bull-elephant plucked some particularly succulent leaves from the near-by trees, and again tried to feed the dying animal: the leaves remained protruding from her half-open mouth.

" According to Mathers a signal now seemed to pass between the bull and the calf—for suddenly the calf darted for its mother's body and began to nuzzle for one of her teats. Very feebly the cow-elephant moved one of her legs to give the calf easier access: her flanks heaved. For several minutes the calf sucked frantically. Then it scrambled to its feet. Calf and bull stood, watching silently for a good five minutes. Then the calf retreated a few steps. The bull-elephant lumbered forward. He lowered his great head and pushed at the rear end of the cow

134

until she was bunched up, belly to the ground . . . And do you know what he did then?"

Cartwright paused and stared round him belligerently.

" He had one more resource open to him," he said, very softly. " Mathers doesn't know whether by then she was dying or already dead—but he mounted her!"

There was a moment's silence, then somebody laughed. Cartwright crashed his fist down on the near-by coffee table: his face was crimson as he bellowed:

" How *dare* you laugh! I will *not* tolerate such obscene behaviour in my house!"

At that moment I almost felt that Cartwright was of my party without knowing it.

Not that he had forgotten Trudy during his recital—it always was a recital, quite unprepared but couched in rolling phrases delivered with a great sense of drama. He had, in fact, kept his eyes fixed on her throughout, with a curious intentness. As soon as he had finished, moreover, he announced, in a loud, challenging voice, that Trudy had agreed to sing.

Renée seated herself at the grand piano which occupied one corner of the room, and Trudy took her position facing her audience. It was evident that the three of them had made their plans beforehand, at some stage during the course of the evening.

There was nothing in the least unusual about a musical conclusion as such. Quite often, in fact, Cartwright engaged well-known professional performers to round off his parties, and I was, in fact, in consequence more than a little embarrassed for Trudy's sake, especially as I knew that Renée would be a barely adequate accompanist.

I need not have worried. Trudy had brought no music of her own with her, and had picked out from Cartwright's large but miscellaneous selection a few of the best-known, not to say, hackneyed, *lieder* and arias. But these she knew well, and in fact their very familiarity heightened the surprise she sprang on me.

I already knew, of course, that Trudy's voice was potentially a fine instrument, but I hadn't realised how far she had advanced in learning to make proper use of it. I had expected something technically good, but still at the promising stage—and at the same time, as far as delivery was concerned, rather mechanical,

perfunctory, and even slightly mocking. What I was quite unprepared for was the power and conviction in her voice.

I stared at her dumbfounded as she stood there in her sari,
very upright in a little circle of light thrown by a standard lamp.
Her breasts rose and fell with an ease and naturalness such,
it seemed to me, as I had never seen before. As it happened the
light played straight on to the white column of her throat, so
that it rippled, as if reflecting flames. The pure notes rose out of
it as easily as if they were taking wing. For the first time I
realised, with a sense of shock, that Trudy had begun to lead a
secret life of her own. I was seized by simultaneous sensations of
exultation, delight, and a poignant hopelessness and despair.
Glancing at Cartwright, I saw that he, too, was staring at Trudy
with a kind of awe-struck, baffled longing.

I think everyone present shared to some extent in these
emotions, and when she had finished there was a long sigh,
followed by a burst of enthusiastic applause. There were shouts
for her to continue, but she ignored them. Very quietly she
walked across the room, and sat next to me, with a
demure expression on her face, and one eyebrow quizzically
raised.

But that was not the end of what was, for me, a momentous
evening. Trudy's recital was followed by that strange moment
when the whole structure of a party suddenly begins to subside,
as if someone had pulled the stopper out of an air-bed. It's the
moment when you know for certain whether you have enjoyed
or hated it; whether you are refreshed or exhausted; whether
you have eaten or drunk too little or too much; and what
exactly is the taste in your mouth. It's the moment when the
room you're in settles down to its real shape and dimensions,
and all the furnishings fall into focus with a jerk, as if after an
earth tremor. It's the moment when you take in the state of
your clothes and your person, and catch sight of your face
in a mirror with feelings of relief or despair. And it's the moment
when, probably for the first time, you take stock of the company
as a whole.

At the height of any gathering of this kind it's only the
people who accidentally impinge upon the field of your vision
who really register. You are oblivious of everybody else's presence, and if you leave before the unwinding process has taken
place it's quite easy to pass someone in the street the next day

without a sign of recognition, though you have just spent some five or six hours under the same roof, in the closest proximity, eating out of the same dishes and drinking out of the same bottles.

The dying embers of Cartwright's party were accompanied by what he insisted on calling " libations " or some " tisane ", the recipe for which he had, characteristically, found mouldering at the back of one of the shelves in his college library. The brew had a sweetish, rather sickly taste which strangely enough, however, did not fight with the rest of the contents of one's stomach, and took the last edge off one's party-time euphoria in a most soothing and benevolent manner.

Barley water was obviously one of its main constituents, and I was reflecting as I put my cup down that this gave it a flavour vaguely reminiscent of the kvass I had drunk, years before, in the Russian Old Believers' village in Brazil, when I caught sight of a couple at the other end of the room in Russian costumes. I suppose I might have been dimly aware of them in the corner of my eye for some time, so that it was they who had started the chain of association.

At any rate, the man was wearing Cossack boots, baggy trousers, long tunic, and tall fur cap, the woman an embroidered blouse, multi-coloured skirts and petticoats, and a coloured scarf wound round her head. And at the same moment I realised that the pair of them were also studying my *gaucho* costume with more than ordinary interest.

I got up and walked across the room in a dream. The circular movement of my life, of which I have always been aware, seemed to impress itself upon my consciousness more strongly than ever, like a wheel rising to cut across traverse lines. The other two must have felt the same, for after a quick look into my face to make sure that they had not been mistaken, they showed no particular surprise.

" Yes, Tanya was sure it was you," Ivan said, with a quick clasp of his small, bony hand. With a shock I realised that I had never thought of her with a name. I suppose I must have heard it before, but it had simply not registered. To me she had always been " the Russian girl ". Even dressed as she was now I still found it difficult to think of her in any other way. She was still in part a wavering emanation of an experience made mysterious by tropical heat, remoteness, and the fumes of kvass.

137

As if I was looking through a pane of beaded glass I saw again the interior of the Old Believers' hut, set down so improbably in the heart of Brazil: the rough furniture: the huge stove: the bearded, long-haired Russians in their archaic costume: the embroidered curtains and hangings: and the alcoved bed. Inside my head I could hear the ghostly echo of a balalaika, throaty Cossack love songs—and the soft voice of the Russian girl.

I could hardly believe my ears when I heard myself saying, in banal, everyday tones:

" What on earth brings you two here?"

Tanya gave me a half smile, half ironic, half rueful:

" Yes, we do seem to meet in unlikely places . . ."

Ivan, too, gave me one of his quick smiles, like a shaving cut off with a particularly sharp knife. " It's the first time we have been to one of Dr Cartwright's oh so famous parties," he said, " and almost certainly the last."

With a nod he got up and made for the long table which served as a bar. He looked more hard-bitten than ever— indeed, I almost said " frost-bitten ", for his body seemed smaller, sparser, as if withered by cold. He seemed to be holding it in, as if, like one of those Japanese dwarf-trees, some force was being savagely compressed within artificially miniature limits. The expression on his face, too, was more sardonic, thrown into relief by a strange greyish pallor of the skin and indentations round his mouth, so deep and distinct that they looked as if they must have been stamped in by machine.

When he reached the table he surveyed the litter of bottles. He shook first one, then another, and grimaced. He found a half empty glass and began to pour the dregs from the bottles into it.

Tanya—though it still seemed odd to apply something so specific as a proper name to her—caught my eye, and looked away. " We haven't answered your question, have we?" she said. " Well, Ivan is a sort of colleague of Dr Cartwright's—he's attached to the same college. He lectures in Russian now . . . We didn't know you knew Dr Cartwright. It really is a *mundo pequeno* you see!"

" A small world indeed! And what do you do?"

" I teach Russian too—some Portuguese as well—at a less exalted level, of course."

" You have no family?"

138

" No . . . Ivan did not wish it . . . It hasn't been that kind of marriage."

It seemed perfectly natural to be talking in this way. The passage of time made us strangers in one sense, but privileged strangers: it felt as if we were partisans in the same campaign, between whom it was only proper that intelligence of a most confidential nature should be exchanged as quickly as possible.

" And you?" she asked, turning her grey eyes on me for the first time: they were larger and more brilliant than I had remembered them. Perhaps it was because her features were thinner; the girlish plumpness had left her cheeks, bringing out the oval shape of the face; the flush had gone, too, and her skin now had a kind of silvery luminosity. The plumpness had also gone from her neck and shoulders: her body seemed slighter, almost frail. The effect was not of a blossoming that had passed its peak, but rather of one that by shedding the outer petals had revealed the real shape and essence of the bloom.

I accepted these changes, too, as well as those of circumstance and milieu, which were, I suppose, startling enough, without surprise, as if they were merely a change of clothes.

" And me?" I said, suddenly remembering her question. " Restless, restless. I've lost my way somewhere."

" Ivan is restless too. You and he are alike in some ways—but he seems to revolve on a pin-point."

" You are happy with him?"

" He's a good man. He is kind and loyal. But he says he lost his capacity for happiness a long time ago—and I don't know how to give it back to him . . . I think perhaps it's wrong to say he 'lost' it—that means you might find it again, doesn't it? He himself says it withered prematurely. He is not a man who recovers from suffering. It shrinks and confines him, immediately, and for good."

" Have you lost yours, or has it, too, withered?"

" No, I think I've only lost it."

" You don't seem very sure about it."

" For a long time I thought that . . . that dreadful time in Brazil had withered me inside too. But I feel now it only sent me into a kind of tunnel—you know, a tunnel with a lot of twists and turns, but opening into daylight somewhere . . . And I'm not unhappy—only aware of not being happy . . . I

139

mean, I feel sometimes that I'm capable of another way of living. It is stupid to talk of happiness anyway: that's just a—well, a kind of bonus you might or might not get . . . I suppose I'm really talking of fulfilment, whatever that means!"

" What does one do?"

" I told you. I'm not really unhappy. I accept. Besides, I'm loyal too . . . But you—you don't sound as if you were happy either?"

" No. I really am *un*happy. But I know I *oughtn't* to be: there is something I ought to do, or that ought to happen . . ."

" Perhaps it's best to drop the ought and trust to the happen . . . I was going to ask you if you and Trudy had children?"

" Don't ask me that question! It upsets me. I don't know why. I suppose mine isn't that kind of marriage, either. But . . . but it upsets me."

" I'm sorry . . ."

" No, no it's all right—*you* can ask me anything, but somehow I have to answer how I feel . . ."

" Perhaps it's her voice that is growing."

" What a strange thing to say! You haven't heard her sing before, have you?"

" Oh no, of course not—but there's certainly something happening *there*, isn't there?"

" Yes. Yes, I suppose there is . . ."

Ivan rejoined us. I had been watching him out of the corner of my eye. He had filled and emptied one glass after another. He had done so without any appearance of enjoyment: indeed a grimace had crossed his face after every glass, not surprisingly, perhaps, in view of the extraordinary haphazard mixtures that had gone into his glass. He had undoubtedly drunk a great deal, but he appeared perfectly sober; the alcohol seemed to act like a caustic, drawing his body and personality into an even more bitter knot. But the pallor of his skin had increased, and there was a grey, powdery look round his mouth.

We talked in a desultory way for a few minutes, then crossed the room to Trudy, who had just disengaged herself from a circle of admirers. Cartwright was in close attendance, a spaniel-like expression on his face, so at variance with his usual look that I nearly burst out laughing.

140

Trudy had seen me talking with Ivan and Tanya, so she greeted them without any particular surprise. Her manner was rather like that which one adopts towards an old school-fellow whom one hasn't met for years—a friendly curiosity in the presence of someone who once played such an important part in one's life, combined with a total disinclination to renew the relationship.

Not long after this, the party began to break up. Ivan went off to collect his car, which he had been obliged to park in the next street. Trudy had refused the offer of a lift, explaining that she liked to walk after she had been singing: this was perfectly true—it was the only sign of tension I ever saw in her.

While we were waiting outside the house for Ivan to return, Trudy discovered that she had left a scarf behind, and went back to get it. All the other guests had dispersed by now, so that Tanya and I found ourselves alone for a few minutes. Immediately we turned and clasped each other's hand.

The suddenness and apparent inevitability of it took me completely by surprise. There had not been as much as the fraction of a second's reflection or hesitation. The movement was simply *there*, as if we had plucked it out of the air. It only lasted a few seconds, but I felt as if the touch of her hand was the end of a clue that reassured me of the existence of a labyrinth I had left too precipitately and for no good reason.

Trudy re-emerged from the house, attended by a bobbing, weaving, simpering, bowing Cartwright, and almost simultaneously Ivan drove up. The car was a surprise. It was large and obviously powerful. But somehow it seemed to me extraordinarily ugly. In part this was perhaps because the colour, a kind of muddy ochre, made me think of a staff car, and this in turn conjured up pictures of desolate battlefields and mud-filled trenches. The huge bonnet rose in a menacing mound, like a dugout; the various pipes which coiled round it struck me as especially sinister, as if they might be used to dispense poison-gas. I held open the door, which seemed ridiculously small for so large a car, for Tanya to climb in, with a sinking of the heart and a curious feeling of distaste. The roar of the engine made me shudder. I would not have thought it possible to feel that way about a piece of machinery, as if it were somehow corrupt. As the car shot round the corner I half expected it to collapse into fragments, like a heap of dried mud.

141

Trudy and I walked home in silence. Trudy, though, was in a noticeably serene frame of mind. I say noticeably because I was struck by the contrast with her normal passivity which was almost entirely negative. She had the suggestion of a smile on her lips, as she walked along humming one of the arias she had sung at the Cartwrights.

When we got home she surprised me further by being in bed before me, and when I drew back the bedclothes I was astonished to see that she had not put on her night-dress. This was the closest she had ever come to open invitation. For a moment I was quite shocked. I wanted to cover her up, to say, "No, no you can't do this—this isn't like you at all!" But it was impossible to associate that statuesque, perfectly proportioned body with vulgarity or lewdness. In any case there was no further response. She didn't actually go on humming aloud, but I was convinced she was doing so inside her head. As once more I pumped myself into that warm, beautiful flesh I seemed to hear somewhere inside my own head a long-drawn-out wail, like that of a wind across the desert. I might have been no more than some apparatus at a service-station for re-fuelling the tanks or re-charging the batteries. When it was all over and she lay beside me breathing evenly, peacefully asleep, the same half-smile on her lips, I suddenly felt a burning spot in the palm of my hand, where Tanya's hand had touched it.

I think it was the end of a thread into the neglected labyrinth that had burned into it. But I didn't follow it. I was held fast by my obsession. A few weeks later, in fact, Trudy and I were on the move again. I had got myself transferred to Paris. I suppose I ought to explain (though I've no intention of going into details) that I was by now doing pretty well in my role as free-lance, free-booting contact-man and agent, in what is cryptically known as import-export. The role still suited me. It always seemed to supply me with sufficient funds to do the things I wanted to do, as well as ample opportunities for roving when I felt restless. In this instance, though, it was Cartwright who had provided the initial impetus.

He was round at our flat very early one morning a few days after his party. When I opened the door to him he darted eagerly inside, then stopped short when he saw that Trudy wasn't there. I had difficulty in not laughing aloud. Perhaps he sensed it, for he transferred his gaze to me. He took in my dressing-gown and pyjamas and generally tousled appearance, with avid expression in his eyes, his head thrust forward.

When a few moments later he heard Trudy moving about in the room next door he looked relieved, then angry, and began to pace up and down. When eventually she appeared, wearing a long lime-green negligée affair, trimmed with swansdown of the same colour, his eyes nearly popped out of his head. She gave him a cool nod, and sat down at the table, where I had already arranged the breakfast things.

Trying to keep a straight face, I invited Cartwright to join us. He seated himself, very stiff and upright, opposite Trudy. I sat down beside him. I held up the coffee-pot, but Trudy shook her head, and leaned forward to help herself from the jug of orange-juice. The negligée fell apart revealing the upper halves of her breasts, framed in the lime-green swansdown. They smelt like newly-baked bread. She made no attempt to pull the ends of the negligée together, but sipped at her orange juice, both hands cupped round the glass, regarding Cartwright curiously and dispassionately. Then, looking him straight in the eyes, she said: " Well? "

Cartwright flushed. " I wanted to thank you for singing to us the other night," he said, in a harsh, constricted voice. She nodded. " As a matter of fact it gave me an idea," he went on.

" Oh yes?" Trudy said politely, taking another sip at her orange juice.

" Alex Stangroom is a friend of mine," he said. " I'm sure I could persuade him to arrange a public recital for you."

Trudy put down her glass and helped herself, slowly and deliberately, to toast and marmalade.

" No, thank you," she said, when she had completed the operation.

Cartwright glared at her. " I beg your pardon?" he said.

" I said: ' No, thank you '."

Even I was startled. Stangroom was a name to conjure with in the musical world.

" Why ever not?" I asked.

" Oh, I'm not ready for that sort of thing yet," she replied, helping herself to another segment of toast. " I shall know when I am," she added serenely. She picked up the morning paper. " Excuse me," she said, and began to read without another glance in Cartwright's direction.

143

Cartwright sat for a few moments, very still, his jaws moving as if he were chewing the end of a cigar. Then he got to his feet. With a solemn expression on my face I escorted him to the door. When I got back into the living-room I broke into a bellow of laughter. Trudy lowered her newspaper and regarded me intently: her own face was quite unsmiling.

But Cartwright was back the next day, and during the following weeks rarely a day passed without a visit or a telephone call.

I was always present during his visits, but he didn't seem aware of it. He seemed to regard me as an annoying but unavoidable adjunct to the situation like the furniture. For my part, I was always grave and correct, with a hint, even, of unspoken sympathy in my manner. Inside I was bubbling with suppressed laughter. Somewhere inside myself I was ashamed of it, but I could not help it: I enjoyed watching Cartwright's inevitable discomfiture: I enjoyed watching the reddish gleam in his eyes as anger and pride battled with desire.

But one morning, quite suddenly, I experienced a revulsion of feeling. I answered the door-bell as usual and admitted Cartwright into the little hall, but when he made to push past me into the living-room (the door of which I had closed behind me), with his customary brief nod, I barred his way.

" I am Trudy's husband," I said, very softly.

He switched his gaze from the closed door to my face. At first his expression was merely impatient. Then it changed to a kind of furious, baffled astonishment. He struggled fiercely as I seized him by the scruff of the neck, twisted him round, opened the front door with my free hand, and threw him, face first, down the half dozen steps that led to the first landing.

He fell heavily on his hands and knees. He remained in a kneeling position for several minutes, breathing heavily, his head hanging, nearly touching the floor. Then, very slowly, he got to his feet and turned to face me, as I stood, very still, looking down at him from the doorway of the flat. He held his hands awkwardly, as if the wrists were paining him. His right trouser leg had been torn at the knee, and the knee-cap, covered in blood, showed through. There was a graze down his left cheek. The two of us stood gazing at each other, without speaking a word. Then he turned and hobbled, slowly, but with considerable dignity, down the stairs.

When I had closed the door of the flat I switched on the light in the darkened hall and examined myself in the mirror. My face was stiff and heavy. I was grinning, and my teeth showed very white. But when I switched the light off I remembered the set of Cartwright's shoulders as he had hobbled down the stairs, and I felt sick.

Trudy and I were off to Paris the next day. We always travelled light and we always rented small furnished apartments. Trudy, as always, accepted the sudden move without question. She knew exactly who to seek out in Paris in order to continue her singing lessons.

*   *   *

It has been raining from the moment I opened my eyes this morning. The downpour has that peculiar English persistency —so different from that anywhere else, and especially from the savage onslaught of tropical rains, a guilty letting of water, attended by a guilty melancholy, as if apologising for incontinence.

But though the light is dim, somewhere behind it there is another light, and that is beginning to change. I can tell it when I study the wall of my room. It is as if the decorators had just done it over, one pastel shade lighter. In that tiny gradation are stored up seed-time, harvest, bud, blossom, bees, honey, and the heat and murmur of summer.

I tried to explain this to the young nurse just now. She was helping me fasten the buttons on my dressing-gown. From time to time I confess to having some difficulty with buttons. On these occasions my hands tremble and the joints get knotted and clumsy.

What I can't stand, of course, are the clickings and cluckings with which most nurses perform this kind of service. Imagine me, a man, standing there while some girl, young enough perhaps to be my great-grand-daughter, the nape of whose neck is as fresh as a new-peeled nut, kneels to fasten my buttons as if I were an infant about to go to school for the first time! It is a humiliation I could not endure—which is why I am permanently bed-ridden as far as this hospital as a whole is concerned.

It is different, of course, with this nurse. She can help me

145

fasten those buttons without being in the least insulting. She does it in a comradely way, as if I were a soldier who had been recently wounded in battle, or an Arctic explorer whose fingers were incapacitated by frost-bite.

Sometimes she is refreshingly bad-tempered about it.

"Damn these buttons," she said this morning. "Why d'you want to be such a nuisance? Why must you use this stupid dressing-gown, when there's a perfectly good one with a cord provided for you?"

"It's *you!*" I snapped back. "Why *d'you* have to be such a clumsy bitch? . . . And you know I don't like the standard issues!"

And I put my hand quite roughly on her shoulder, and we both muttered under our breath, as we made our way to the window.

I think it's at these moments that I love her most. It is then that I feel most fully a man. I love her with the mind of a man, and the body of a man. I have not become, for her, a thing, a mere collection of human parts—and she acknowledges it. To feel love in the flesh is not necessarily to act love in the flesh. If I were younger, or if it were more seemly, I would take her in my arms and pierce her with tenderness and passion—and that, too, she knows and accepts. We have not said anything about this, of course, but we both know where the glow between us comes from: we both know it is there.

"You and your nonsense about the light," she grumbled on this occasion. "It's a dreary, dismal March day—and it's my day off! *Look* at it!"

We were standing at the window now. There wasn't a lot of wind, just enough to slant the rain a few degrees and send it swilling across the grey-black asphalt, as if someone were sweeping it with a mop. Enough, too, to make the branches of the trees stir a little. The branches caught my eye.

"Don't you see what's happening to them?" I said.

"What—another of your daft fancies?"

"Don't you see the green?"

She peered through the rain-splashed window and shook her head.

"You have to focus twice," I told her. "It's just a faint flush, as if someone with green paint on their fingers had drawn them along the branches . . ."

" Oh, help! Not the poetical stuff!" she said with a grimace, but she peered through the window again.

" It's moss," she said accusingly. " Dirty old wintry moss!"

" No, it really *is* the first green!"

She gave me a grudging smile. " You have sharp eyes—for some things," she said.

" What do you mean—' some things '?"

" What I say. You know where you are, and what you are— on the whole. You don't deceive yourself— much . . ."

" My mind's clear?" I asked her without embarrassment. We discuss these things, too, as if they were symptoms of an accident, like battle-fatigue or snow-blindness.

" Except for one thing," she replied, after a moment's reflection.

" What is it? Is it anything ugly or offensive?"

" No—I would tell you if it was."

" But isn't it something I ought to know?"

" Oh yes, you *ought* to know it!"

" Then you must tell me!"

" I couldn't do that."

" For God's sake—why not?"

" Because you are a man, a living man!" she said angrily.

" You must find it out for yourself!" she added, more softly. " I wouldn't insult you by *explaining*!"

" Explaining what?" a voice said behind us. We turned and saw that young Cartwright had come into the room.

" How dare you come creeping up on us like that?" the nurse flung at him.

He blushed. " I'm sorry. I did knock first." Then taking in the fact that I was out of bed and standing upright:

" I say! Do they know about this?"

" Mind your own business!" she snapped at him, then added: " If you breathe a word outside this room you'll be sorry!"

" Oh, yes—no, of course not . . . not if *you* say so . . . nurse."

He blushed again, hopping about first on one foot then the other, as if the soles were swollen.

" As a matter of fact," he continued, in a halting voice, " I was looking for *you* . . ."

She hunched up her shoulders and tucked her hands under her cloak: her mouth set in a severe line.

147

" Indeed?"

" Well, er, yes . . . It's your day off, isn't it?"

" And how, pray, did you know that?"

This time he gave an impish grin.

" Easy! I looked at the roster on the notice-board."

" Yes?"

" It so happens I've got the day off too . . ."

" Oh yes? Interesting for you."

" I was wondering . . .?"

" You were, were you?"

" I've got these two tickets . . ."

" Really?"

Holding herself very stiff and upright she made for the door. Young Cartwright held it open for her, then skinned through it in pursuit.

They had both, apparently, completely forgotten my presence. I was left standing at the window. I made my own way back to the bed and sat on it. I managed those bloody buttons myself, swearing, with great vigour and even greater enjoyment, over each one of them. I felt in the best of spirits . . .

I wonder what it is, though, that she wants me to find out for myself? If it's so obvious to her, I can't for the life of me understand why I don't know it myself. I suppose a bit of my mind has gone sleepy, like an old pear . . . But to have to discover something about oneself, at my age! It makes me feel twenty—no, thirty—years younger!

*   *   *

Trudy and I had been in Paris about a month—in a top-floor flat off the Place de l'Opera, when I had one of the sudden rages which, during that period of my life, used every now and then to rush through me, like an express train through a tunnel. I had been cheated over some consignment or other, I remember, but for some reason it was only when I was back home that I broke out. For a few minutes I strode up and down smashing everything I could lay my hands on. Trudy sat on the divan, with her feet tucked under her, the score she had been studying still in her hand, the still centre of the cyclone. She didn't speak or make any attempt to stop me. At the very beginning she snatched up one or two of her personal possessions on the table beside her and pushed them behind the cushion she was leaning against (a few moments before I booted the table across the room) but apart from that she didn't move. Her eyes followed me, though, switching eagerly to and fro, as if she was watching some esoteric game. Sometimes her eyes, gleaming excitedly, would alight on an object before I had noticed it myself. After a while she seemed to be actually directing me, though without in the least reducing the tempo or fury of my assaults. At the end of it, she said, very mildly, " We shall have to replace all these things, of course," and immediately returned to studying her score. I cleared up the mess myself.

I felt much better afterwards—except for the fact that I found that, for the first time in my life, I was impotent.

Trudy didn't become petulant or sweet or forgiving; she didn't become resigned, or good-humouredly understanding— reactions I would have found tolerable. She said nothing at all, and gave no overt sign that she had noticed anything different in my behaviour.

But one day, about a week later, she said: " Madame Mohl " (that was the name of her singing teacher in Paris), " Madame Mohl says that my voice has lost its edge a little "—and she looked straight at me, her large, candid eyes very wide.

" Damn Madame Mohl! " I said.

At the same time, Trudy did modify *her* behaviour. That is to say, she got into bed as usual, lay on her back with her arms languidly raised, clasping the back of her head as it lay on the pillow, the wide sleeves of her night-dress falling back to reveal the smooth, creamy undersides of her arms—a sight which, in normal circumstances, would have been sufficient to send me half mad with desire.

She would lie like that for about as long as it usually took for me to complete my love-making. Then, as if she had a timing-device under the pillow, she would turn over on her side and fall into a deep and tranquil sleep.

After a week or so, however, I suddenly decided that there was a secret but positive, and perhaps even passionate, avowal in this pattern of behaviour, and with tears of mingled grati- tude and ardour, my potency miraculously restored, I resumed my ministrations. I persuaded myself that a responsive tremor ran through her body, and in an access of excited hope I began

149

to believe that I was about to break through to the complete union for which I craved, and that a new chapter in our relationship had begun.

Evidence was quickly forthcoming that I might not be mistaken. Whereas in the past my bouts of love-making had been entirely on my own initiative. Trudy now took to retiring to bed herself at the most unexpected times, and of giving oblique notice of her intentions.

" I think I'll have forty winks," she would say, yawning and stretching, so that the lines and curves of her body disposed themselves like those of a Matisse drawing. Or: " I think I'll do my breathing and relaxation exercises." Or, during one period when she became mildly interested in the various Eastern philosophies which were going the rounds of Paris at the time: " It's time for my *physical* Yoga "—with just the slightest emphasis on the adjective.

True, when, after a decent interval I would go into the bedroom myself, I might really find her sleeping, or lying on her back taking deep breaths—or even with her limbs twisted and coiled like the branches of a well-established wisteria, a spectacle which always struck me as unutterably poignant, and almost unbearably provocative.

But she was always prepared to break off whatever she was doing, even sleeping, with the utmost docility. It was also true, I had to admit, that I was aware after a while that there was no noticeable change in the quality of my own sensations. I still wooed her painstakingly, desperately, and then, when I could hold back no longer, threw myself upon her in an agony of desire. But the gratification still lagged behind both the stimulation and the performance. I still felt myself shooting into her, not with joy but a thud of despair, as I were directing a bullet against my own heart.

Still, I told myself, it was only a matter of time. Often now a half-smile would touch her lips, not indeed of actual pleasure or satisfaction, but at least of approval.

This went on for quite a long time. It nearly always took place, I noticed, in the mornings or afternoons—a circumstance which I continued to interpret as an indication of a positive preference on Trudy's part, and therefore an omen full of promise. Until, suddenly one day, the horrible thought struck me that it was all following a time-table.

At first I refused to believe it, but the nagging suspicion persisted.

Then one day, after Trudy had left the house, I found she had left her diary in an unlocked drawer of the bureau. I went through it carefully, noting the times and dates of her appointments with Madame Mohl. Surely I could not be mistaken? Surely Trudy's morning and afternoon retirements for " relaxation " preceded her singing lessons in a curiously suggestive manner? What is more, she had entered brief notes against these appointments. Most of these were straightforward enough —" Good today—kept larynx down perfectly "; " a decided improvement "; " timbre needs attention "; " must work harder on diaphragm control "; " still tending to flatten top notes "— and so on. But surely some of the other entries were, if somewhat baffling, humiliatingly suggestive? Thus one of them read: " Slight falling off—step up usual routine? "; another, a few days later, " yes—distinct improvement "; and yet another which caused me to tremble, " Performance improving—in ratio, perhaps? " And finally, what was I to make of: " relaxation further improved: passage far less restricted "?

Feverishly I searched back through the earlier entries until I found those belonging to the period of my impotence. " Disappointing ", I read; " a definite falling-off "; " sounded almost guttural today "; " too dry and parched "; " needs more liquidity "; " must find remedy "; " further discussions with Mme Mohl. Surely her suggestion is ridiculously far-fetched? "; and " Perhaps Mme Mohl is right—worth trying ".

It might be supposed that these apparent revelations would have rendered me impotent again. Not at all. I became a man of iron. I ploughed Trudy's compliant flesh with redoubled vigour and determination, and as the seed poured out of me in ever greater profusion, I muttered under my breath: " Let's see what Mme Mohl makes of *that*! "

I had the idea that I was being very clever about this, as if I were a secret agent laying a particularly subtle trail in order to entrap suspect traitors.

Perhaps it was a case of telepathy, but Trudy herself began to refer to her teacher more frequently than she had done before.

" Madame Mohl was very pleased with me this afternoon " . . . " Madame Mohl congratulated me this afternoon " . . . Madame Mohl this, and Madame Mohl that.

On one occasion, after a spell of particularly potent activity on my part she reported: "Madame Mohl tells me that I've made ' quite remarkable ' progress! She says it's just as if some ' new force ' had flown into me . . ."

"Then I hope she knows where it comes from," I interrupted slyly, with a sharp look at Trudy's face. She stared back at me in astonishment.

"She'll do well in opera," I remember telling myself, "her acting is first-class too!"

I took to researching into those books which deal with the more recondite aspects of anthropology and sexology. I picked up many curious and fascinating items of information. I learned, for example, that throughout the ages, and in many different parts of the world, the restorative and stimulating properties of semen, whether swallowed, rubbed into the skin, or absorbed in the usual manner, have been held in the highest esteem.

I went to London to continue my researches, feeling more than ever like a secret agent hot on the trail, and with the idea of perhaps extracting a more scientific opinion from Cartwright. We had exchanged a few letters, of a perfectly amiable nature, which had made no reference to the circumstances of our last encounter. Perhaps he wanted to keep a line open to Trudy, though as far as I know he had made no attempt to contact her personally.

He made no reference to it, either, when I called on him, and he didn't, to begin with, mention Trudy's name. I led up to the subject that was gnawing at my mind with what I thought was considerable cunning, softening him up by resurrecting certain old jests of a learned but scabrous variety, of which I knew he was particularly fond, then proceeding by way of such fascinating hotch-potches as Burton's *Anatomy of Melancholy*, and less decent though highly literary publications known only to a sophisticated élite—to which he was equally addicted—in order, finally, to stimulate his own flow of curious and esoteric anecdote.

Eventually the opportunity for which I had been waiting arrived, and with an air of the utmost innocence I said:

"Is there anything in these tales about the beneficial effects of sperm upon the female physique?"

"But of course," he replied irritably (I had cut across one of his favourite monologues). "A woman needs a small, but

152

regular supply of male hormone if she is to look and feel her best. Surely it's a cliché that a woman with a really satisfactory sex life positively *glows* with health?"

" Well, I can think of another reason . . ."

" Another reason for what?"

" For glowing with health—without benefit of sperm. After all, so do I."

" So do you *what?*" He was darting his head at me in a fury of exasperation.

" So do I glow with health afterwards," I lied.

" Yes, yes of course! But can't you be serious for once?"

" I've never been more serious in my life . . . The male hormone, then, it does a woman good in a purely physiological sense?"

" Yes."

" Absorbed in the usual manner?"

" Yes—though of course it has also, through the ages, been the so-called secret ingredient of all the most exclusive and expensive beauty preparations."

" Ah!"

" There is a snag, though . . ."

" What is that?"

" It tends to encourage moustaches!"

" And the larynx?"

" What *are* you talking about? On the upper lip, of course!"

But then he stopped abruptly. " Trudy!" he said, in a husky whisper. " It's Trudy, isn't it? Do you want to ask me something about you and Trudy? Tell me, tell me! Yon can ask me any-thing! Anything!" And he seized my arm and began shaking it. I shook him off and hurried away. I no longer felt jealous of Cartwright: I was too absorbed in the new phase of my servi-tude. In any case he was in chains too.

The servitude lasted for several years yet. I no longer felt a living man, with a man's needs and desires. But the mechan-isms continued to work, if anything more faithfully and efficiently than ever—in spite of the fact that Trudy's body was no longer real to me. I still found it aesthetically beauti-ful, but it was no longer her body so much as the force of my suspicions that primed the machine to action. I slowed it down or speeded it up at will, all the time intently studying her face and her eyes for any tell-tale sign that might confirm

153

these suspicions. At the moment of climax in particular I watched her: I would stare so intently into her eyes, indeed, that in this respect at any rate she became aware, and took to dropping her eyelids the instant I took her in my arms, so that she looked more tranquilly alabaster than ever.

All the time, too, I took careful note of her professional progress. Her diary had disappeared from the bureau, and she no longer discussed her singing with me. But by then she had advanced to such an extent that it was easy to obtain information. People were beginning to talk about her. She had given a number of public recitals. There were paragraphs about her in the papers—always favourable and gradually becoming enthusiastic. I didn't go to the concerts myself because she asked me not to do so, but I stood outside the door of the room where she had installed her piano and listened to her practising—and knew that the newspaper reports had spoken the truth.

There was a new fullness, richness, and assurance about her voice. It, at least, was warm and alive. At first I felt a secret thrill of pride. " *I* have a part in this! " I would tell myself, " It is really *my* creation! " I felt that her voice was a child we had made between us.

But this emotion was soon followed by another, which filled me with anguish and self-disgust. I was *jealous* of her voice.

Then one day, at breakfast, she announced, quite calmly: " I've decided to leave you."

She was sitting, as she usually did, with her elbows propped on the table, her coffee cup held between her two hands, as if it were a chalice. Her last recital had been a great success, and she was breaking into opera—or rather, opera was coming to her. She was, in fact, fully launched—and so, given the state of mind I had been in for so long, I suppose I ought not to have been particularly surprised by her announcement. But my heart gave a thud as if someone had just swung a sledge-hammer at it. There was at one and the same time a haze before my eyes, and an absolute clarity of focus upon Trudy's arms, bare almost to the shoulders where the sleeves of the kimono she was wearing that day had fallen back.

I can really see it. It is not just a vivid memory: not a case of seeing " as clearly as if it happened yesterday ": it is re-enacted, not recalled . . . The kimono is of black silk with a rising-sun motif on it in gold thread; the silk of the lining is apple-blossom pink; and Trudy's arms rise out of the sleeves as if they themselves are fleshy blossoms that curve over at the top, as she holds the cup, like honeysuckle; and her mouth is poised over the cup like a humming-bird poised over a flower. She draws up the coffee (it's a full-size cup, she doesn't like those minute thimble-deep ones) in little sips, with a slight sucking noise . . .

When, however, several minutes had passed without a whisper from me, she set down her cup and, swivelling round in her chair, stared at me in surprise.

" You've gone quite pale! " she said accusingly.

" Wouldn't you? "

It was an idiotic question, but she considered it intently for a moment. Then she shook her head abruptly: " No! "

" But why? "—an even more idiotic question.

" I can't see why you should go pale," she said in a musing voice. " After all, you must have realised that it was no longer necessary . . ."

" *What* was no longer necessary? "

" Why, our marriage, of course! "

" No longer necessary to whom . . . to what? "

" I don't understand . . ." She frowned.

" No longer necessary to your . . . to your *larynx?* "

" What a peculiar way to put it! . . . It's true, though, that it's standing in the way of my career . . ."

" Standing in the way! You were glad enough of it before! It gave you what you needed—what your voice needed! . . . Ah yes, and don't imagine it won't happen again! Don't imagine you won't need it again! It might crack, dry up, go dead—and *then* where . . . who . . . who would . . .who would . . ."

" *Stop* it! What are you saying? What do you mean? For heaven's sake *control* yourself! "

" Control! "

" Surely you can see that the time's arrived when I must be free? "

" Free for what? . . . Free for whom? " Then in a small, trembling voice— " Free for Cartwright? "

Trudy stared at me in even greater astonishment.

" What an extraordinary thing to say! Are you drunk or something? Naturally I mean free to develop my career—to

155

make the best use of my voice. It's going to be a full-time job now: I haven't time for other distractions."

" ' My voice '. You mean ' *our* voice '! Don't you see . . ."

" I don't want to listen to you any more. You're talking nonsense. You know I don't like being put out at breakfast-time." She spread out her fingers in a loving, luxurious gesture, and once more lifted the coffee-cup to her lips.

" I tell you what, though," she said after a few sips. " I think *you* need to be free too!"

She left the next day, taking her belongings with her. I returned to England a few days later. For a time I thought she might be going off with Cartwright, in spite of her denial—for when I disembarked at Dover a very odd thing happened.

As I was going through the crowded dock area, as noisy as a market-place, another column was coming in, and suddenly, half-way along, I saw Cartwright. He saw me too, but although he stared hard at me, he gave no sign of recognition. Everything, it seemed to me, went silent. The two columns shuffled along without a sound, as if ankle-deep in dust, inch by inch, until Cartwright and I were staring into each other's faces. We were separated by no more than a few feet, but we spoke not a word. Cartwright's face was white, that chalky whiteness you only see in red-heads: the hair itself had a curiously bristly look, as if he had just had a crew-cut.

Very slowly, still staring at each other, we began to move apart. At the last moment Cartwright turned his head and his lips curled back over his pointed, nicotine-stained teeth: his lips were colourless: for a moment I thought he was sneering, then suddenly I realised that his expression was one of terror —and in the same instant I felt a prickling at the nape of my own neck. We were both convinced that we were staring into the faces of ghosts or döppelgangers.

Immediately the uproar started up again round my ears, as if wax inside them had broken, and I tried to break out of my queue and join the one going in the other direction. But it was the busiest part of the season, and the whole area was packed with passengers, porters and officials. It was some time before I could retrace my steps. I searched the quaysides, the gangways and the ships themselves until the last whistle went, but I couldn't find Cartwright.

156

I didn't think of staying on one of the steamers until it was too late. Cursing myself for my stupidity, I rushed to the booking-office, only to be told that I wouldn't be able to get a passage on the Dover-Calais route for another forty-eight hours. I bought a ticket and hung about, without eating or sleeping for the rest of that day and night.

At eleven o'clock that morning Cartwright himself came through the barriers.

"She doesn't want either of us," he said the moment he caught sight of me, as if continuing a conversation that had started only a few minutes before. He gave me a look of intense hatred, and I returned it with interest. Nevertheless we boarded the boat train together, and travelled up to London sitting side by side in the same carriage. Our hatred and jealousy seemed the only stability that was left in the world . . . The hatred and jealousy faded away in time, but through force of habit the bond remained, like the rusty couplings of railway carriages marooned in a siding.

Not that either of us had any cause for jealousy. During the next few months I avidly devoured gossip columns on both sides of the Channel, and I'm sure Cartwright did the same. But there was not the slightest hint that Trudy was involved in any other liaison. At first this puzzled me and I began to entertain all kinds of wild ideas about her private life, and to suspect her of powers of duplicity and secretiveness which a moment's reflection would have reminded me that she didn't possess. It wasn't until a number of years later that I was able to grasp the truth, and even then it needed a distancing not only of time, but also of space and of a whole series of special circumstances.

*   *   *

It happened in Lisbon, in the early stages of the Second World War. By then I was already past the age of the call-up—as were Griffiths and Cartwright, though all three of us volunteered for active service. Griffiths could have become an army chaplain, but when he insisted that he wanted to become an ordinary soldier he was turned down. Cartwright was rejected on the grounds that, as a distinguished scientist, there was more important work for him to do elsewhere. I wasn't in close touch

157

with them at the time, but I did hear through mutual acquaintances that neither of them accepted the decision, and that they had succeeded in getting work directly related to the war effort —though at the time I didn't know its nature.

For my own part, my knowledge of Spanish and Portuguese, combined with my unusually complex network of business contacts, persuaded someone or other in some department or other that I would be useful in the shadowy and ill-defined sphere of so-called Intelligence. I am not referring to the atmosphere that is supposed to surround this kind of activity. It really *was* shadowy and ill-defined, for the simple reason that neither I nor those who ostensibly controlled me had the slightest idea what exactly I was meant to be doing. I was called a commercial attaché, and in fact I worked so hard in that capacity for a time after my arrival in Portugal both I and everybody else more or less forgot that I was intended for any other function. I had just been inserted in a convenient niche in case I should turn out to be useful, at some unspecified time and place, for other equally unspecified purposes. It was by no means an uncommon arrangement. I met at least a dozen other people at one time or another, of various nationalities (including the enemy ones), who were in exactly the same situation, and I know for a fact that several of them were never once called upon to emerge from behind their covers. The cover, in fact, became a cosy reality, the other an eventuality at various times exciting, menacing, sinister, boring and eventually so remote that it was no more than a faint nagging, like that of a queasy tooth.

My arrival in Lisbon had, in any case, produced a giddy sense of unreality. The blitz had been in full swing during the three or four days I was dashing round London making my preparations—marshalling my various commercial contacts, visiting City offices, export depots, merchant banks and so on, collecting my papers, both authentic and forged, and receiving my briefing, both actual and potential.

For security reasons I was not given my departure date or my itinerary till the last moment, and this entailed a dash across London in the black-out. It was a particularly dark night, which made the beams of the searchlights look hard and compact in outline, as if they were bands of illuminated metal, and which gave the red glow over dockland an additional ferocity, as if London's heart was slowly but inexorably burning away under a black tarpaulin.

The ride in the commandeered taxi was a hazardous one, with no light to guide us beyond the tiny slits through the papered-over headlights, and an occasional gleam when a rising searchlight momentarily picked out the mounds of broken glass along the pavements, like ice swept to the roadside in an Alpine town, and I only just caught the train for Poole Harbour.

It, too, was blacked-out of course. There was bombing at intervals along the line, so that the train proceeded by fits and starts, on several occasions stopping for an hour at a time, very still and silent in the black well of the countryside, like an animal flattened against protective vegetation until danger has passed. There was no restaurant car, and by the time we got to Poole I was giddy from hunger. I was also too exhausted to eat when I got on the plane.

It was an old Sunderland flying-boat, which heaved and pitched in every tiny spiral of air. To make matters worse it had to turn sharply after an hour's flight (so clumsily that I expected it to fall to pieces then and there from the strain) and sneak back to Poole Harbour. Enemy fighters, it appeared, were lurking somewhere over the Channel. Several VIPs, the steward hinted, were on board, though for all I knew I was supposed to be one of them myself, and we were all of us agents about to be thrown into various niches in the event of a use being found for us. At any rate there was no conversation, and we regarded each other with suspicion, hostility, or distaste.

When eventually we got going again I fell into a deep sleep, which itself seemed an extension of the black-out I had just left, but in which I was still conscious of being hurtled to and fro like a boulder thrown down a mine-shaft.

And then, suddenly, there was another and bigger bump, followed by a skeetering noise that might have been made by giant skates on ice, and I opened my eyes on a scene of such brilliance that at first I thought I must still be dreaming.

Everything was white and sparkling; the sun on the Tagus, the white sails scudding past; the uniforms of the Portuguese sailors detailed to supervise our disembarkation. The friends, relations and officials waiting for the passengers a little distance away looked as if they were assembled for Henley Regatta or a cricket match at Lord's—blazers, white flannels, summer suits, panamas; flowered dresses, parasols, and floppy wide-brimmed hats, and all of it under a steady, blazing sun. They all looked incredibly healthy and bronzed. In my drab English suit, crumpled and covered with dust, I felt as if I had that moment crawled from under the rubble of a bombed-out building, or spent the night trying to sleep in the Underground.

I was met by a young attaché from the Embassy—unbelievably dapper and clean-looking, in spite of the fact that his pink little nose was peeling. I allowed him to usher me into a waiting taxi, with what seemed to me indecent haste, as if he was ashamed to be seen in my company. I even allowed him to give directions to the driver in the most atrocious Portuguese I have ever heard; and I was so tired myself that when I tried to intervene I found that I had temporarily forgotten the language myself.

The drive did nothing to restore my sense of reality. Black Horse Square seemed to have the kind of spaciousnes you get in a surrealist painting, as if it were drawing your guts out. The arcaded buildings of the custom house, the post office and the various ministries had the luminosity, at one and the same time sharply-edged and shimmering, which you find in Venice. The Rua Augusta, by contrast, seemed incredibly narrow, but its jumble of glittering shops and its crowds of pedestrians seemed even more unreal. I felt I was in the grip of some hallucination that had taken me back in time and space. None of this, surely, had any connection with the war-shabby Europe I had left behind.

The feeling was even stronger when, a few hours later, after a sleep which was more like a plunge into unconsciousness than ordinary slumber, I looked out of the window of my room in the little hotel in which I had been temporarily installed, on to a little square dominated by the statue of the great Portuguese poet Camoes. As if my appearance had operated an unseen switch, lights sprang up everywhere; first in the *praça* itself, and then, above the feathery tops of the trees, in long brilliant parallel lines along the Avenida da Liberdade. I jumped back, reaching automatically for the black-out blind, then remembered that I was in a neutral country, and looked out again.

The lights multiplied, above, below, at every conceivable

angle, like a basket piled high with illuminated fruit. Pulsations of sound came up to me: chattering and laughter from the pavement cafés, the clatter of sandalled feet on cobble-stones, the clanging of the trams, the hooting of taxis, and threading in and out, the wailing of *fados* sung by a woman with a particularly throaty voice from a nearby park. Both the sound and the light, it seemed to me, had an exaggerated, frenetic quality.

This was accentuated by the fact that inland the lights ended abruptly, without any outriders, as if a whole segment of them had been simultaneously dowsed by a wave of blackness—while in the seaward direction they thinned out gradually, like so many fiery palm-trees straggling down a sloping beach, to be swallowed up in an immensity which one sensed rather than knew to be the Atlantic Ocean.

The sense of impermanence was overwhelming. These, it seemed to me, were not only the last lights in Europe, but the last before a final and total extinction, a sliver of brilliance before the sun dipped below the horizon, for the last time. Even so, it was not, it seemed to me, a last manifestation of vitality; in my exhaustion of body and mind, half of them still hovering somewhere among the bomb-sites of London, I felt it rather as the phosphorescence on the edges of an organism that was already moribund.

I closed the window and sat on the edge of the high, old-fashioned bed. I had spent much of my life abroad, and as a rule I adapted to new places and surroundings easily, quickly, and with enjoyment. It was not, moreover, the first time I had been in Lisbon. But now I felt as disorientated as a middle-aged package-tourist plunged for the first time in his life among utterly unfamiliar sights, sounds, smells and tastes, and yearning with all his soul for fish-and-chips and a cup of tea.

In fact the meal that had been sent up to my room some hours before still lay, barely touched, on a tray: the chicken soup, with its globules of olive oil, and its rice sunk to the bottom of the bowl like a sediment; the fish cakes of *bacalhau*, to which I am normally very partial; and the chunks of kid, had all filled me with nausea. Even the fruits piled high in the wicker basket, though they were all familiar to me, and would have seemed like manna from heaven in rationed England, seemed utterly alien. So, too, did the dark, ornately carved furniture—

the uncomfortable high-backed chairs, the wardrobe like a baroque church porch, the towering head-piece of the bed on which I was seated, and the tiles, blue, white and yellow tinged with orange, round the wash-basin.

But suddenly my eyes alighted on one object in the room which was unequivocally English. It was an old-fashioned radio set, of ugly design and cheap, highly varnished wood, and with a piece of curly fretwork over the speaker. It was the kind of set you would have seen in tens of thousands of British homes at the time, on the shelf of every café, Nissen hut, air-raid shelter, canteen, and Air-Raid Warden's post. Just to look at it made me hear Big Ben, the air-raid sirens, and the slurred echoes of Winston Churchill's voice.

The almost aggressive different-ness of everything else made me lean over and turn the knob. For a few seconds there was a lurching, slithering sound, like that of melting ice sliding down a slope. Then suddenly, a woman's voice emerged rather faint, but with such distinctness and clarity, such self-contained perfection, that it seemed as if the surrounding atmospherics were the raw materials out of which a cameo had been carved. I turned up the volume control and the pure, thrilling notes flooded the room, welling up, it seemed, from floor to ceiling, and reducing the cacophony outside to a kind of reed-like irritation.

It was the first time I had heard Trudy on the radio. I had, in fact, taken pains to avoid doing so, though as she became increasingly famous it had proved quite difficult, especially after the outbreak of war, when she had joined ENSA and was in great demand at concerts for servicemen, at a period when the closeness of death and the day-to-day austerities of living had alike provoked a genuine hunger for sustenance of a kind that would normally have been scoffed at.

She was now singing a selection of arias from the better-known operas, but with that professional devotedness, at one and the same time obsessive and joyous, which is the hall-mark of the true artist, and which has the power of re-creating the familiar in all its original freshness.

I listened spell-bound. It was as if I were hearing Trudy sing for the first time. So in a sense I was. The various layers of unreality that had enfolded me ever since I left London, and now the consciousness of the hundreds of miles of darkened earth

162

and sky and water which lay between her voice in my ears and its source, all seemed to isolate that voice to a quite extraordinary and magical degree. Encapsulated in its wooden box, it seemed to have the passionate wholeness of a newly created entity.

Not that I thought of it as disembodied. On the contrary, as I listened the feel, the smell, the texture of Trudy's body came back to me with the most poignant vividness. As if I were once again lying beside her, my eye seemed to run along the contours with a sensation that immediately communicated itself to my finger-tips and made them long to follow after. In my mind's eye I could see, too, the rise and fall of her breast as she stood in front of the microphone in that distant studio, the slight hunching of her left shoulder, followed by a faint upward flutter of the arm and an uncurling of the fingers—no more laboured than the swaying of a branch—as she rose to her topmost notes—and, above all, the quiver, then the swelling, of her throat.

Suddenly I understood. Her voice *was* her sex, her self, her life. I experienced a brief pang of the old jealousy, as I wondered whether it had always been so, and whether I had been partly—and merely—instrumental in bringing it about. But a moment later I had an overwhelming conviction that it *had* been so from the beginning, that through the years voice and body had been searching for each other, until they had become one. In a last flash of recollection, even more vivid, almost transfiguring, I saw the beautiful contours of her naked body, and saw them moulding her voice, as it moulded them.

I lay on the bed and burst into tears of mingled grief and thankfulness. Then, without even taking my clothes off, I fell into a deep and dreamless sleep, impervious to the clamour around me.

I woke to a morning that seemed incredibly fresh, and exciting, and new. The noise outside was just as deafening, except that the *fados* had been replaced by the yells of the fish-wives and the clatter of their wooden sandals as they struggled up the steep slopes of the side-streets, their flat baskets on their heads. But the noise had become a challenge, and a restoration of vitality and hope.

I leaped out of bed and stretched. The air I took in was warm and sticky, heavy with the compounded smells of fish,

163

olive oil, cheap wine, garlic, and human bodies, but it flowed soft and healing through my lungs. My body was as full of the joy and sense of power as when I was a young man, all those years ago in Brazil. I felt free again, and not only that, but as if, by some extraordinary act of mercy, I had been snatched back in the nick of time from a path I had strayed so far along that I had no longer been able to realise that it was utterly alien to me, and had been set down again on that other path which sprang from the centre of my being. I felt as if after years spent among false gods, I had returned to the true faith. I felt not merely restored, but as if I was beginning life all over again.

* * *

Thursday has become rather a special day in my calendar. I get two visitors then—the nurse, and young Cartwright as well. Whether they plan it or not beforehand I don't know. They don't arrive together, and they always affect the greatest surprise when they encounter each other in my room. Perhaps they look up each other's rosters of duty and make their deductions from that.

The first time it happened they were embarrassed by each other's presence and couldn't bring themselves to address a single word to each other.

It's one of those days of wild wind which seems to tear off bits from the fabric of one's existence—desires, regrets, guilts, tossed higgledy-piggledy across the sky among bad-tempered birds, and leaves, and scraps of paper, and drops of rain that seem to have bounded off a hot plate but have somehow got frozen in the process. It doesn't affect me so much, of course; but it's the sort of weather that always upsets animals and young creatures.

"It goes right through me!" the young nurse said with a shudder, as a fresh gust slammed against the window—the three of us were standing there as usual, looking out.

"Me too!" young Cartwright chimed in, a little late on cue.

"It makes me want to scream," she went on.

"Me too!" said young Cartwright.

"I'm right out of kilter today, anyway. I suppose . . .?" She trailed off into an unspoken question-mark, obviously directed at me—I had been doing one of my wise-old-man pontificating acts.

" Me too! " young Cartwright chimed in, a little late on cue. She ignored him and continued to look at me with one delicate eyebrow raised, but a decidedly ironic gleam in her eyes.

" It's like a magnet," I said. " This kind of weather, I mean. It pulls up the parts of you that are all loose nuts and screws."

" I feel like that most of the time! "

" Me too! "

" Then you are not living the life you are meant to lead," I said sententiously.

" Oh, how that sort of remark infuriates me! How does one know what *is* the right sort of life?"

" It keeps nagging away at you. Don't you feel it?"

" Of course I do! . . ."

" Me too! "

" Anyway, is it *one* kind of life you're talking about? I mean, is it the same for all of us? Are you talking about getting converted or something?"

" Of course not," I said, " Or at any rate not to one particular religion—but everybody has an inner faith, which must be discovered and lived by."

" Have you?" I thought for a moment.

" Yes, I have, though I lost it for a long time and had to find it all over again."

" Well, I suppose I'd better start looking! "

" Me too! " young Cartwright added, with unexpected fervour —though from the way he looked at her it was obvious where his search was going to start.

" Come on, little Sir Echo," she said to him, not unkindly, " We'd better get this old bag of bones back to bed! "

*   *   *

For several months I worked at my job as a Commercial Attaché in Lisbon in a perfectly normal way. As normally, that is, as could be expected in a country which was supposedly neutral but most of whose high-ups seemed to be praying for an Axis victory.

Lisbon was a strange place during the war, filled with the

165

flotsam and jetsam of half a dozen nationalities: rich playboys who had escaped from the Riviera; decaying aristocrats and princelings; pacifists; deserters from one armed service or another; drifters; refugees; diplomats—and business men of every variety.

The business men were for the most part a pretty shady lot, out to make a quick profit from the war by every conceivable and inconceivable means. I was used to dealing with this type —indeed I had already met a number of them when I was in Paris. Some of them were also secret refugees from Nazi-occupied Europe, living on forged papers, and striving to make enough money to silence informers, and perhaps bribe their way across the Atlantic. I soon learned to pick out the edge of desperation in their hagglings, and though they were every bit as ruthless as the rest I made a point of favouring them whenever I could.

I was so busy with genuine commercial work, in fact, that I had almost forgotten that I had any other function, and when one day one of the suave young men from the Embassy—it might have been the same one who had met me off the plane, but as they all looked exactly alike, wore the same old Etonian ties, and had the same old Etonian voices, I couldn't be sure —came up to me in the English Club and said casually, as we were both at the bar waiting for a drink, " It would be a good idea, old boy, if you tried your luck at the Casino tonight " I didn't pay any attention, assuming that this was a somewhat eccentric way of making conversation. It was only when I was half way through dinner that night that, reflecting that I rarely visited the Casino and wasn't in the least interested in gambling, the significance of his remark suddenly struck me.

I hurried through the rest of my dinner, picked up a cab and drove out to Estoril. It wasn't the glossy package-tour place that it is now, of course. No strings of coloured lights, no stacks of hotels shaped like inverted shoe-boxes, and facing the curve of the bay like giant dentures. Just a stretch of asphalted promenade, lit by a few electric standards among the palm trees; a white, one-storied clubhouse on the beach where one could change before bathing and shower after; seldom more than a score of coloured sunshades or canopies scattered at wide intervals in the soft, creamy-fawn sand, which on particularly hot days was so agitated by the sand-fleas that it looked as if it were on the boil. What hotels there were, were expensive but discreet. There were plenty of white one-storey villas, shrouded by palm trees and creepers, but no blocks of flats. On the other hand, the advent of the polyglot Riviera sets had scandalised the older members of the various European colonies and the local inhabitants alike. The exiguous bikini (though that term hadn't yet been invented) caused a special sensation. The Portuguese authorities in fact had just banned them, insisting on one-piece costumes with skirts reaching a regulation length down the thighs (for men as well as women), and what is more, sent policemen on to the beach armed with tape-measures to make sure the regulations were being obeyed—a much coveted duty. What is more, in mixed company you weren't allowed to lie down, but had to sit uncomfortably upright hugging your knees. The proprietors of the floats and row-boats did a brisk trade: the bay was as calm as a mill pond and a hundred yards out one could discard one's Victorian style swim-suit and do some sunbathing. The policemen had binoculars and used them assiduously; but it was obviously in their interests to turn a blind eye.

And of course there was the Casino, far back from the front, behind a long rectangular garden of formal walks and shrubs, on moonlit nights oddly reminiscent of the Taj Mahal. But it was very different inside then; with its deep leather chairs, red velvet curtains, and red plush alcoves and balconies it was more like an Edwardian club or theatre than the giant ice-cream parlour it has since become.

During the day time it was cosy in a lush but unostentatious way, something like the interior of Fortnum and Mason's or Harrods, and mostly populated by elderly ladies with careful coiffures and so many protuberances on their fingers that it was impossible to tell which were rings and which knuckles; and elderly gentlemen in tussore suits and white-and-brown shoes, still talking in the idiom and still swapping the fast anecdotes of the 1920s. The latter included a real English lord, with elder-berry-veined nose and nostrils and a monocle which he had some difficulty in keeping in place owing to muscular atrophy. All of them looked as if they were en route for Cheltenham, Harrogate, or Baden-Baden—which they probably were.

After dark it was a much more animated scene. The elderly ladies and gentlemen were still there, recognisable beneath

167

further layers of rings, scarves, fringes and flounces, or in dinner-jackets of impeccable but antique cut. But they were over-shadowed by more inspiring figures with exotic-sounding names or titles, whisked in by chauffeur-driven black limousines from outlying mansions: tall gentlemen with black imperial beards and moustaches and eyes hidden, it appeared, behind whole series of retractable grey eye-lids; and equally commanding ladies with far more impressive encrustations on their fingers, and further jewels glittering in their purplish-brown hair, in the lobes of their ears, and at their wrinkled, orange-coloured cleavages. They were accompanied by slender young men, with pale handsome faces and motionless black eyes, and young girls with platinum-blonde hair, silvery skins, and eyes like polished enamel, all standing in various mysterious relationships to their elders. It was an extraordinary sight to watch them clustered round the gaming tables, like the cast of some pre-war French film—or, rather, as the evening advanced and even the deadest eyes began to glitter, and as I remembered the blackout and the bombs I had not long ago left behind me, like so many crabs clinging to the last black and glistening rock to rise above the storm.

Ensconced at the most expensive of the tables, and appearing perfectly at home in the theatrical setting, were Ivan and Tanya. Somehow I managed to keep a perfectly straight face. At first I couldn't understand why I felt so surprised. It wasn't even a particularly startling coincidence: after all, if I had been sent to Lisbon because I spoke fluent Portuguese, the same could just as well apply to them. I hadn't any doubt that they *had* been sent, and that the purpose of my visit to the Casino was to contact them.

As I played I examined them out of the corner of my eye. I could see now what had startled me. Their clothes, it was true, were much more elegant than anything I had seen them wearing before. But the real disguise lay in the fact that they were almost *too* recognisable. A touch here, a touch there, to hair-line, eyes, nostrils or lips had brought out what was most characteristic of their features. The features were unmistakably theirs, but oddly accentuated, like engravings on copper, and lacking any of the lambency of their real selves. The difference was like that between the reflection of a familiar building in water, and in ice.

168

One of the effects was to bring out their Russian-ness. Gesture, word, intonation, were naturally authentic; there was nothing in the way of a performance about it; but they gave me something of the feeling that I've had in the presence of nationalistically inclined Welshmen or Scots—that they were almost too good to be true.

Obviously they were habitués, and highly valued ones: indeed they more or less held court during the rest of the evening, receiving with charming but slightly bored smiles a whole string of newcomers presented to them by other regulars. When my turn came to be introduced—by the young man from the Embassy, who, with his perfectly cut but featureless face and dinner-jacket had seemed so much a part of the scenery that I hadn't registered his presence until he popped up at my elbow —I was quite prepared for the Count and Countess which accompanied their names.

Before I had time to recover my inner equanimity at having been the recipient of the same polite blankness as everybody else, the young man from the Embassy whisked me off in his car. But there were other visits to Estoril and other apparently chance encounters, at the gaming tables, or in the little swimming pool, with its balcony and high, ornate ceiling, which was suspended at the heart of the Casino buildings like a globule of green jade; or on the beach or esplanade; or at the English Bar in nearby Mt. Estoril—until it had been thoroughly established that I was a bona fide new acquaintance. By then I had a good deal of difficulty in reminding myself that Ivan and Tanya were not what they pretended, especially as it turned out that they really had been placed in a villa near Biarritz a couple of years before the outbreak of war, so that they could join the stream of wealthy refugees escaping from irritating war-time restrictions to the haven of a neutral country which might not have the same civilised amenities, but at least possessed a similar climate.

I suppose I have to explain that their main assignment was to organise the Portuguese end of the escape-route from France, along which all sorts of people were passed during the war, from airmen who had been shot down to members of the Resistance or their English contacts, and various specialists, potentially useful to the Allies, who had been stranded in France by the speed of the German advance. My reluctance in this matter has

169

nothing to do, at my age and at this distance in time, with the Official Secrets Act, but is entirely due to my distaste for the whole business. It is true that many activities which then seemed necessary, and even natural, in retrospect appear as the ingredients of a fifth-rate cloak-and-dagger comic opera. But I felt it even at the time. I had become accustomed to a heightening and exaggeration of the atmosphere in my encounters with Tanya. I see them now as a challenge I had, some time or other, to face, a shell I had to break through. But the ambience in which we now had to meet seemed ridiculous and unreal.

To begin with the three of us never had a chance of talking to each other alone. This didn't bother Ivan. Part of the mystery about him indeed was explained, when I learned that this sort of work was not new to him: he had apparently undertaken various secret assignments in the years immediately after the Russian Revolution. Besides, he really was an emigré Russian of noble family. He entered into his role with evident enjoyment. He still didn't smile, and he drank almost continuously, but he was happier than I had ever known him. He had found something closer to his kind of reality than anything he had known for years.

I was at least able to *look* at Tanya. Her face and figure had the same fluid but tranquil quality I always associated with her, but they could not obscure the peasant contours of her cheekbones. Perhaps she was aware of it; from time to time I detected a flicker of uneasiness in her eyes. For the most part, though, she conscientiously followed Ivan's lead—and in order to do so held herself utterly aloof from the past, and from me as a man who had played a part in it. I was, at this stage, no more than the stupid *persona* I had been forced to assume. But both of us felt the strain.

I've forgotten many of the details of the adventure (if you can call it that) which followed. I did try to recall them, but unlike those of our escapades in Brazil, they bored me, producing none of the excited sense of re-living a whole segment of my life. They were the repetition of a pattern, only in a crude and perfunctory form. I look upon them now as so much rubbish that has to be got through before I can get to my own reality again . . .

About this forgetfulness, though, can it be the callousness of old age? The adventure ended in tragedy for one of us. I could,

I suppose, make the excuse that it is the tragedy that makes me forget, but in my heart of hearts I know this isn't true. My memory has been selective, retaining with perfect ease the events that affected my own life, and the restoration to my true self that resulted from the tragedy. Perhaps the callousness was there at the time too, camouflaged by civilised habits: it is only children and the very old who recognise the essentials of their own survival and aren't ashamed of them . . .

I know that some time that winter I was sent to Oporto, ostensibly in my official capacity, and from there proceeded, on what was supposed to be a short holiday, to Coimbra, where—surprise, surprise—I was to run into Ivan and Tanya again.

Coimbra was the right place for that kind of rendezvous. Perhaps it was the students in their long black cloaks who gave it a romantically secretive atmosphere. There was something reminiscent of Venice about it, a kind of mixture of the sinister, the poignantly beautiful and the vulgar. It was in fact bitterly cold, but a clean, crisp cold. The moon was brilliant, so that the shadows of the cathedral, and the university library and buildings, with their sweeping curves and balustrades and flights of steps, and the reflection of the ruins of Santa Clara in the Mondego, incredibly still at this time of the year, had the sharp-edged, hypnotic clarity of a Canaletto.

The house we met in might have been a Venetian *palazzo*. It was one of the buildings that had survived the earthquake of 1755: big and heavy, fort-like in shape, with ornate facings and a huge doorway and portico, embellished with numerous coats of arms, and constructed of a buttery-yellow stone that looked as if it, too, had been immersed in water for the past three centuries.

It was now a superior sort of guest-house, run by the widow of an impoverished grandee, whom everybody called Doña Rosa. The Embassy had seen to it that we were the only guests.

At meal times we sat shivering in our overcoats on uncomfortable chairs, whose back towered over us like scaffoldings, round a vast refectory table in a huge dining-room. Doña Rosa presided at the far end of the table, behind an array of Swiss, Italian and German patent-medicine bottles. We could have talked quite freely there, as the only words of English Doña Rosa possessed were—with a gesture towards the bottles—

" my liver ". But it was so cold that the food chilled in its passage from plate to lips. It seemed even colder than it was because of the tantalising presence of a massive stone fireplace, bulging with carvings and armorial bearings which, however, contained no fire for the simple reason that there was no chimney. It had been installed by one of Doña Rosa's forebears, who, at the time of the Peninsular Wars, had been going through an English phase.

A few rugs were scattered here and there, but they were lost on that vast expanse of flooring. The boards were waxed and polished, but they had shrunk with age. Cold air seeped through the numerous cracks between them from the stone-flagged hall below, so strongly that if it had been gas one could have put a match to it and had a hundred rows of burners.

As it was the only warmth came from the tiny *fogao*—a kind of earthenware dish on legs, filled with wood embers—which the maid placed under the table at the beginning of the meal. It did no more, during the fifteen minutes or so it took the embers to die down, than produce a slight tingling in the toes. Even so, our legs kept a gool deal warmer than the upper parts of our bodies; the walls were threequarters covered with tiles which, in summer, would have kept the room beautifully cool, but were now like squares of polished ice. We felt as if we were inside a giant-size igloo.

The only place where we could have our wretched conferences in reasonable warmth was in bed. It was, in fact, a common winter custom in the area, but the first time Ivan led the way into his and Tanya's bedroom and solemnly pulled back the coverlet of the huge bed I goggled at him in amazement.

" For God's sake, it's freezing! " he said irritably.

" Of course," I replied, and I climbed into the bed, still in my boots and overcoat, and seated myself at the far side, against the wall. Tanya followed, and then Ivan. There were some five minutes of violent shivering and a thrashing of limbs as we tried to snuggle as close as possible to each other, like animals in a litter. Ivan brought out glasses and a bottle of *macieira* from the bedside cabinet. The cheap brandy tasted like cleaning spirit, but gradually the shivering stopped and we began our discussion.

Again the whole thing seemed so preposterous that it made little impression on my memory. The gist of it was that we were supposed to be touring the district as holiday-makers, with Coimbra as our base, and that at some stage we were to pick up two Englishmen who had been passed along the usual secret escape route from the French Pyrenees; they would be smuggled across the Spanish-Portuguese frontier at a spot opposite Fuentes de Onoro, on the Spanish side. Perhaps it was more subtle than that: I just can't remember. Perhaps in any case it wasn't: I do recall from this chapter of my experiences that nearly all the successful stratagems *were* startlingly obvious; usually it was the subtle ones that failed.

One brief snatch of conversation alone come back to me.

" Why," I remember asking, " go to all this trouble of collecting me?"

" We want to be on the safe side," Ivan said.

" That sounds very flattering—but I don't follow."

" Oh, we've been told you know the two men."

" Who are they?"

" I've no idea."

He stopped abruptly and reached for the mottle of *macieiria*. The only other thing that I remember is that I was conscious of the shape and scent of Tanya's body beside me, and that when I tried to take another swig from my own glass I had to put it down because I had expected the taste of kvass.

*   *   *

Fog this morning. A greasy London fog which leaves a chill trail, flecked with soot, on sills and window panes, and seeping through the cracks seems to corrode the hinges and catches as I watch. The sulphurous tang that also seeped into the room drowned the ether-and-disinfectant hospital smells, at the same time it accentuated the smells of my own body. I felt as if I were swathed in dirty cotton wool, and I threw off the bed-clothes as if that was what they were composed of. I didn't mind the fog though. I don't mind what kind of weather it is, or any of the sensations, however unpleasant, it brings. Weather is the medium in which all those creatures out there through my window are living and breathing. I can feel them breathing.

Seated on the edge of the bed I remembered, with a savage

173

intensity, the wholesome dirt of the past. The caked mud and sweat after some game, swilled away in the languor of a hot bath or shower. The sweat, itself like hot water, pouring down my back as I scrambled up a rock-face, or swung an axe at the base of a tree, or paddled desperately against the current of some Brazilian stream. Above all, the film of love-making, floating away in the bath-water like the skin of a snake, but leaving the glow and the scent intact beneath.

Oh, what joy it was to remember using my body to the full! To push it, exulting, beyond its limit; to force another spurt out of aching limbs, another gasp out of burning lungs, another gust from flesh apparently satiated! I longed to burn away the last granules of energy then and there. I rose on my toes and spread out my arms; for a moment the years fell away; I felt the muscles and sinews of a young man inside my soul, flexing and tensing; my lungs filled and I felt as if I were about to crow like the cockerel that used to get me out of bed when I was a young man, to gather mushrooms out of the curling morning mists, to poach in forbidden streams, to run, mindlessly, on and on across the downs, through tall grasses that slapped at me like wet towels, through woods still dark enough for the night creatures to scuttle alongside me in panic or curiosity, or to keep secret assignations in mowing grass where every blade still dripped with dew, until the strengthening rays of the sun dried them and the sweat on our bodies alike.

I determined to get away from the hospital at once; to take to the roads; to tramp until I had exhausted the last dregs of my manhood; to die, under the sky, in some ditch or hedgerow.

I strode over to the wardrobe, still propelled by the muscles of sixty years ago, and threw open the door. I began to pull out my clothes. I recognised them, but I couldn't believe they really belonged to me. Their old man's smell astonished me. Soon, though, I told myself, there would be more sweat in them and a good deal more dirt. They would be permeated by the fog, by damp leaves and straw, rain, and wood smoke. I flung the clothes in a heap on the floor and began undoing the buttons of my pyjama jacket, but then the door of my room was suddenly thrown open. I was so startled that I staggered and fell.

I must have had a momentary blackout, for the next thing I

remember was that young Cartwright and the nurse who reminds me of Tanya (even more so today for some reason) had helped me to my feet, and I was standing with an arm draped round each of their necks. I could still feel the young man inside me though; he may have retired into my soul but he's still there.

"Don't let *them* know," I said, with a jerk of my thumb in the direction of where I imagine the hospital authorities have their offices.

"We must get a doctor!" young Cartwright said, in a trembling voice.

"You *are* a doctor!" the nurse told him, with withering scorn.

"Yes, *of course!*" young Cartwright replied, as if the idea had only just occurred to him. "I mean, I'd better report it!" I gave a violent shake of the head.

"Don't you! Don't you!" the nurse snapped at him. "If you do, I'll never speak to you again!"

"Well then," he said, trying to sound in command of the situation. "We'd better get him to bed . . . so that we . . . I can examine him."

"I intend to go on standing!" I said, finding my voice for the first time, and delighted to hear how fierce it sounded. "In fact I want to walk to that damned window!"

There was a pause while young Cartwright tried to propel me back to the bed and the nurse (with assistance from myself) resisted.

At last he gave in, and the three of us, skirting the pile of clothes still lying on the floor, made our way to the window. Outside the fog was thicker. At first I could see nothing at all. Then shapes began to loom up; a human figure hurrying past; a square van; a moped; in the distance I could just make out a group of trees, huddled together like cattle. Their outlines wavered; they formed, dissolved, re-formed, like ghosts trying to materialise, or bodies that have not quite turned into ghosts. I stared at them for a long time. I stared at them as if I had accidentally stumbled upon a work-room where the mysteries of matter and spirit were being sorted out as casually as if they were bits of material in a dressmaker's shop.

I heard young Cartwright utter an exclamation. He had just discovered that on the way to the window my shirt had wound itself round his ankles. I began to laugh. At once the girl burst into tears.

175

" Oh, did you want to go?" she sobbed. "Did you want to get away so much? Outside? There? I'll help you! Oh, I'll help you if you really want to go!" Then, darting a fierce look at young Cartwright, "And I won't let *him*, or any of them stop you!"

Young Cartwright flushed. He looked as if he too were about to burst into tears. I am glad I thought of going. If I hadn't been interrupted I'd have done it too. But it occurred to me that I've still got a bit of real living to do in here. Suddenly I found that the use had come back to my limbs. I disengaged their arms from around my shoulders, and stepping quickly to one side propelled them towards each other before their arms had had time to fall to their sides.

*   *   *

It was still bitterly cold when we began our tour. My heart sank when I saw Ivan's car. It was a replica of the Bugatti he had owned in England, every bit as ugly and dangerous looking. Moreover, it had no hood, but with the help of multiple rugs and scarves and socks and gloves we were a good deal warmer inside the car than inside our grand boarding-house. Besides, I sat in the back with Tanya, and as we drew away with a jerk and a roar that threatened to crumple a few more yellow flakes from the stone doorway, and brought Doña Rosa and her neighbours running to their windows, I felt Tanya beginning to relax, as if she were edging her way out of a straight-jacket. Her closeness filled me with a sensation that was akin to the slow gathering of desire, but much more inward, as if a gradual unravelling process was taking place inside me.

I can't remember the exact route we took, though not this time for the same reason. I no longer saw our surroundings as the trappings of a fifth-rate melodrama. But at the same time they impinged upon my consciousness in a series of quite separate scenes: the white peaks of the Serra da Estrella, their slopes streaked with slate-blue and orange rock, the tops of the trees throwing off powdery snow, turned by the sunlight into swarms of blanched fireflies; a glimpse of Luso, its pink and white houses trailing like creepers down the slopes; the silver coils of the Mondego, and vivid segments of the Atlantic, caught at intervals from the Serra de Busaco; and the deep, rich greens of cypress, oak and cork in the ancient convent woods of Busaco

176

itself. They were real, but they flashed past sharp-edged and bright, like picture-postcards whirled round on a stand.

The kaleidoscope effect was in part due to the reckless speed at which Ivan drove. But I seemed to be able to register the scenes through which we passed at two different speeds: at eye-level, as swift as the episodes of a dream; inside me very slowly, as if by some act of patient and loving creation.

It was several days before it struck me that this process was the reverse of the unravelling sensation I had experienced when we first set out. Then suddenly I began to feel that the pieces out of which my life had been constructed during the past ten years had all been pulled apart and laid out afresh, preparatory to being reassembled on quite a different pattern. Tanya meanwhile seldom spoke, but I knew she was beside me and aware of my presence. The purpose of our expedition faded into an unreal background.

One day our circuitous route brought us to the government run hotel at Busaco—a vast structure, built in the Manueline style, which enclosed the ruins of the thirteenth-century Trappist monastery and was surrounded by magnificent woods. Inside it was beautifully appointed and cared for—and superbly heated. It was also very English; we were given tea, cucumber sandwiches and crumpets dripping with butter, in front of a huge log fire.

The manager looked more like a Portuguese politician with his regulation black suit, white shirt, grey tie, and black patent-leather shoes, and his regulation narrow face with its sallow complexion, blue chin and jet black hair shot with silver streaks. He was very polite, with just a hint of contempt in his manner for those who could afford to enjoy the flesh-pots of *his* country while their own were at war. As we left he produced a morocco-bound visitor's book. As I signed I noticed that the name above ours was that of a well-known English resident at Sintra: he had visited the hotel two days before.

Outside the hotel Ivan pronounced: " Now we must get to the frontier as quickly as possible." The car shot forward, and for the next few hours I was in such a state of panic, as we hurtled along the sides of mountains and round hairpin bends at the edges of precipices, that it was some time before it occurred to me that it must have been the signature in the visitor's book that was responsible. Presumably it was the signal

177

to Ivan that our two compatriots were about to be passed across the Spanish frontier.

At last we reached a spot on a deserted mountain road, almost facing the frontier. The car mercifully screeched to a stop, and we got out. Ivan raised the bonnet and started doing something to the engine with a spanner. Tanya began to stroll along the edge of the road, picking wild flowers. I stood beside Ivan, staring across the valley.

" Do you see anything?" Ivan asked, still bent over the car. The valley was covered with tall ferns and green scrub, which ended abruptly at the foot of a steep hillside, clothed in dark conifers, about two miles away. As I watched I thought I saw two figures emerge from the trees, stare across the valley, and then strike out more or less in our direction.

I reported what I had seen to Ivan. " You will find binoculars in the glove compartment," he told me. " Take them out, but keep them under your overcoat. Then climb down the slope here until you are below the level of the road. Keep your binoculars trained on those two, and as soon as you are quite sure you can identify them, let me know."

I did what I was told, and a few minutes later had installed myself in a small hollow behind a rock, some dozen yards below the road. I focused the binoculars in the direction where I had last seen the two figures. But now I could see nothing. We appeared to be the only occupants of the landscape. In the still, cold air the only sounds were the tap-tap of Ivan's spanner and, at some distance, but clearly audible, the sound of Tanya's voice as she hummed some Russian song. Although my fingers clasped round the binoculars felt like slivers of ice, the sun was quite strong; the rock in front of me was warm against my chest and I fell into a half-sleep, in which I dreamed that I was one of the pieces in some sort of game, the object of which was to escape from the huge, shiny board scattered with numerous obstacles in the form of curiously shaped concrete posts and pylons, into a muffled mauve and green countryside beyond.

A moment later my forehead struck the rock in front of me. I shook myself and took another look through the binoculars. I kept them to my eyes for several minutes, but could see nothing. I had decided that I must have been mistaken, and was just about to return to Ivan to tell him so, when suddenly

178

I noticed a bobbing movement among the ferns, about half way across the valley. I kept the binoculars trained on the spot. A moment later the tops of two heads appeared—or, rather, two hats, one of them a black beret, the other a black trilby. There was something decidedly comic about the way they bobbed along, like floats on the surface of a stream. At the lowest point of the valley, the hats disappeared below the level of the ferns, but then, as the wearers began to struggle up the nearer slope, reappeared, bobbing up and down more jerkily now, as if thrown by an inexpert juggler.

A moment later, two foreheads also appeared, and then two faces. I stopped chuckling so abruptly that I bit my tongue. Frantically I swivelled the little wheel on top of the binoculars in order to get a better view. I stared through the lenses intently and unbelievingly for several minutes. Then I unslung the binoculars from around my neck, and although by now I was shaking with silent laughter, remembered to conceal them beneath my overcoat, before I scrambled to my feet and raced back to Ivan.

"What in God's name are you laughing at?" he asked. I waved my hand helplessly; I was almost suffocating from the effort of keeping my laughter under control, though in fact the road and the surrounding countryside were so deserted that it would hardly have mattered if I had let it out.

"Well, *do* you recognise them?" Ivan asked irritably.

"Oh yes!" I spluttered. "Oh yes, I recognise them all right!"

Ivan closed the bonnet of the car and stood upright. Tanya stopped her humming and began to stroll back towards the car, as a lorry, loaded with cork, suddenly appeared round the bend of the road, but it drove on without slowing down; it was the only vehicle to pass during the whole proceedings.

Tanya resumed her casual stroll along the verge, stopping every now and then to pick a flower or grass. She reached the car and slowly climbed into the back seat, leaving the door facing the valley open.

There was a faint scrambling sound below us. Ivan went to the verge and waved his hand. The scrambling stopped. He looked carefully up and down the road, then waved his hand again. The scrambling noise was resumed, at a faster tempo. A few minutes later the beret and the Anthony Eden trilby appeared above the verge of the road, level with our feet. They were followed by two faces. The eyes beneath the hats goggled like grapes being squeezed out of their skins when they alighted on me. Their owners hesitated, as if they were tempted to turn tail and run back in the direction from which they had come. For my part I was having such difficulty in keeping my laughter under control that I could only stand there swaying helplessly, while Ivan leaned over the verge, extended a hand to each of them in turn, jerked them up on to the road, and pushed them into the back of the car.

It was only when the car was roaring away that I let loose the bellows of laughter which otherwise, I was convinced, would have been heard all the way to Madrid, and when I turned round to examine the occupants on either side of Tanya more closely I was seized by a fresh paroxysm.

Cartwright was the more presentable of the two. The Anthony Eden hat quite suited his foxy, wedge-shaped face. On the other hand the studied seediness of the rest of his outfit struck me as excruciatingly comic: the frayed edges to collar and cuffs; the stains on the grey waistcoat and spats; the dandruff on the shoulders of his shiny black topcoat, with its nibbled velvet collar; the scalloped bottoms of the pinstripe trousers; the cracks in the patent-leather shoes; and above all the shabby sample-case, redolent of cheap ladies' underwear, celluloid practical jokes, and inferior rubber goods.

But he presented nothing like as grotesque a picture as poor Griffiths, with that black beret perched on top of his large head, above the episcopal looking chops and double chins. The disguise, moreover, had not entirely obliterated the clerical flavour. The roll-neck fisherman's jersey he was wearing was also black, so that one half expected to see a dog-collar hidden somewhere among the chins, in spite of the rope-sandals, the haversack, and the sliver of a Gauloise apparently gummed to a corner of his mouth. " I don't see the joke! " he burst out indignantly when eventually I fell silent from sheer exhaustion.

" Don't! Don't! For God's sake don't speak as well! " I gasped, holding my stomach, which was aching so much that I wondered whether I had given myself a rupture, and for the rest of the long drive back to Coimbra, they both sat very still and severe, though every now and then throwing apprehensive glances over their shoulders, as if they feared I might stop the car and exhibit them at the roadside as a knockabout act. And I still had to endure the spectacle of them solemnly clambering into the big bed for a midnight conference. It broke up in confusion when I was seized by another storm of laughter, which eventually dragged Tanya in its wake.

Looking back at it now, the grotesque reappearance of Cartwright and Griffiths at this juncture strikes me as a kind of comic epiphany. They were a pair of pantomime undertakers come to bury a dead self. In consequence I couldn't help feeling grateful to them. They had given me the first unequivocal laughter I had known since the day I married Trudy. The tears they sent streaming down my cheeks seemed to melt the last residue of that old pain and grief. The tearing at the muscles of my face and diaphragm was a switching of points that had been rusted up for years. It contorted and emptied my body. It was like birth.

I wasn't fully aware of it at the time. I had learned that exterior events, whether solemn or comic, ordinary or grotesque, are the hieroglyphics of an inner history, but I had been out of touch with my own inner life for so long that my perceptions were blunted. In any case it's only when you get to my present age that you can see that your life isn't one but half a dozen stories, sometimes confluent, sometimes spilling into all kinds of different directions. It's like a team of trace-horses, and if the leader breaks loose, or gets stuck in a bog, the others gallop off wildly, usually spreading destruction in their wake. Still, I look upon that advent of Cartwright and Griffiths, and even its unreal melodramatic setting, as the real beginning of my re-generation.

I made it up to them the next day, by keeping a perfectly straight face while we discussed our plans. I had to keep my eyes studiously averted, though, when a few days later they appeared in the garb of two of Ivan's playboy friends and I took care to keep my eyes fixed on the countryside as we drove back to Estoril. There, by a planned accident, they ran into the rich Englishman from Sintra who had signed his name in the visitor's book in Busaco, and who now greeted them as long-lost friends and whisked them off to his vast, tree-shrouded palace, to be lost all over again. I believe they were homeward bound on a Sunderland flying-boat within a week, and before the month was out they had both been transferred to Cairo.

I did try to find out the details later on. But when I pumped

Griffiths he wagged a fat finger at me and boomed: " State secrets, dear boy! Sworn to, ah, secrecy! "

He was still enjoying the cloak-and-dagger stuff so much that I didn't have the heart to press him any further.

I also asked Cartwright. " Can't remember! " he snapped. " Had other fish to fry! " then added, with unexpected bitterness. " And so did you! "

I'd forgotten that Cartwright had made another set at Trudy, who was in Cairo at the time, giving a series of concerts for the troops—and very popular they were. He had made a fool of himself, too, pestering Trudy with flowers, and presents and passionate avowals, and eventually creating a scene in a night club that couldn't be overlooked by the authorities. He had been sent back to England in disgrace, and spent the rest of the war in his laboratory. After the war Trudy married her impresario, very rich and old enough to be her father. It was purely a business arrangement, I imagine, but I am told they were very amiable together.

Cartwright's jab at me was perhaps meant as a reminder that I, too, had quitted my grand secret-service career under something of a cloud. When I got back to Lisbon I resumed my ordinary commercial work and found that I was busier than ever. No one mentioned my absence or the reason for it, and I was sent on no further assignments. Perhaps the powers-that-be had heard of my proneness to laughter and decided it was a security risk.

On the other hand, Ivan and Tanya were still in the thick of it. It would have looked altogether too obvious if I had broken off contact with them straight away, and so there was no objection to my meeting them from time to time. But I was expected to tail off the acquaintance by degrees. Instead, I took to visiting them whenever I had a spare moment, and showed no sign of regulating the habit. This did not bother Ivan, one way or the other. He always greeted me politely, with his odd, bitten-off smile. But he never spoke out of his assumed character, and if I tried to engage him in personal conversation, his face immediately closed up, and he fell silent. His new persona seemed to please him far more than the old one: he retired inside it as if it were a tent, and closed the flap. He wanted no company other than a bottle. Towards Tanya his manner was unfailingly courteous and gentle, but the gentleness had no warmth, as if it were the product of some mental resolution or code of honour. The real man seemed to be shrivelling away, like a body behind a sarcophagus.

But Tanya still had to relate to the persona, still had to play her own part, and she was finding it more and more of a strain. I tried to get her away from it by taking her swimming or boating. Away from the beach, she would suddenly become gay and relaxed, talking and laughing as if she had just been released from a vow of silence. But we were seen by one of my young men from the Embassy, and I was given a severe reprimand, to which I responded with derision and, I have to confess, considerable ribaldry. I had in any case decided that my presence was becoming too much of a strain for Tanya, and that for the time being I must keep away from her. For one day, as we balanced, at either end of a float, the paddles across our knees, the sights and sounds of the beach apparently a continent away, wrapped round in the rays of the sun, the mask she had managed to maintain until this moment suddenly cracked; her face was scored with lines, as if the broken pieces had cut into it. Tears welled into her eyes and trickled down the cracks. I leaned forward and overturned the float. As we clung to it I put my arm round her shoulders: I kissed away the tears and the drops of salt water together.

Not long after this Ivan and the Bugatti went over one of the corkscrew bends near Busoca. He wasn't on an assignment at the time. He and Tanya were on leave, spending a week-end in the hotel. It was the first time he had agreed to take time off since they had come to Portugal. He found even the slightest relaxation of his role which this entailed intolerable. On the Saturday night he had got up without disturbing Tanya, and taken the Bugatti out of the garage. A goatherd had seen him roar past " as if he was chasing the devil ".

As it happened I was in the neighbourhood at the time on business, and Tanya telephoned me when Ivan did not turn up for breakfast. By the time I reached her, the police had already arrived with news of the accident. I was with her when she identified the body. It was badly mangled, but the face was unmarked. The pallor had an intense stillness, like that of china. The features seemed to be a pattern painted on. Even the grin was expressionless.

I helped Tanya clear up Ivan's affairs. I can't remember what

183

happened to the rented villa he and Tanya had been living in. I can't remember what happened to Ivan's effects . . . Yes, there must be callousness in my inability to remember, but I don't think there was callousness in our behaviour then. It was simply that Ivan had vanished out of our lives as completely as if he had been a lighted room and we had switched off the light. We were left outside. We went everywhere together. It caused a scandal, of course; the Embassy didn't like it, either, but it was some time before they insisted that we leave the country. Certainly there didn't seem anything wrong about it to Tanya and me. It had happened naturally and, it seemed, inevitably. In public, of course, Tanya kept up the pretence of being the Russian count's widow, but we weren't much in public, and Tanya's services were no longer required by the Embassy. I think we only spoke of Ivan in a personal way on one occasion, when Tanya suddenly said: " He was a kind man. And that was very brave of him, because he didn't really believe in kindness."

" He had made himself a code," I replied.

" Yes, that was all he had. It was all I knew of him. The man had died long before I met him."

There was one respect, though, in which Tanya and I were wary of each other. We had both been hurt, at the centre of our beings. We had both travelled a long way from that centre, leaving it bruised and ailing. The odd circumstances of our first meetings, and of our reunion in Portugal, got in the way. We were no longer young. We were close, but still not intimate. We were not yet living together as man and wife.

We felt passion rising in us like a tide tugging at the moorings of a boat, but we couldn't bring ourselves to slip the hawser. We were terrified of being disappointed—or was it of being overwhelmed? But terrified, first and foremost, of self-deception, of finding that something, which we were convinced held the ultimate secret of being, was ordinary and commonplace after all. It would make no difference to our being together. That was now taken for granted. But suppose we found we had lost the capacity for intense experience? Suppose we tore aside the curtain and found behind it, not a sanctuary with an altar, but something impossibly humdrum—a cupboard for discarded luggage, say, or a telephone kiosk?

But then a colleague of mine, who lived with his wife in a small chalet in Parede, on the line from Lisbon to Estoril and

Cascais, was unexpectedly ordered home, and as he expected to be away at least until the end of the summer, he offered to rent the chalet to us.

That chalet was not only the most romantic place in my life, but also the most holy—and I'm not going to apologise to any of the clever dicks about the adjectives. Not that Parede itself was a distinguished looking place. It hardly qualified as a separate place at all. It was too close to Lisbon to have acquired any special character of its own. On the other hand, it was too far away to be called a suburb. But it felt like a suburb all the same, as if the environs of Lisbon had suddenly stopped with a jerk, throwing a bit of themselves forward, like a wave hurling a clot of spray.

It was inhabited in the main by small government functionaries, minor tramway officials and bank clerks, who worked in Lisbon, couldn't afford to live farther down the line (and certainly not in Estoril), but fiercely cherished their commuters' privacy. They weren't very sociable, and the few rickety tables outside the single grocery store cum café were seldom occupied—though the smell of the long strips of *bacalhau* flapping and rustling under one's nose, more like old hides than dried cod, may have had something to do with it. But for the most part the inhabitants of Parede preferred to hurry from the little railway station, down the sandy avenues with their rather bedraggled palm trees, through their iron-scroll front gates, and into the shady, not to say, gloomy, privacy of their own homes.

In this respect the houses of Parede were quite unlike those of any suburbia I have known. They really *were* private. This was all the more remarkable in view of the fact that they were quite close together. At first glance, too, they looked as if they were all exactly the same size and built to the same design. Perhaps they were, and perhaps it was only the curve and slope of the roads that made each of the houses stand slightly askew to its neighbours, so that when you got close you saw that the doors and windows of one house were set at a slight angle or on a slightly different plane to those of all the others nearby. It was, in consequence, practically impossible for anyone to overlook anybody else. At the most there would be a fleeting glimpse of head and shoulders on the short path to the door, quickly obscured by shrub or trellis-work, or projecting porch.

185

I have never seen so much ingeniously disposed trellis-work, or as wide a variety of bushy and concealing shrubs and creepers. At the same time there were no gardens in the English sense of the term—nothing to bring commuters out at week-ends with mowing machines, hoes and shears, and thus to peer at each other through gaps in the hedges. There were only a series of little paved squares, with perhaps a couple of urns, or a sun-dial, or a stone seat—for decoration, not sitting in, though the lizards used to dart in and out the cracks—and growing, apart from the shrubs and creepers, little more than an occasional cactus or a very sickly rose bush. What gardening was necessary was performed for the most part by a little old woman, her back bent like a question-mark, who plodded beside a donkey, equally decrepit and loaded with an assortment of gardening implements, among which old fashioned besoms predominated.

In many cases privacy was further protected, either by ex-tending the porch or by building a kind of glass tunnel on to it, the inside of which was a riot of tropical vegetation, so that the returning commuter could dive into his home like a seal disappearing through a hole in the ice. In addition to all this, the doors were as solid as those of medieval keeps, and all the windows were heavily shuttered.

The little, one-storey house Tanya and I moved into was, if anything, even more private than the rest, because it was the last of a curving row, facing on to a hillside, bare and empty apart from a few rows of ancient vines, some gnarled olives, several clumps of brown fern, a couple of goats and, in his off hours, the old woman's donkey. It was a good deal smaller than most of the other houses, consisting of only two rooms, with a stone-flagged kitchen, and an alcove with a rickety shower, which tended to fall on one's head if treated too seriously. There was the usual paved courtyard in front, with its full quota of trellis-work, and a wall rising and falling in Manueline curves. There was a further grand architectural feature in the shape of a tall, covered gateway, so out of proportion to the wall (which could easily be vaulted over on its down-ward curves) that it had the appearance of a triumphal arch or twin totem poles. The words " Chalet Tomaso ", surrounded by various scrolls and flourishes, were inscribed on blue, yellow, and red tiles, set into the right-hand pillar.

186

Tanya and I fell in love with the Chalet Tomaso straight away. It smelt fresh and dry inside—indeed several lizards inhabited it—except for the area round the shower, and the musty smell there was a wholesome one, emanating from a well sunk into the tiny yard at the back, which provided us with all our water. The well was erratic, so we used to fill great earthenware pitchers, which we kept in a row in the kitchen. We did our cooking over small earthenware stoves similar to the one which had warmed our toes in Coimbra. If I close my eyes now, I can smell that blend of burning charcoal and damp earthenware; it is the most beautiful and evocative I have ever known.

What we loved best of all about the Chalet Tomaso was its patio. It faced on to the hillside, and it was filled with sunshine all day long. At the same time, with its smooth stone-slab flooring, its stone alcove and seat, and its dense screen of vine leaves, and the branches of the vine coiling and twisting overhead like an exuberant fan-vaulting, it was always cool and shaded.

The larger of the two rooms opened on to this patio, through french windows fitted with green-slatted shutters and a mosquito mesh. We made this our bedroom. We kept the big, old-fashioned Portuguese bed, with its huge mattress and bolster, both of them so densely stuffed with straw that they were nearly as solid as wood. But the English furniture in the house we stored in the cellar, replacing it with the traditional Portuguese peasant furniture—cane-bottomed chairs and stools and a low table, painted black with designs of sweet-peas and convolvulus; a wardrobe and chest in scarlet with pink roses; a sideboard in green with white lilies. When we took some of these pieces back with us to England, they looked impossibly gaudy, and the cheap wood soon warped and split. But in the Chalet Tomaso, with the blue sky and sunshine making an equally vivid patchwork through the vine leaves, they looked exactly right. So did the brilliant striped rugs we scattered over the bare stone floors, and the ornate pieces of china and earthenware which we bought at local villages and fairs.

I could go on describing the details of that little house for hours—I could live inside my memories of it, indeed, for the rest of my life. There are times when I wonder why I don't. It is only this deep conviction within me that one must go on living in the present and preparing for the future, however

187

brief it may be, combined with the nagging sense, caused by what the young nurse said the other day, that there is still something I have to discover, something I have to learn, that prevents me.

But the Chalet Tomaso is bound to mean more to me than any other place on earth because it was the scene of what, in my kind of belief, was my own authentic miracle in my life.

It happened on our first night there. We had sat in our little patio far longer than we had intended. It had been a very hot day and it was still warm, though not unpleasantly so, in spite of the fact that there was little air and the stars were for once almost blotted out by the lingering heat haze. The full moon, though, was not completely quenched, and light spilled over, too, from the skyline of Lisbon, only a few miles away.

The darkness was a purplish-black colour. It seemed never to be still, to come tumbling through the gaps in the canopy of vine-leaves above us and then to crowd round us, a ghostly yet palpable presence. We could almost imagine that it had a blood stream of its own. But the whole night pulsated. The distant lights did not twinkle, they throbbed, and when they began to go out, it was impossible to think of them as simply extinguished; rather, they died away, slowly and gradually, like fading heart-beats.

As they did so, we were conscious of our own. We had become nervous of each other. We tried to go on talking, but in all that blackness and stillness it seemed wrong to talk aloud. Whispering, on the other hand, is only for confidences; it makes small talk impossibly stilted. We fell silent. We groped for each other's hands, but failed to find them. We sat apart on the stone seats of the patio. I could only dimly make out Tanya's shape, and I could not see the expression on her face. But I knew her eyes, too, were staring into the darkness, and that she too was thinking that for years we had both been living lives that were alien to our true natures, and that perhaps it was too late to change them. We knew that we could only return to our real selves through our bodies; but we no longer trusted our bodies; we were terrified to hand ourselves over to them, in case they should fail us.

It was another hour before we suddenly got to our feet, impelled by the same resolution. This time our hands did meet, but mine felt big and clumsy, hers small and tentative. Her

188

fingers closed on mine in what had begun as a gesture of re-assurance, then had turned into one of dismay.

I pushed open the french windows and we entered. While Tanya was undressing I busied myself hooking back the windows and making sure that the frames of the mosquito mesh met properly. I checked and re-checked half a dozen times. By the time I had finished Tanya was in bed. I took my own clothes off in a rush, left them lying on the floor, and, alarmed at the whiteness of my own body in the darkness, hurriedly climbed into bed beside her.

We lay on our backs, staring up at the ceiling. We held hands again, firmly this time, but more like comrades than lovers. At first the darkness pressed close. Then suddenly it began to crumble, like the undersides of a mushroom. We could just make out each other's faces. We smiled at each other, in an apologetic, rueful fashion. We still couldn't speak.

Yet I knew we couldn't just turn over and go to sleep. For one thing we were both wide awake, like two people committed to a vigil. It was not a case of greed, or opportunism, or eleva-tion of will over instinct. The desire was there, somewhere, but hidden, apparently beyond my reach. I felt we were like separate elements waiting for the right catalyst.

At last I took her in my arms. I felt clumsier than ever, as if I might break her bones. I passed my arms behind her shoulder-blades in a loop, as if I were gathering a sheaf of corn. She sighed and trembled. I half raised her from the bolster and crushed her against my chest. She seemed to fall away, as if she had turned into dew. Then we were lifted up and tumbled over and over in the warm waves.

But it was not right. The union which I knew was somehow, somewhere, attainable between us, had not taken place.

Everything had happened which is supposed to happen. We should have been satisfied, but our bodies knew that we were not. There was a discord somewhere. Sad and resigned, we sought each other's hands, trying to comfort each other. We were gentle and loving, and not the least resentful. But what we had experienced was a second-best. I knew our bodies and our souls were capable of something more. At the same time I seemed reconciled to the idea that the heart of the mystery, wherever and whatever it was, was not for us. We would believe by an act of will, but we could not hope for revelation. The

189

old belief which I had touched in my youth had eluded us, it seemed, for ever.

It was then that the miracle took place. My body, I had supposed, was tired, dispirited, seeking only sleep and the recuperation of sufficient energy to face another day with its mundane concerns and responsibilities. And then, suddenly, a voice inside me seemed to say: "No! It has not passed—this is the crucial moment of your life—take it!" very loud and commanding, as if the words were banging against my chest.

A moment later I found myself lifted up and turned—thrown, almost, towards Tanya: there is no other way of describing it. I was aware of no decision, no act of volition on my part. I was possessed by a force beyond my conscious control. As I took Tanya in my arms again she let out a cry, part startled, part fearful, part joyous. She stared up into my face as if she could not recognise it; as if there was indeed a power in the depths of my being who had taken over my body and was looking out of my eyes. He owned every inch of me, every muscle, sinew, nerve and vein. There was no possibility of fumbling or discord now. Limb flowed to limb, bone locked to bone; flesh sealed to flesh. I was hardly aware, even, of my own potency as, supremely confident, my hands both holding and caressing her shoulders, it found its own way, powerful, thrusting, insistent, yet tender and receptive, endowed with intelligence entirely its own, purely instinctive, yet aware of the exact moment, to a fraction of a second, for surrender to a complete and overwhelming forgetfulness.

This time it was as if we were swallowed up in the velvety blackness. Still clasped in each other's arms, we lay there for what seemed centuries, healed and restored to the remotest corners. We were separate, yet fused together so completely that I really did feel that our flesh had become one, veins and arteries mingling like confluent streams, the ganglia intertwined as inextricably as creepers on a wall. The experience was so overwhelming, so far-reaching, that it seemed as unique as any revelation. The uniqueness and the completeness gave me the feeling, almost, that we belonged to some species which mated only once in a life-time, achieving in that single, central drama, the plot, and its unravelling crisis, dénouement, and final resolution. It didn't seem possible that such an experience could ever be repeated.

In a sense it was true. The perfection of union was with us to stay, but the miracle itself, the transfiguring moment, was unique and therefore unrepeatable. But it was for both of us the hinge, the centre of being. Without it we would have yearned, for the rest of our lives together, for a satisfaction we secretly knew existed, but which we would have despaired of ever discovering or achieving. With it, we always knew, during the inevitable intervals of the ordinary and the mundane, of separation, sickness, or simple recession of desire, what was possible between us. There was always a goal, a standard, a lodestar. With that knowledge, it was unthinkable that either of of us should ever seek to replace our relationship, any more than those who have been granted the mystical experience of godhead could contemplate changing their faith.

*   *   *

I awoke this morning in a jagged frame of mind. When life is foreshortened as mine is the range of rightness and wrong-ness—morally and spiritually speaking, I mean—isn't so very wide. All the more reason to keep it clear, to make the right judgements. But I knew the moment I opened my eyes that there was something badly wrong somewhere. Something I had left undone. Something I had to learn, had to *see*. What can it be? It keeps tugging away at the back of my mind like a dog trying to break its chain . . . I am aware of a falsity somewhere, some kind of self-deception, some error. Not a big one, I think; something pardonable, perhaps even endearing in view of my advanced years and circumstances—and therefore utterly disgusting to me, an abnegation of my manhood . . . For I want to die as a man, not as a creature neutered by illness and age. That is the one thing that is left in life for me to desire— and I pray for it fervently, passionately. I pray to the god of the senses.

It is too late, even if I wanted to, to pray to any other. It is the only god I have discovered for myself, and normally I am deeply content to have found him. It's easy never to find anything to live by or to, making do with habit or rote, or utter emptiness. Better to have found something than to pass one's life in indifference, arrogance, or theory. Better to remain faithful to one god, even if it is the most squat and ugly of them

191

all, an emanation of the primeval swamp, than to wander in a wilderness. And all gods are intermediaries.

But this morning all this seems the most arrant nonsense. What have I been doing but elevate self-indulgence and appetite into a hollow and pretentious system in order to gratify my vanity? This inner wrongness which gives me no rest but which I cannot lay my hands on, like a splinter lodged in my flesh, makes even the greatest certitude of my life suddenly shabby and suspect. It is horrible how one grain of poison can affect the whole organism, how quickly the whole tenor of one's being can go into reverse, how quickly the destructive principle can take over.

There is no shading off from one to the other. It is all or nothing in matters of faith, a direct transition from ecstasy to filth. The voice which speaks to me of my old belief in general and of my relationship with Tanya in particular, however exaggerated it may sound to the outsider, expresses the truth as far as I am concerned, and is wholly good. But the voice that is taking over scoffs at the most sacred of my feelings, turns them inside-out, and reduces them to a horrible vulgarity . . .

" Oh, so you have made a philosophical erection on the differentials of fucking, have you?" it says. " All very grand, but you know, all it boils down to is the simple and—believe me, far from elevated—fact that some fucks are better than others!"

I am terrified that this voice is taking possession of me, that I shall die to the sound of its mocking laughter . . . If only I could find that hidden " wrongness " . . . I must search, search, think, think . . . If I could find it, it might be the catch to release the trap-door and send the devil tumbling back into the cellarage . . .

*   •   •

It's two days since I wrote the last entry. I think that's right. It may be longer—the blackness of the pit obliterates time as effectively as those crowded dreams which seem to comprise an epic, but take up a few minutes only. In other words, I fell into the cellarage myself. But I found the secret at the bottom. I know what it is that has been bothering me. I have discovered what I had to discover. And it has blown the

192

blackness sky-high. My whole being is suffused with happiness.

The process of discovery began yesterday afternoon, while young Cartwright was visiting me. I had a sudden collapse of some kind. Fortunately I was sitting on the side of the bed, and all he had to do was to pull back the bedclothes and scoop me back under them. He didn't do it very tidily. His hands were shaking. Obviously I didn't entirely lose consciousness, because although I was lying at the bottom of this very deep, black pit, I was aware of it and, moreover, I could look up and out of it, as if through a periscope, at what was happening above, and I could hear everything too, just as if I had a receiver plugged into my ear.

Young Cartwright was pulling at my pyjamas, and prodding at various parts of my anatomy. He got into a state of panic. He caught hold of my wrist and dug his thumb into it as if he wanted to break through the bones and sinews—in fact I've still got a bruise there. In fitting the ends of his stethoscope round his ears, he knocked off his spectacles (I don't know whether he really needs them, but apparently he can't feel professionally grown-up without them). He caught them in mid-air, tried to hook them over the ends of the stethoscope, naturally failed, pushed them into their case—and then dropped the case as he tried to cram it into the pocket of his white coat. He dabbed all over my chest with the stethoscope, as if he were franking a pile of envelopes. Then he drew the stethoscope away and laid first one ear then the other over my heart, muttering to himself as he did so. The muttering turned into something not far off a whimper as he raised his head again, and I longed to be able to reach up and pat him comfortingly on the shoulder.

Then he jumped to his feet, accidentally kicked his spectacle-case across the floor, swore, and tore open the door. I heard him jabbering frantically down the wall-telephone, which is somewhere in the corridor outside my room.

Everything went very still and dark again, but some time later I became aware of a murmur of voices. I couldn't hear everything that was being said: the words came in short bursts, as if a heavy sound-proof door was being open and shut.

" Everything! I've tried everything!" I heard young Cart-

193

wright say, in a wailing voice. Then came the indistinct rumble of an older and decidedly irritable voice. There was a kind of rustling noise as if somebody was rummaging among dead leaves. I thought I felt a faint jab somewhere on my arm. I was aware of other fingers, firm and unhurried, tapping at my body, then of a stethoscope applied expertly and confidently. The irritable voice spoke again. I couldn't catch what it said, but I heard young Cartwright reply:

"Yes, of course I have! I've done everything I've ever been taught! Everything!"

The irritable murmur again, a sharper edge to it now. Then young Cartwright:

"But I tell you I don't know *what* it is! I can't find anything wrong—except that . . . except that . . ." He sounded as if he were about to burst into tears. And then I heard the irritable voice, very clear and distinct this time: "You young fool!" it said, "Can't you recognise the symptoms of dying?"

It was then that the blackness dispersed, and I was lying on my bed again, in a flood of light. The Registrar, or whoever it was, was striding to the door, with young Cartwright at his heels. The door closed. A small hand was slipped into mine. I squeezed it. The pressure was returned.

"So *that's* it!" I said. The young nurse was looking down at me with shining eyes. With eyes shining like that she looked more like Tanya than ever. "Yes!" she cried, "You see? You have found out! But you needed to find it out for yourself, didn't you? Tell me I was right to let you find out for yourself!"

"Of course you were right."

When she left the room, I pushed back the bedclothes and examined my body for myself. There was no scar of any kind. There had never been an operation. There was no operation to come.

I want to sing and shout for joy. It is a wonderful thing in itself, at my age and in my situation, to have had a mystery to search for—and to have discovered it! I feel like Christopher Columbus. I have opened up a new world.

There is no disgrace in any of the ills that flesh is heir to. But to invent them, that is a different matter. Why did I do it? What lies behind it? One of the fantasies of senility? A doubt somewhere, a sense of guilt, a desire to be punished for some unknown impiety? I can't answer these questions, but I know

that the discovery of my self-deception has removed the last
obstacle in the way of complete surrender to my own kind of
faith. I am fully restored, taken back into the heart of the
mystery. I have conducted my own operation. I have cut out
the wayward growth in my vitals. I am whole again in body and
soul. And I am glad, too, and proud to be dying of ' natural
causes ', by the simple wearing away of time and experience.

* * *

There isn't time and I haven't the energy to set down the
story of the rest of my life, even if I wanted to—which I don't.
I have been impelled, for my own sake, to relate those parts
of it which must have been most meaningful to me—to me, and
nobody else—otherwise I wouldn't have recognised the impulse
or yielded to it. I haven't the slightest wish to go over what I
have written, to see if it makes sense to anybody else but me.
It reassures me of the underlying pattern in my life. It has
restored my sense of wholeness and that is all I am interested
in . . . Except perhaps that I have the fancy that the young
nurse has been reading these papers. I shall tell her she can
have them . . . Yes, she *must* take them. I don't want anybody else here to pry into them . . . But she will understand.
Perhaps she will make young Cartwright understand too . . .
Perhaps they will see the pattern of it all together . . .
   It is Tanya, of course, who is the centre of that pattern. But
I've no wish, either, to say much about our life together after
our marriage, just after we left Portugal. It is private and sacred
to me, and much of it is therefore incommunicable. One man's
idyll is usually meaningless to another. A happy marriage
doesn't lend itself to communication through words. The impulse
to write, in somebody like me, only applies to that which
is incomplete and unresolved.
   The word happiness, in any case, is altogether too facile.
The fullness of our relationship had tragedy in it as well as joy.
There are some passages in it which I should find too painful
to recall in any detail . . . Especially the death of the son we
made between us during our miracle, our only son . . . It
seemed a ridiculously casual sort of death—a car whose brakes
failed on a zebra-crossing . . . The boy was fifteen . . . At first
I thought we would never recover. In a sense there was a part

of us which never did—but we had to learn to let that part of us wither away and die and fall into the grave beside our son. It is the only way to recover from grief of that sort—to accept that the only true tribute to the dead is a partial death of oneself, and the burial of that part, and the determination to go on living with the remainder, fully and without looking back, in the belief that a truncated self can also grow new branches . . . But the learning of those lessons is another story altogether, and it doesn't belong to the particular process of self-discovery I have been attempting here.

In fact there is only one scene I feel the need, an overwhelming need, to recall. Perhaps it is because I am in the same place myself, with Tanya and our son, after all these years. My heart leaps at the thought, like a signal drum . . .

Even so I don't want to go into all the circumstances that led up to it . . . It was several years before either of us realised that anything was wrong. I couldn't fail to notice, of course, that Tanya was growing thinner, and that there were things that taxed her strength. But we didn't pay much attention to it for a long time. It was Cartwright who eventually advised me to take her to a friend of his at the Royal Marsden Hospital. The diagnosis was leukaemia. She had all the treatments that were available. For a long time the disease progressed so slowly that we were able to build it into our lives, accepting it as an inescapable fact, like the weather. It made us gentler, more patient and loving to each other. We enjoyed being together more and we were seldom apart during those last years. We enjoyed the small intimacies, the day-to-day adventures more than ever. Yes, in some ways it added to our happiness—and happiness *is* the right word.

As she grew weaker she looked even more beautiful. Not only more beautiful, but more desirable. Both of us were full of the most tender desire. She didn't grow thin in the usual way; the bones themselves receded: her whole frame seemed to shrink, but not to shrivel; her flesh was as firm as ever, the skin as smooth. She merely became more light and delicate. At the end she had the fragility of fine paper. Her eyes became even more brilliant, until the whole of her loving nature seemed to flood them.

I felt them resting upon me one night. A glow that passed right through my body, deep into my sleeping soul. As I woke, they shone on me in the darkness. There was a special intensity in their light. I knew what it was at once, and my heart turned over.

"No! No!" I said. I began to weep. The tenderness of the eyes regarding me from the pillow deepened. She smiled and held out her arms. I took her in mine. She felt as light and insubstantial as gossamer.

"No! No!" I said again. "Not yet! Not yet!" Frantically I began to kiss her. I felt my tears on her cheek. "There is something! There must be something I can do!" I kissed her more frantically than ever. I put my hands under her nightdress and found her breasts. They were warm, rounded, beautiful. Her eyes grew wider. They seemed to spill over with light. She smiled, and opened her lips.

"Yes! Yes!" she cried as I went on making love to her, as if it was the first time, with a concentration of tenderness and of love that poured every atom of my body and soul into one focus. "Yes, oh yes, my love!" she whispered. Her body melted before me, revived, clasped itself around me, faded. I do not know at which moment she died in my embrace. The smile was still on her lips. The eyes seemed to go on glowing for a long time.

*   *   *

So my excursions to the window are over. I don't mind, now that I've learned that no matter how reduced the conditions of one's life, life itself need never be empty or static. Even if the body is immobile, the inner life of thought and imagination goes on as actively as ever. And even if the brain is struck, who knows what rich and varied fantasies, like the changing colours of a dying lizard, it is weaving?

In any case, I still have an external life. The sunlight and shadow on the wall is full of life and motion. It would be impossible, watching it, not to know that it was Spring again. Sometimes there is a sudden agitation in the pattern, as the wind outside tumbles a tuft of leaf or blossom, or a bird swoops past. Sometimes the re-disposition of the dappled squares has a slower, more stately movement, and I can sense the passage of heavier substances—an ambulance or a laundry-van in the grounds of the hospital itself, or even a double-decker

197

bus, sunlight bouncing off its red paint and its glittering chrome, beyond the walls. And in between the two extremes, a continuous rippling, like the dancing of a swarm of gnats. All this quite apart from the gradual changes that form the groundwork—the passage of clouds across the sun, followed by its triumphant bursting through the last white threads; and the deepening tones as morning passes through high noon to sunset. It is a whole pageant and if it becomes insufficient in itself, the transition to memory or imagination is so simple and unforced that it cannot really be called an effort of the will . . . And then the ripples of light open out into English meadows and meandering English streams, or into the dense forest mazes and interminable rivers of the New World. The stabs and darts of light repeat the most vivid illuminations of my past; not only the visual ones, but those also of the flesh—the first awe-struck discovery of the body's resources of pleasure and joy, the first discovery of desire, the first discovery of mutual desire and its sharing, and (most awe-inspiring of all) the miracle I shared with Tanya. And the pools of blackness in between become the woodland shrines of the god I have tried to be faithful to.

*   *   *

I don't know whether I shall be able to get this down. I have become weaker during the last twenty-four hours, and the effort of reaching out for pen and paper was almost more than I could endure. The act of writing is like pushing a tree-trunk through treacle, and what I have written will probably be indecipherable. I want to do it all the same. If there hadn't been pen and paper handy I would have found some way of communicating, even if, like the Incas of South America, I had to tie knots in my handkerchief or in one of the sheets. I want to leave a record. A record of the great gift that has been granted to this old believer—a final experience so intense and illuminating, so full, it seems to me, of vindication, completeness, and hope that I feel no sense of sacrilege in accepting it as my true final unction.

I was lying here alone, waiting for the light on the wall to go out . . . It must have been a remarkably still day outside, for the light has hardly shifted at all. No more than an occasional slight stirring, like that of a watchful animal . . . I didn't mind its watchfulness. We watched together, inexorable and even grim, but companionable in our patience. I knew it wouldn't be long, and I was quite reconciled to this mode of dying . . . But suddenly the door opened and closed, very softly, and the young nurse was standing by my bed. I couldn't see her very clearly; her uniform made a white blur, shining at the edges like a lamp in fog; and the outlines of her face kept blending with those of Tanya. But the hand that found mine and clasped it was firm and warm. Then as it was withdrawn, the shape became blurred again, at the same time as it began to quiver, and its outlines swelled and contracted, like those of a cell that is about to divide, or a chrysalis that is on the verge of bursting. Then the shape became still again. The whiteness was replaced by a kind of pearly opalescence.

Then suddenly everything became distinct. She was standing there with her breasts bared. I gave a cry, and my arms leaped from the bedclothes. She came closer. My hands reached out and closed over her breasts. They swelled beneath my fingers. The nipples tightened. I could feel her eyes fixed upon me. At first I was frightened to look into them. But when I did so their expression was grave, almost solemn. They did not contain the slightest suggestion of patronage or pity. She looked at me as a woman looks at a man; not an old man, or a man in need of this or that—but, simply, a man . . .

I don't know how long she stayed there. I closed my eyes in an ecstasy of wonder and joy, and when I opened them again she had gone. But my fingers were still alive with her touch. And from deep inside me my whole manhood grew erect, as if stone had taken wing, and the landscape of my years was complete.

About the Author

GILBERT PHELPS began writing when he was at elementary school. After winning scholarships to grammar school and Cambridge, and various spells of teaching, he joined the BBC West Region in 1945, and produced "The West in English Literature" with Dylan Thomas, Cecil Day Lewis, and John Betjeman. He produced the first Talks series on the Third Programme. From 1950 to 1953 he was Supervisor, Educational Talks, in London and producer for the Third Programme. He subsequently became Chief Instructor in the BBC Staff Training Department. After working as a script editor in the BBC Television Drama Department he left the Corporation; after tutoring for a time at University College, Oxford, he now devotes himself full-time to writing.

Gilbert Phelps is keenly interested in the theatre and the cinema, and likes to swim, travel, watch cricket and football. He is married, and has a son and daughter and three stepsons. In addition to his novels (the most recent of which was the highly praised *Tenants of the House*), he has published short stories, poetry, travel books and several volumes of literary criticism.